THE DIAMOND BOGO

AN AFRICAN IDYLL

ROBERT F. JONES

Skyhorse Publishing

Books by Robert F. Jones
Blood Sport
The Diamond Bogo

First Skyhorse Publishing edition 2015.

Skyhorse Publishing books may be purchased in bulk at special discounts for sales promotion, corporate gifts, fund-raising, or educational purposes. Special editions can also be created to specifications. For details, contact the Special Sales Department, Skyhorse Publishing, 307 West 36th Street, 11th Floor, New York, NY 10018 or info@skyhorsepublishing.com.

Skyhorse® and Skyhorse Publishing® are registered trademarks of Skyhorse Publishing, Inc.®, a Delaware corporation.

Visit our website at www.skyhorsepublishing.com.

10 9 8 7 6 5 4 3 2 1

Library of Congress Cataloging-in-Publication Data is available on file.

Cover design by Rain Saukas

Print ISBN: 978-1-63450-228-3
Ebook ISBN: 978-1-63450-887-2

Printed in the United States of America

for
BILL WINTER
The best
of the last
of them

"*What is the use of our feeble crying in the awful silences of space? Can our dim intelligence read the secrets of that star-strewn sky? Does any answer come out of it? Never any at all, nothing but echoes and fantastic visions.*"

— *H. Rider Haggard*

PART ONE

THE LAST SAFARI

PROLOGUE

All day the two Samburu ran across a high plateau, loping
through the cool fog, looking back now and then to see if
the pursuit was gaining. The one with the spear wound in
his thigh had weakened, the slash opening and closing
with every stride like a toothless mouth. But there was no
tongue in the mouth, only wires. His name was Korobo
and, from time to time, he snatched the upper branches of
a shrub to chew the tender bitter leaves. He did not mind
the taste. This was *miraa,* the khat of the Arabs, a mild
narcotic with a slight lifting effect, but now, six hours after
the Tok lance had opened his leg, with six hours of thorn
underfoot, six hours without meat or water, no narcotic
on earth could ease the lion bite of his pain. The khat,
however, kept him going.

They should have known the Tok would be there, in
that dry, eroded donga on the far end of the known world.
They had come upon the remains of a giraffe, the belly

3

hide slashed wide as only the Tok spearheads cut in this country, the charred shinbones split lengthwise by a stone-headed Tok club and the marrow lapped out by harsh Tok tongues. But the *wazee*, the elders of their tribe, had said for years that the Tok were finished—*na kwisha!*—wiped out by the cholera and the snail disease, the survivors hounded out of the country by the guns and trucks of the Wazungu. Other young *morani* of their village had hunted this far west, into the high plateaus of Kansdu, and seen no sign of Tok for a generation. But when they discovered the giraffe kill, the two young men had paused, suddenly sobered by the implication. The Tok were small but strong as baboons, few but fierce as wild dogs, cannier than a wounded buffalo. And crazier than a *m'zungu* with a belly full of gin.

They had discussed the matter, squatting over the still-warm ashes of the Tok fire, poking at the bones with their thornwood knobkerries, shivering their spears in nervous reflex, the iron laurel-leaf tips still sheathed in their cowhide wrappings, looking out over the empty country ahead—a cold green country, this, high above the Samburu plains and the welcome heat of home. But Machyana had prevailed, he being the older of the two. To Machyana's way of thinking, it would be cowardly to flee the Tok without even seeing them, two hyenas slinking at the cough of a lion. They would follow out along the Tok sign until they had at least caught a glimpse of them, then run for home and a war party. The Tok were small and slow. They could not run with Samburu morani. But Machyana had reckoned without Korobo's spear wound. . . .

The Tok came swarming from the donga like soldier ants, dozens of them, their voices deep as drums and their huge heads wobbling as they ran. Their pointed ears shone white in a pearly light and their huge, furry penises—always erect—swayed to their waddling gallop. Spears filled the air, and before the younger Samburu could turn, one was boring straight at his chest. Korobo brought down his club in a vain effort to bat the iron away, but the point hit him on the front of the thigh, its force diminished only a bit by the gesture. He could feel the metal grate on his thighbone. Then they ran.

Fast at first, with the fear pouring through them, the Tok grunting at their heels, but slowing after a while as the blood flowed from Korobo's leg, then the pain crawling in to replace it. Machyana stayed back, though he could easily have outdistanced the pursuers, and once even dropped behind to skewer the leading Tok with his spear. The spear took the Tok through the throat, but the ugly little creature merely stopped, smiling, then exhaled a stream of blood through his broad twitching lips. He would not even fall. The others whooped and scrambled to catch up.

From time to time, so fast were they moving, they ran unaware on herds of game. Gazelles pronked off in haughty outrage, staring back as they bounced to safety. A flock of helmeted guinea fowl zigzagged with them for a while, one even brushing the wounded man's foot as it dodged, panic-stricken, unthinking, away from pounding danger. Buffalo moved sullenly aside, wreathed with squawking, feathery haloes of tickbirds. It is good country for buffalo, Korobo thought. He was weakening swiftly now and his mind, protectively, had shifted gears from the imminence of his death to more prosaic matters. Some good *dume* in that herd, he thought. Good bulls. I must tell Winjah about them when next he comes to Tinga.

And that thought gave him hope.

If Winjah were here . . .

But the Tok were gaining now. Looking back over his shoulder, he saw that there were at least nine of them in the forefront of the pack, with the rest strung out as far as the horizon.

If Bwana Winjah . . . Yellow-haired Winjah with his bundook. Yes, maybe he has come up since we left the village, maybe he is hunting here even now, with his Wazungu friends, the weak white men, fat, but with guns. It could be.

Machyana dropped back again to urge more speed, but there was none left in the speared man. Machyana gestured behind to the Tok, running steadily with their lumpy, awkward, tireless waddle, their lances and their stiff penises swaying in ugly synchronization, their wide grins . . .

If Winjah—reaching out through the fog, reaching out half a day's run to kill with the mere flash of his pale eyes, much less his rifle. Yes. Running, Korobo imagined it: the green truck growling over the next hill, its windscreen flaring through the fog with that beaded gleam of wet glass, then Winjah out of the truck, all corduroy and cool, no bundook even, stopping the Tok with a hoisting of his hand, a flash of his eye . . .

And then he saw it, actually saw it. The flash of the windscreen, of the eye. There, in that tangle of thorn off to the left. The flash of glass like spear points in the dark. With a yell of jubilation to alert Machyana, the speared man broke into a final sprint, his pain forgotten now, swallowed up in his surge of joy, and bent his course toward the thicket. Behind him he could hear the bone whistles of the Tok exulting—Gone to ground! Gone to ground!

Hah!

And as Korobo neared the thicket, the glass flashed once again, brighter this time, a blue flame out of the black, a blue flame edged in red and green. It must be Winjah, the speared man thought, pounding now toward the spikes of the thicket, it can only be Winjah, only . . .

It was a buffalo. A great, wide, dark buffalo, broad of back and horn, scabbed and dung-caked of belly—a buffalo unlike any Korobo had seen before. Between the swooping arc of its horns gleamed a huge bright stone, sharp as the sun on wet glass and deep with changing colors. For a long instant the man and the beast stared at one another. The light from the stone picked the man's eyes. Then the buffalo exploded out of the copse where it had lain throughout the afternoon, black and awful in the instant, and felled Korobo with one quick thump of its boss. Without breaking gallop it turned on the leading Tok, all nine of them, and killed them in as many seconds. The rest of the Tok stopped, turned, and fled the way they had come.

But Korobo was not dead. The buffalo trotted back to him, sniffed, then lay down with its scarred knees across the speared man's belly and began to lick his face. The rasp of the buffalo's tongue peeled the hide away in long raw strips. The buffalo licked and licked until the creature beneath its knees was dead, and the salty flow of tears mixed with blood had run dry. Then it grew bored and moved off after the browsing herd. The sunset light, having burned away the fog, now fired the great prism mounted between the bull's craggy horns and flashed forth multifaceted beams of red and gold and lightning blue.

Machyana, who had observed all this from a perch in a tall umbrella acacia, climbed down and made off toward the east, toward home, weeping along the way for his dead companion. Or so he told it later.

At first, no one believed him.

1
THE HUNTER AT HOME

Winjah sat on the patio of his farmhouse sipping tea and surveying the morning. Below him spread all of Africa, or so it often seemed to him on mornings like this—the forest-clad mountain slopes swaying in a slow, indecipherable rhythm to the dawn breeze, while farther down the land began to spread into the brindled brightness of the vast game plain, then disappear into a forever of heat haze. Sunlight blazed on the ice fields of Mount Baikie, two thousand feet above him, but the tea groves and pyrethrum fields of his plantation still lay in partial shadow. Already his farmhands were at work. The sound of their singing and the hollow ring of pangas cutting brush rose to his ears. It was good to be home, for however short a time. And the time was short indeed.

A man of middle height and years, with sun-bleached blond hair and sun-wrinkled blue eyes, Winjah was perhaps the best professional hunter still working in this

far, game-rich corner of Africa. His full name was William
Henry Olliphant Wynton, but the tribesmen of Kansdu
had a difficult time with the harder consonants, hence the
nickname. He even used it on his business cards: "Winjah:
Hunting & Photographic Safaris, P.O. Box 163,
Palmerville, Kansdu." It was simple and direct, like the
man himself.

The house, though, was far from simple. Winjah had
supervised its construction out of native hardwoods and
fieldstone over a four-year period, between safaris. It was
a perfect replica of the Lake District cottage in which he
had been born, and from which he had fled to war and
other killing some twenty years earlier. The last days of the
English adventurer, those, and he had lived them to the
full. Korea and Malaya first, the blooding, and then
Africa—where blood seemed part of the air. The house
itself was almost a museum of his adventures, the
half-timbered stucco walls covered with Masai spears and
Rendile shields, Suk knobkerries and Turkana wrist
knives, the beaded leather skirts and redolent snuffboxes
of men he had killed and women he had loved. Elsewhere
hung the heads of his finer trophies: okapi, mountain
nyala, sable antelope, a Rowland Ward's class
scimitar-horned oryx, puku and topi, bongo and dibitag.
He'd killed them all—one of each species known to
African taxonomy. The eyes of these trophies stared
bright and unblinking in the gloom. Each day a servant
girl dusted them to keep the glass eyeballs shiny.

Wherever the walls lacked heads or weaponry or tribal
art, they were filled with books. Winjah had grown into the
world without benefit of higher education, a lack he had
rectified by voracious reading. He was particularly proud
of his Africana collection: leather-bound volumes, many of
them long out of print, dealing with African exploration
and big-game hunting, tribal folkways and military history,
art and natural history. Here Mungo Park rubbed covers
with Alistair Graham, Samuel Baker with James Mellon.
Neumann and Baldwin and Frederick Selous (both
volumes), Karamoja Bell's taciturn memoirs, Richard

Meinertzhagen, Teddy Roosevelt—Winjah had them all, had read them all. Many of the books bore marginalia in Winjah's emphatic hand, corrections or amplifications of facts borne out by his own hard experience, or in some cases simple exclamations of delight—"Egad!" "Ah!" "Indeed!"—when an earlier writer had caught the quick bright wings of Africa by just the proper pinion. Whenever he hunted a new region, Winjah brought with him a work by an earlier traveler. But in recent years, as the hunting played out and the trek to the game took him deeper and deeper into the blanks on the map, he found few books to accompany him. In his early years, he had kept a detailed journal, replete with sketches, of his travels and kills. No longer. Too many hunters he knew had been expelled from Kansdu, and other newly independent African nations as well, their property confiscated with no recompense, on the strength of "evidence" culled from their journals and distorted in court by sly though barely literate government prosecutors. Twenty-three hunters had been ousted from Kansdu alone since the tiny country achieved independence three years earlier. Only half a dozen remained. Yes, Winjah thought, the time is short.

He finished his tea and walked behind the house to the storeroom, where his safari team was loading the trucks. They would take off this morning and set up camp at the edge of the Tok Plateau, so that by the time Winjah arrived with the clients a few days hence the camp would be shipshape and ready for action. The lads smiled as Winjah came up—he was a good bwana, considerate, patient, and he paid well. Winjah checked the tanks of the Bedford lorries for petrol. Frequently the Africans would load in perfect order, rotate the tires impeccably, polish the windscreens to a high gloss, and then put water in the petrol tanks. Or vice versa. But today everything was in its proper place and Winjah praised the men in a loud enough voice that their women could hear. At the last moment, though, he checked the ammunition safe, a battered green steel box lashed deep under tenting in the back of the lead lorry. It was empty save for spider webs.

Winjah turned bleakly, his shoulders slumping with exasperation. The men giggled nervously. Then Lambat, the head tracker, sprinted for the house and the ammo stores.

For twenty years it had been like that. Winjah cursed to himself as he walked away. You tried to teach them, and they learned, but they never coordinated the bits, never caught the spark that made the engine run. Africa.

Well, this would be the last time out, the last safari. If it worked. Since the young Samburu, Machyana, had come to him three weeks earlier with the tale of the huge buffalo with the bright stone in its forehead, Winjah had reached his decision. Time was short, the government was moving in on all Europeans who remained in the country. General Opolopo Bompah, the former sergeant of infantry who now served as Kansdu's President, had made it all quite clear. He wanted the hunting rights for himself, the ivory and the rhino horn and the hides. To hell with hunting for sport, or for tourist dollars. The quick money was there, on the hoof, and Opolopo would take it.

Winjah had exercised extreme caution in organizing this safari, to prevent Opolopo from learning about the buffalo with the stone in its head. Pondering the list of his earlier clients, looking for one he could trust on this dangerous and important mission, he had settled finally on Bucky Blackrod, an American journalist with whom Winjah had hunted a few years earlier. Blackrod was a good shot, brave enough, and his journalistic credentials would cover the real intention of the safari: Who would bring a scrivener along on so precarious an expedition? Winjah had outlined the plan to Blackrod in a letter which other clients had taken out of the country for him after their safari had ended. They would go into the high country of the Tok Plateau and secure the valuable "trophy," then exit across the border into the Sudan. Blackrod would procure Sudanese visas. With the proper amount of baksheesh, it should be no trouble to smuggle the stone out to Amsterdam, where it would be sold and the profits divided. Winjah left it to Blackrod to bring along at least two other clients, reliable but rich if possible. If one were a woman, that would be even better for deceptive purposes.

Winjah strolled back to the patio, whistling "North to Alaska," the Johnny Horton song. It stuck in his mind. That's where he would go, once the affair of the Diamond Bogo was completed. North to Alaska. He'd always wanted to try his hand at gold prospecting, kill a moose or two, catch salmon from the front porch. Yes, North to Alaska.

But once he had poured himself another cup of tea and sat back on the overstuffed ottoman, he felt a chill creep down his back. The books glowered at him from the shelves, the trophies glared. Even the spears and knives winked, it seemed, in a forbidding manner. On the posts of teak that supported the patio roof—the roof he himself had raised on one of his rare visits home, during the rainy season—the bleached skulls of Cape buffalo stared empty-eyed under their great, sweeping black horns. Buffalo he had shot on this very property, some of them, as he hacked it from the wilderness. On his forehead he wore the scar, pale and shiny, cut by one of those horns when the bull rose up, long after it should have been dead, and hooked him. This was his land.

But I must leave, he said to himself. There's nothing for it. All that work, all that blood, the opening of new country. Who could have imagined it would end so swiftly? The spoilers have it now, and we are out. He sighed and sipped his tea. It was tepid. He called the girl.

She came with hot tea and the morning post. In it was a letter from Blackrod.

"*Jambo,* Bwana," it began. "Herewith my check in the amount of $8,500 for the safari we talked about on the telephone the last time you were in Cairo. We'll be arriving in Palmerville on the Pan Am flight from New York about noon on the 15th June. I'm sure you'll find my companions just fine for our purposes—a bit of hunting and a lot of photography. They are Donn and Dawn McGavern, a wealthy young couple from Montana who have never been to Africa before but are eager to see it.

Later, they would like to meet General Bompah, of whom you have spoken so highly, and perhaps Donn—who is an avid photographer—could do a few sensitive portraits of him for publication in America. In any event, we are all eagerly awaiting this chance to see the beauty of Kansdu firsthand and admire the marvelous progress being made in the 'Africanization' of that lovely country. I will certainly do a few stories about it for major American publications. Sorry for the brevity of this letter, but I'm busy packing. Best. Bucky."

Winjah smiled as he put down the letter and picked up the check. He had told Blackrod to stop payment on it just before he left New York. That way the bloody general wouldn't get the money. Though he would get Winjah's farm and all that went with it. Blast his grasping hide. Let's see—the 15th June? That gave Winjah three days to cull his collection of books and memorabilia and pack the few he could afford to take with him. Well, it would make the days pass faster.

Overhead, a weaverbird fluttered onto the patio and perched on the horn of a buffalo skull. It cocked its head, the eye diamond-bright, and squawked querulously.

Bloody Africa, Winjah thought.

2
THE WANDERING Y

Both Donn and Dawn woke up grousing that morning.

"It's all your fault," grumped Donn, walking toward the marbled gloom of the atrium bath.

Dawn shook her long blonde tresses, first in slow amazement, then in waking awareness that the argument, begun last night over stars and Three-Eyed Toad, was still raging.

"No, it's not," she piped, sleep creaking in her delicate, always timorous throat. "It's the heavens!"

Donn groaned piteously in his W. C. Fields voice as he slid back the door that opened the bathroom to the weather. Mother of pearl, he thought. No. Mother of toilet seat. The sky was iridescent at this early hour, a tumble of black-bellied clouds paling to blues and gleaming grays, a whole rolling skyscape washed through with the clean whites and yellows of a northern sunrise. The sun had not yet topped the horizon. The morning star winked balefully

between the clouds. Venus, you bitch. That was the trouble
between them now—that fucking horoscope.
Horrorscope, he cussed to himself, then yelled it aloud to
the morning. Cattle raised their heads and stared.

"Your mother!" howled Dawn in retort.

"What?"

"Well, she's the one that insisted."

He pulled the shower curtain with its Basho haiku
plastic impregnated silken furls and adjusted the Magic
Fingers shower head while he framed his rejoinder.

"And you resisted?"

Silence, except for the upwinding purr of gushing
water. He stepped under the tepid downpour and let it
pound him, gradually turning the valve until the
temperature was almost unbearably hot, feeling the steam
open his night-clogged, oft-broken nose, then switching
the knob hard left and bracing for the icy shock. He could
almost hear his pores snap shut, like so many tiny clams.
He counted slowly to one hundred in Japanese—ichi, ni,
san, chi—as his *sensei* demanded, then shut off the shower.
At his mother's urging, strange woman now in her waning
years, Dawn had had her horoscope charted for the month
ahead: the month they would be on safari in Kansdu. A
local astrologette had taken first crack at it—Iris
Kornshok, pig farmer and mystic, dung and stars, the
cosmic swineherd. Her prediction: extreme danger from
water, darkness, mysterious disappearance.

"If you go," she told Dawn in no uncertain terms, "you
won't come back alive."

Dawn forked over two hundred bucks and squirmed
in the seat of the silver Porsche Targa all the way back
home.

Donn forwarded the chart to a higher-priced
stargazer he'd met once at a coke party in New York, along
with a check for half a grand, and asked for a second
opinion. *Pronto!* The reply, though couched in language
more elegant than Iris's was nonetheless corroborative.
"Grave danger surely exists," wrote this stellar consultant,
"yet it need not interfere with your travel arrangements.

Keep in mind that the peril of the moment pervades the
universe. Wherever your wife may be during the month
ahead, she stands equally vulnerable to the verdict of the
heavens. The stars are fixed, as is the threat they pose.
Should she stay at home, in the seeming safety of your
domicile, the powers of the planets, the strength of the
stars will not be lessened. Water: She might bang her head
in the shower. Darkness: She might fall down the stairs in
the night. Mysterious disappearance: She might crash her
car, after dark, into a bottomless quarry pool. . . ."

"Or catch her tit in the garbage disposal during high
tide in the black of the moon, you astral asshole," grumped
Donn as he emerged from the bathroom, toweling himself
savagely.

Dawn lay curled in the fetal position on the rumpled
king-sized bed, her china-blue eyes abrim, as Donn
reentered the bedroom. His anger and frustration eased at
the sight of her, as it always did. A beautiful woman, she
was like so many of them: fearful. Either it hardened
them, he thought, or it turned them timid. I suppose the
timidity is better. Makes it easier to love them.

"What are we going to do?" she asked. "About
Africa?"

Donn and Dawn had traveled widely for persons their
age, and to the wilder parts of the world. On tours
organized by the Audubon Society and Eric Lindblad, they
had visited lands as remote as Antarctica and the Falkland
Islands. Once they had studied the bird life of the upper
Orinoco, amidst the headhunting tribes of Venezuela. The
only headhunters they saw carried transistor radios and
begged for chewing gum. Their favorite, though, was the
trip to Scammon Lagoon in Baja California, that wild
extension of plastic Los Angeles that belongs to macho
Mexico but, since the highway went in, is rapidly turning
to a junk sculpture of beer cans and ticky-tack. There they
had seen the Pacific gray whales at their mating, the
barnacled turbulence of cetacean love. Donn took a
photograph of a male gray, rolling on its back in an ecstasy
of foreplay, with its phallus flailing at the sky like *Pequod*'s

mainmast. He had written a poem about it, heavily symbolic, titled *"Chubasco."* One day it would be published.

They traveled the wilder parts of the world as their parents and grandparents had done the Grand Tour—it was expected. They went into the world with open minds, wide-eyed, sufficiently heeled. They sought sophistication and charm, not in the Louvre or the Uffizi, but in the tapestried halls of nature. They preferred the tapirs and coatis of the Costa Rican selva to all the sprites of Nymphenburg, the scream of the toucan or the chirrup of the rare Andean bee-hunting blackchat to the sweet voices of those castrati who had so charmed their forebears. Indeed, the world—even its wildest parts—was safer, more comfortable now than the most civilized corners of that Europe their ancestors had toured. Apart from the odds-against chance of a hijacking or a terrorist bomb in the lobby of a fine hotel, there was little to fear, little to cause discomfort. Donn had often told Dawn that, in the political climate prevailing in the late-twentieth century, the wild regions were certainly safer than the so-called civilized ones.

Now, though, he must comfort her again. Like most children of wealthy parents, she had been taught from toddlerhood to fear kidnaping; like most beautiful girls, to fear rape. These fears, he knew, overwhelmed even her fear of death. So he lay beside her and calmed her and caressed her, then made easy, reassuring love to her. Preprandial love, their favorite kind.

"Africa," he said later, when her muscles had relaxed. "I've got to think about it."

After breakfast (Lebanese orange juice thick with brewer's yeast, a dozen vitamin pills, eggs Benedict that oozed gently to the silver, the ham cut and cured in their own smokehouse from their own pigs, purchased from Iris Kornshok along with wisdom, and two piping-hot cups of mocha java), Dawn turned to the dishes while Donn went out for his morning survey of the ranch. Today it was not just routine: He had to ponder the chart.

But it's never just routine, he thought, walking out into the late May morning. Five hundred acres spread before him, out from under the beech woods that shaded the house—The Wandering Y. Donn McGavern, Prop. Yes, the Wondering Why Ranch. Obscured just enough in the naming to keep his friends guessing, and himself as well. All his life he had kept them guessing—first with the guns and horses, then with the football and the race cars, now with the words. Quick-draw artist, rodeo rider, Big Ten linebacker, sports car champion, poet, novelist—what more could a rich boy do to answer the wondering? Well, he'd plugged himself thrice through the calf and right foot while slickening his border shift. He'd busted both collarbones on Braymers. He'd left fragments of his kneecaps on the playing fields of Ann Arbor and Columbus and Madison and Lansing. And his nose all over Turn Nine at Riverside, coming down into that ungodly hairpin there that still woke him at night sometimes, seeing the wall come up in his dreams as some see the earth while falling asleep. And the words rode him still, roweling, blasting, hitting hard without footsteps, blowing the doors off his mind when he least expected it.

The dogs bounded out to greet him, Norwegian elk hounds, hirsute basketballs of caninity that could leap from their toes and lick his nose without reaching apogee. The horses nickered as he passed the corral, shaking their elegant, bony heads at him, great umber orbs now dark in the vernal light. Donn broke into a canter of his own, running out toward the road and then hurdling the fence, cutting through the sweet young alfalfa, as the horses pounded beside him, inside the fence. Down the row of shivering poplars. His own long blond hair flew like their manes, and his nostrils caught the air as hungrily. Down to the lake, now, with the horses left behind him, he paused to watch the stippled surface as he caught his breath. Bluegills and pumpkinseeds rising to the early midges. He would skip writing this morning, go back up to the house, and assemble the slim five-and-a-half-foot bamboo Orvis, an ounce and a touch of delicacy, and cast to sunfish all day long—the two-weight line snickering through the guides, laying out straight and fine over the pale washed nests, the #32 Black Gnat tied by Harry Darby just ticking the water. Dancing lightly on its tiptoe hackles. Then the subtle slurp of a half-pound bluegill ingesting the fly, tipping up, then down again with the same balance as a big brown trout, aquatic blimp—but exploding as the point sunk home with the fractive energy of an Atlantic permit . . . yes, Donn thought, for the hundredth time, if you could breed a bluegill up to thirty pounds, you would have the permit's peer. . . .

Like hell you would, he thought angrily. And like hell I will.

Ah, but the stars—water, darkness, mysterious disappearance. What to do? He dropped to the lotus position, heel tucked deep in the yoni place, back straight, hands loose in his lap, thumbs to forefingers, palms up, and waited for the answer. Staring down into the lake, he felt his mind begin to clear, the murk of the moment settling out while his consciousness grew slowly pellucid like the lake water itself. Words rose like feeding fish from the layered lake bed of his mind to bubble at the warm and sun-washed surface. "It is the stars, the stars above us, govern our conditions." That was *Lear,* Act IV, Scene iii. But hadn't Shakespeare scorned that very fatalism elsewhere in the play? "This is the excellent foppery of the world, that, when we are sick in fortune—often the surfeit of our own behavior—we make guilty of our disasters the sun, the moon, and the stars; as if we were villains by necessity, fools by heavenly compulsion, knaves, thieves and treachers by spherical predominance, drunkards, liars, and adulterers by an enforced obedience of planetary influence."

Yeah, the stars as cop-out. Donn was not even certain that he believed in astrology. What was it John Fletcher had written in *The Honest Man's Fortune* (1647)?

Man is his own star, and the soul that can
Render an honest and a perfect man

Commands all light, all influence, all fate.
Nothing to him falls early, or too late.
Our acts our angels are, or good or ill,
Our fatal shadows that walk by us still.

Very existential indeed, Donn thought, but existentialism
is passé. It's mysticism now. Charts and Chings and
Suchlike Things. (And I'm a poet and don't even know it.)

Astrology had come with the new life-style Donn had
adopted after the near-fatal sports car crash in California,
come with it free of charge, like a vest with a new suit.
Recovering from the multiple fractures, suffering the
endless operations to restore his face to something vaguely
like its previous contours, he had discovered that, while he
was going roundy-round in fast cars, his friends had all
turned hippie. They switched him on to dope—grass at
first, then coke and psilocybin, mescaline and three-eyed
toad. Amphetamines to storm the brain, stunning downers
to sooth it. Words had come washing up from the
wreckage of his previous life, the flotsam of a rigid
structure gone aground on a reef of dope, and idly he
began piecing them together, until one day he discovered
he was a poet. A hip poet. Hair to his elbows, pining and
posturing like some latter-day Oscar Wilde, though
without the faggotry. He'd taught high school English for
a while, playing scar-faced guru to a bunch of midwestern
yahoos who couldn't make the football team, blowing gage
behind the boiler room, quoting Basho and Rilke and Gary
Snyder while living in *Winesburg, Ohio.* The college lecture
circuit wasn't much better. He came on between Tim
Leary, crepuscular in his chemical satori, and one David
Smith, a jolly jock turned freako who swam channels, ran
through deserts with mushroom-blasted Mexican Indians,
dove into Mayan death wells, and generally proved that
even a long-haired doper could have muscles. And balls.

One night in 1968, during the height of the Vietnam
hassle, Donn and David Smith had emerged from an
auditorium on the campus of a small border-state college
only to be confronted by a horde of likkered-up, prowar
hard hats. Six longhairs already lay shattered on the

concrete under the flagpole, writing and whimpering under the torchlight in pools of blood, puke, and busted teeth. David walked straight up to the biggest redneck, grabbed him by the nuts and the shirtfront, lifted him face high, and bit off his nose. Then he tossed the redneck into the crowd, chewed up the nose—great gristly crunchings—and swallowed it. Nobody bothered them.

"How the hell did you do it?" Donn asked him later.

"It was easy," Smith said. "My chart was right. Also, I didn't really swallow the nose. Just tucked it in my upper lip till we got to the shadows."

Clever.

But our chart is wrong, Donn thought. Or at least hers is. If only Blackrod hadn't invited them on the safari . . .

Donn had met Bucky Blackrod, the sportswriter, a year earlier at Indianapolis during the race weekend. It was Donn's first visit to a racetrack since his crash and he had intended it as a therapeutic visit, a chance to exorcise the demons of the Riverside Wall. Instead he had fallen in with Blackrod. They had boozed on the banks of the Wabash, trampolined with hookers on the beds of the Speedway Motel, guzzled beers and skinned their knuckles in the White Front, that den of dirty-nailed iniquity on Sixteenth Street where the wrenches and the race fans congregated before the big Memorial Day blowout. Walking to the track one morning, stunned after a night of rowdyism, they had seen Art Pollard kill himself in the short chute between Turn One and Turn Two. The car hit the wall, spun, hit, spun again, then burned in a pale, flickering methanol glow. Donn's eyes felt as if they were melting like candles in his skull. Blackbirds squalled in the ash trees.

"It wasn't so bad," Bucky said. "I've seen them in pieces."

Bucky Blackrod was crude and corpulent. He drank too much and smoked even more. At night he snored like a congress of Caterpillar tractors; during the day he mined his nose and crotch with pawky, smoke-stained fingers. But Bucky knew his stuff. He could bore from within, giving Donn introductions to car owners and their women whom Donn, with his new hippie shyness, would have approached only with stiff trepidation. There was something compelling, almost reassuring, about Bucky's insensitivity—an American armor that glinted through the rust. Also, he wrote fairly well. Blackrod's first and only novel, *The Bruxist,* had gotten good reviews. It was about a journalist who wept a lot and gnashed his teeth over the cruelties and inequities of the modern world, and the exploitation of that world by the press. When the journalist-hero finally got tough enough to rebel, symbolized by a physical attack on his managing editor in which he tried to chew the man's throat out, he discovered that gnashing had worn his teeth down to mere stubs, ineffectual as his rage. Bruxism.

Blackrod's current proposal was for the three of them—Donn, Dawn, and Bucky—to go on a month-long safari in Kansdu, a small African nation as yet unpolluted by hunters. It would be largely a "foot safari" on horse- and camel-back into country few white men had ever seen, much less hunted.

"It'll be the Last Hunt, Donny Boy," enthused Bucky over the phone. "Game as thick as anything Selous ever saw. Elephants that would throw Arthur Neumann and Karamojo Bell into a dead faint. Savage cannibal tribes lusting after Dawn's tender titties; dusky maidens with filed teeth and twitching tails. Diamonds gleaming on the hillsides, gold nuggets rolling down the stream beds. Plenty of *bhangi* to smoke, and good cold Tusker beer every night around the campfire while the jackals howl and the simbas cough in the writhing dark. How's that, Donny Boy? The sun-scorched plains shimmering like sleeping lions, the snowcapped light of Kilimanjaro infusing the scene with an astral radiance. All the things you like. It's adventure, Donny Boy."

It would be, Donn thought, rising from the lotus position beside his pond. Cat's-paws wrinkled its watery skin; a bass leaped in the dark-blue distance, swallowing a frog. If I knuckle under to the stars now, I will be their slaves for the rest of my life. He walked slowly back to the house to deliver his verdict.

3
THE GUINEA WORM

"Wait a minute!" said Bucky Blackrod. "I can feel it moving now. Get ready. Okay, nail the bastard!"

A group of drunks lunged at his hairy bare leg, propped on the scarred lip of the bar. Clumsy hands snatched and groped. Irish curses blued the air.

"Missed him!"

The worm had emerged from the edge of Bucky's shin, waving up into the boozy light with its pointed eyeless head—a thin red ribbon fully a foot long. But at the attack, it had once again retreated.

It was a Guinea worm, *Dracunculus medinensis,* an African parasite that had plagued explorers ever since the days of James Bruce, the eighteenth-century Scot who had been the first white man to reach the source of the Blue Nile in Abyssinia. Bucky had acquired his unwanted passenger during a hunting safari in Central Africa three years earlier. Doctors could do nothing about it. The worm was impervious to drugs or medication of any kind. It lived in his legs, migrating from one to the other in a slow tingly crawl occasionally punctuated by a stab of pain, like a hot needle run through his veins. Toward evening, usually, it would emerge from his skin for a look around. But usually, toward evening, Bucky was halfway in the bag, too slow with drink to catch it. Thus the pursuit of the Guinea worm had fallen to his drinking buddies, who found it an amusing game. Unfortunately, most of them were slower than Bucky. Old men—retired cops, laid-off stevedores, elevator operators, cab drivers, just plain bums—they had been drinking since nine in the morning, when Clancy's opened. Clancy himself, a tall, cadaverous, big-knuckled man with a slab of patent-leather hair across his pale forehead, never drank. But even he could not catch the Guinea worm and had long ago given up trying.

"Maybe he's waiting to get back to Africa," Bucky said, ordering another shot to go with his beer. "I'll be over there by the weekend. Maybe he'll come out and go away. Go get himself a girl friend."

"Yes," said Clancy from behind the bar. "I suppose you'd call a female of the species a Guiness worm." He adjusted his leather bowtie as they laughed.

"I still say you should let me try this," said Riordan, the veinous ex-cop. He patted the .38 Police Special in the quick-draw clip at his hip. The butt of the gun peeked out from under a roll of fat in a dirty shirt. "He can't be quick as a bullet. We'd let him come out with the bar as a backdrop and I'd blow his soddin' head off."

"Clancy wouldn't care for that," said Bucky, tossing off his rye. "And anyway, Riordan, you'd probably blow my soddin' leg off."

Riordan bridled, his red face going purple as the others chuckled.

"For thirty years I was the best pistol shot in my precinct," he growled. "From the Bowery to Fort Apache, from Harlem to Sheepshead Bay. I could do it, Bucko me lad."

"A sawbuck says you miss," piped Schultheiss, the crippled ex-elevator jockey. He slapped the ten-spot on the bar. Others chimed in, laying singles and fives on the pile, arguing odds and laying off one another's bets. Bucky peeled a twenty from the inside of his roll—expense money for the upcoming safari—and smoothed it atop the pile.

"Half the pot goes to Clancy, to fix the bullet hole," he said. "And the cops. All right, Clance?"

The bartender walked to the door, looked up and down the street, then pulled the shades.

"We can say it was a holdup man," he said.

"Shhhh," said Bucky, pulling up his pants leg. "He likes the quiet."

The other drunks staggered off away from the bar. Riordan drew the pistol and crouched on the hardwood floor, clearing a space for his shoes in the sawdust. He held the pistol in a double-handed grip, his elbows locked and lying across his knees, the muzzle far enough away from Bucky's bare leg to avoid flash burn. Clancy poured a shot for Bucky and another for Riordan. The Irishman shrugged it away. He wanted to be dead calm.

Silence fell over the saloon, apart from the odd hiccup—Maynard the onetime bicycle racer. They heard a siren go up Eighth Avenue. They heard two hookers giggle down the avenue. Flaherty, who had flown thirty-six missions as chin-turret gunner in a B-17 during World War II, struggled to stifle a beer fart. They waited.

The Guinea worm poked its head out of Bucky's knee. It swayed in the dim light, retreated a bit, then emerged slowly. It came out like a cobra from a fakir's basket, weaving to a music beyond the range of human ears. It was actually quite beautiful—slim, sinuous, graceful almost, a nearly translucent red, like a living thermometer. It hypnotized them with its dance.

Riordan shot.

They all jumped at the bark of the revolver. Bottles shivered on the bar. The clouded mirror shifted an inch to the left. Clancy's black leather bow tie took a ride on his Adam's apple. Flaherty cut his fart.

The Guinea worm, minus its head, whipped back into Bucky's knee like a snapped rubber band.

Later, walking up Eighth past the fag movie houses

and the hooks and the muggers, who paid him no attention because of the blood and beer stains on his clothing, Bucky thought that the Guinea worm would either die inside his leg and rot there, or else grow a new head. It would probably grow a new head. It was that sort of animal. Anyway, he hoped it would. He had come to like it.

He was glad to be heading back to Africa. New York had gotten boring in the past few years. Everybody whined, or snuck around behind your back. Even the muggers were yellow. They cut first and took your money afterward. But they didn't bother him because he was too much of a slob. Only the grungiest of whores would have anything to do with him. He used to be a good-looking guy, but now he was getting fat and he didn't care about anything anymore. The job bored him: It was games. Politics put him to sleep. He liked to read, but he could do that anywhere. He carried his own music inside his head. His movies, too.

In Africa everything was strong and it changed all the time. Everything bit. He knew that inside his fat and his lethargy there was a thin, eager young man waiting to be unzipped. The Guinea worm had told him. He knew that once he got to Africa, the man inside would jump out and go running over the game plains, buck naked, with the Guinea worms waving a weird dance around his ankles.

He could see the buffalo ahead of him, through the heat haze, its huge black head shining, shimmering, waiting.

4
KRAZY GLUE

"The entire affair is shrouded in mystery," said Treacle. "I have it on the best authority—and of course I cannot disclose my source—that even the Russians are puzzled as to how he brought it off. Hmmm, hahhhh, diddlediddle. Haven't a bloody clue. All that is known for certain is that the stone was mounted between the horns of the largest Cape buffalo known to man. And that Rokoff then released the creature—the Mbogo ya Almasi, as the Kaffirs call it, the Diamond Bogo—in a patch of wild country near the secret site where the stone was found."

Winjah listened in silence on the veranda of the Baobab Bar & Grill in downtown Palmerville, contemplating the bubbles in his glass of Tusker beer. Tony Treacle, an expatriate Fleet Streeter and Old Africa Hand, hummed and diddlediddled a while longer, contemplating the firm buttocks of passing European girls. It was a good year for tourism, this. Slim, wheat-haired Swedish flickas and pudendally perfect German *Mädchen* sinuated the sidewalks in front of the New Clapperton Hotel, their unrestrained breasts wobbling enticingly through diaphanous and provocatively titled T-shirts. JERSEY MILK BAR. Treacle shivered uncontrollably as the harmattan brought to his nostrils a whiff of girl-crotch and Lady Dior. Perhaps with the few quid he should realize from the story of the Diamond Bogo he might . . .

"And what of Rokoff himself?" The white hunter had looked up from his beer and was staring, with a playful smile, at the daydreaming journalist. His eyes, even in this relaxed mood, were unflinchingly hard—like blued steel, thought Treacle, like gun barrels, shivering again though this time not with lust. The hunter's mighty thews rippled beneath the sun-faded corduroy of his bush jacket as he leaned forward on the table. His tousled blond locks shook beneath the push of the desert wind. A handsome devil, thought Treacle. More devil than handsome, though, if one were to believe the tales told round the Long Bar at the Chiperone Club.

"Hummm, hah, diddlediddle," said Treacle. "Vanished, one surmises. The secret police have no inkling as to where. Sold out the balance of the stones to Diamang, at a goodly profit, no doubt, and fled the country before the United Front's victory. Murdered his Kaffirs before he left—Kiratu, the chief of special branch, was up there himself, saw the scorched skeletons in the ruin of the bungalow. No doubt to keep them from talking once the Commies came in. As to the location, hmmm, hahh . . ."

"Fiddlefaddle," said Winjah. "He must have left *some* spoor. Where is Kiratu just now?"

"Still here in Palmerville," said Treacle. "Saw him this morning at the ministry. Hasn't a bloody clue."

"So you said." The hunter drummed his hard, broad-tipped outdoorsman's fingers on the table so that the beer bottles rattled. Treacle resumed his perusal of the passing quim. The girls' eyes were a study in themselves. Coming up the broad beggar-and-gift-shop-studded sidewalk from the Palmerville Hilton to the New

Clapperton, walking in pairs for safety here in the heart of the Dark Continent, the girls and their eyes ran a gauntlet of visual inputs ranging from the sublime to the sick-making, each impression limned indelibly in those deep, wet kohl-rimmed orbs. At Abu Said's display window, the eyes would widen with cash-register delight at the offerings within: earrings and necklaces of multicolored semiprecious Kansdu stone, lions' teeth and leopard claws; elephant hair bracelets filigreed in gold for a quarter the price to be found anywhere in Europe or America; razor-sharp Turkana wrist knives for the libbers amongst them; letter and bottle openers fashioned from the tusks of warthogs; exotically carved elephant tusks; heavy, ironshod Waziri and Samburu war spears; delicate snuffboxes hand-hollowed from ivory nuts; wallets and change purses and handbags fashioned from the scrota of buffalo and rhino; gazelle-hide vests and jackets and cute little caps. . . .

Then, in the next glance, shuffling toward her on calloused stumps, his few brown teeth bared in a revolting, deathlike rictus, his leathery writhing monkey's paw extended in supplication, came old Wamatitu the beggar prince, gurgling in Kiswahili—and the girl's eyes would flash terror, desperately out of focus, the delicate feet dance either into the cool incense-scented interior of Abu Said's or on anxiously away, toward the next magnetic shop window. Treacle had timed it once. Each girl was granted precisely 1 minute and 32 seconds in the shade beneath the shop window before the beggars began their crablike advance. That was the deal they had with the shopkeepers. If the girl had not entered the shop in that space of time, the beggar's approach would either drive her through the door, or send her scuttling along to the next one. It was a sound business practice, and the beggars themselves received a share of the profits. Old Abu Said stood at the door, his gold teeth flashing in the dim, and nodded slyly to Treacle. Yes, 'twas a good year for tourism, this. As soon as he got his next check from *The News of the World* . . .

"How big is the stone?" asked Winjah.

"The Rokoff Diamond, mined by Nikolas Nikolaivitch Rokoff in 1961 at a site as yet undisclosed, but probably either in eastern Angola or western Kansdu, three hundred carats of the first water, a blue-white stone of unparalleled clarity, absolutely flawless as they say, valued at last reckoning—that would have been 1970—at four million pounds on the London market, or nearly twelve million dollars American."

Treacle had details like this at his fingertips. That's what being a journalist was all about.

"Be a lot more now, though, wouldn't it?"

"I expect so. Rumor is that Rokoff turned down ten million American for it shortly before the end of the Angolan war."

"Why would he do it?"

"He's quite mad, you know," answered Treacle. "Like his father before him, who played the Tsar's game throughout Central Africa before the Great War, skulduggery of all sorts, then continued after the Revolution on his own, out of sheer wanton perversity. Young Rokoff—he's not really so young anymore, of course, about sixty, I'd reckon—was shaped on the same last. Known as 'the Mad Russian' from Addis to Zimbabwe. His hand evident in nearly every major coup d'état or assassination—except for the CIA ones—from Mogadiscio to Mali. He simply resented the United Front and refused to knuckle under to them. A lone operator like Rokoff need not sell out to the Socialists, like Diamang did, or like Gulf is doing. He packed it in, and knowing he could never get the Big Stone out himself, decided to let it remain where he'd found it—with a bodyguard. The Diamond Bogo."

"How did he procure the buff?"

"His boys—pardon me, his 'men'—had it staked out somewhere in the bush, or at least knew its hangouts. It's a mean, smart sod, this bogo is. Wounded twice by safaris out of Zambia, I hear, and killed five professional hunters already. The latest was Mike Reilly; you knew him, didn't you?"

"Not much of a hunter."

"Well, Mike had a rich bitch from Brussels as a client. She liked to shoot light, nothing heavier than seven-mil magnum. Dropped a *dofu* that went eighty pounds the tusk with that peashooter, and figured that if she could kill elephant with it, why not a mere buff? Well, they stumbled on the Diamond Bogo up around the Tirika Swamp, quite unawares, and before Mike could stop her she'd put one through his paunch and he'd gone off into some high grass. The rich bitch insisted on going in with Mike, and when the bogo came out at them she simply froze. Mike got up ahead of her but before he could shoot, the bloody sod had him. The rich bitch ran out of there, and for the next half hour they could hear the bogo punching Mike through the thornbush, grunting and barking like, the boys said, and Mike screaming for someone to come in and kill the both of them, him and the bogo. But the boys had got the wind up and the rich bitch just sat in the truck slugging brandy. When they went in finally, Mike was in six pieces. The bloody bogo had eaten his face off, the boys said, and his family jewels to boot. All they brought back was his watch—that Rolex he was so proud of, you know? Still running nicely, I'm told. The boys said he was one hell of a bogo, sixty inches if he's a foot, with a boss on him like the bumper on a Bedford lorry. And that great bleeding stone there in the crotch of the boss, winkin' and flashin' like a great bloody star."

"Hard to swallow," said Winjah. "How in hell could that stone stay put, with all the pounding that a buffalo does with his head, just in routine living much less killing people?"

"Humm, huh, diddlediddle," said Treacle. "Krazy Glue. From America. It's so strong that if you get some on your finger and then go to pick your nose, you're stuck like that for life. Wouldn't mind a dab on the old hogsticker though, don't y'know, hmmm, hahhhh . . . but seriously, it's powerful stuff. The lads managed to shoot the bogo with a tranquilizer dart, and then Rokoff chipped out a seat between the horns for the Big Stone. They Krazy

Glued it in there, and I gather it's stuck for good. Rather like the unfortunate couple named Kelly, don't y'know? They always walked belly to belly, because in their haste they used library paste instead of petroleum jelly?"

"Yes," said Winjah, grinning now for the first time during the interview. As an incorrigible limericist, Treacle knew, Winjah could always be reached by means of a five-line stanza of Rabelaisian anapestic trimeter if not by reason. Treacle sensed that the time was right for the question that would make or break his story—and the immediate future of his sex life.

"Are you going after him, Bwana?"

"Wouldn't know where to begin," said Winjah, the gun-barrel eyes resuming their glint. "If Reilly wounded him three months ago in the Tirika, the bogo could be long dead by now, or else skipped across the border into Ethiopia. And as you well know, the last safari that went into Kansdu ended up in the cooking pots of the Tok. The country is virtually inaccessible by vehicle, and nobody wants to pay for a foot safari these days. Too bloody costly. God knows I've no desire to see that country again." Treacle remembered: Some fifteen years ago, Winjah had gone up into Kansdu on police business and come out on a litter, a Tok spear wound through his chest and fevered to the eyeballs. "No," Winjah continued, "I'm afraid Rokoff's Diamond Bogo is safe from me, safe indeed from any sane white hunter."

"But Bwana," Treacle pleaded, his eyes flashing helplessly at the parade of passing pulchritude, "couldn't I at least hint at it, in a story to *The News of the World*? I'm a bit short of funds, don't y'know, hummm, hah. Could be good publicity for the old firm, don't y'see. 'Bwana Winjah May Seek Diamond Bogo.' Big headlines. Lots of customers for next season. Mad Russian. Priceless Gem. Dauntless Pursuit. Mystery Tribesmen. It's got all the elements, Bwana."

Winjah leaned across the table again, and his eyes fixed Treacle as a snake might a mouse. The journalist shivered to his desert boots.

"If I pursue the Diamond Bogo," said Winjah slowly, "and I repeat—*if*—then the last thing in the world I want is publicity. That would bring hundreds of raving, gunslinging madmen from all over Europe and America into Kansdu, all out to beat me to the bogo. Not only would it ruin the last great hunting reserve in Africa, but it would certainly cost the lives of countless ill-prepared idiots as well. It would lead to the destruction, in the long run, of the Tok, who despite their savagery are still an admirable people, not to be mucked about by modern society. And if—my dear Treacle—if one single, solitary word concerning the Diamond Bogo, or my interest in it, should perchance leak from that poisonous pen of yours, I shall track you down just as surely as you're sitting here lusting after those innocent little girls out there on the sidewalk, yes, track you down and skin you out and dip your flayed testicles in a vat of spitting cobra venom. Understood?"

Treacle nodded weakly.

"By the way, old chap," said Winjah. "Here's that fifty quid I owe you. Sorry to have been so tardy in my recompense." He slipped a wad of bills under the journalist's saucer. "You'll take care of the beers, won't you? There's a good chap. Oh, let me introduce you to a friend of mine who's new in town." He waved to a lissome blonde hovering beside the mimosa tree at the entrance to the sidewalk café. The girl trotted over, all hip and honey. "Monika," said the hunter, "I want you to meet my good friend Tony, the best-connected man in all Palmerville. He's agreed to show you the night spots and even take you to the game park. He knows everything there is to know about Krazy Glue. I'm sure you'll love him as dearly as I do. And now, my children, I must be off to the airport. I've clients coming in from America."

Treacle watched the hunter amble over to his battered green Toyota Land Cruiser—the infamous Green Turd, as Winjah called the vehicle—and climb in beside his crew of fierce backcountry trackers. Then Treacle turned to the creamy, eager young lady beside him.

"Would you care to meet my friend Abu Said, the

merchant?" he asked. "Hmm, hahhh?" The girl rose
eagerly, wetting her lips with a slim pink tongue. Her eyes,
rimmed in heavy green shadow, fluttered (Treacle
thought) like the gold-winged diurnal bats that one met
betimes on the game trails of Kansdu. Her breasts
bounced as they walked past the legless, grinning, scabbed,
and gesticulate beggars toward the costly haven of Abu
Said's emporium. BIGGEST JUGS IN TOWN·

    "Diddlediddle," hummed Tony Treacle.

5
IT ALWAYS EXCITES

"I've sent two lorries on ahead with most of the staff," said Winjah. "They'll have set up our base camp by the time we arrive. I'm sure the memsahib will find it quite comfortable." He smiled winningly at Dawn. "King-sized cots, a hot shower, a separate loo for the gentle sex, a spacious mess tent replete with fridge and stereo. Hope you've brought along tapes to your own taste, by the way, as I'm partial to your American country-and-western music, and my modest library is dominated by it. By the way, I insist that Joseph, my majordomo, wear black tie every evening while serving dinner. Candles and wine, that sort of thing. Yet you need feel no compulsion to dress for dinner, as I don't."

Dawn smiled wanly in reply. She was wedged between Winjah and Donn on the front bench seat of the Green Turd as it bounced up the mountain south of Palmerville. Winjah had met them at the airport, whisked them

through customs and immigration, then into downtown
Palmerville for a sumptuous luncheon at Salandini's, the
capital's finest Italian restaurant. Salandini himself had
taken their order. Suave and sardonic, with a horrifically
scarred face that nonetheless retained a dark, almost evil
handsomeness, he was (he explained to her) a defrocked
priest who had turned to diamond prospecting until a lion
had rendered him *hors de combat* in the very forests they
would soon be hunting around Lake Tok. Cannibalism
had been rife in the region back then. Once he had
stumbled on a village below the scarps of the Kan River
where fully five varieties of human meat, mainly
missionary, were for sale.

"American, English, Swiss, and German were retailing
for ten shillings the pound," he said, staring straight into
her eyes. "Italian, however, was double that price. The
meat looked no different, one nationality from the
other—it was all slightly green and dreadfully
fly-blown—so I asked the butcher why so high a price for
the Italian. 'Did you ever try to clean one?' he replied."
Salandini slapped the table with his palm so that the silver
rattled, and Bucky practically choked with laughter on his
fettucini, then grabbed a cheap notebook from his hip
pocket to scribble an entry with his well-chewed Bic. Dawn
dabbed her lips with a none-too-clean napkin and set her
silver aside for the nonce. Her vitello Kansdu had worn an
ominous gloss of iridescent green from the outset.

Right now, as the G.T. clanked and snarled its way up
the mountain road, she was grimly aware of the veal's
continuing activity in her still-delicate stomach, and even
more aware of the sheer cliffs that fell away from the
crumbling edges of the road. The corrugated-steel roofs
of Palmerville glinted toylike below them in the westering
sun, while beyond, to the north, stretched a waste of high
desert—dun and thorn-dotted as far as the eye could see.
Winjah himself seemed to pay no attention to the road, his
right hand resting on the steering wheel as loosely as if it
were steering him rather than vice versa. "The G.T. knows
the way," he laughed as he noticed her apprehension. His

left hand grasped the knob of the floor-mounted
gearshift, stirring it constantly in response to the gradient's
demands. Because of the narrowness of the truck's front
seat, Dawn had to spread her knees on either side of the
shift column. Fortunately she had taken the opportunity to
change from her soiled travel skirt into a smart set of
Abercrombie & Fitch slacks in the ladies' room at
Salandini's, but nonetheless she could feel her labia twitch
anxiously each time Winjah's hand came slamming back in
that direction atop the shift knob. The heel of his hand
always halted a few scant millimeters short of the
vulnerable target. He seemed well practiced in the art.
Donn, still groggy, stared out the window at the awesome
mountains, oblivious to her pudendal peril.

    Blackrod sat up in the open behind the G.T.'s cab on a
wooden bench with the trackers, dozing off from time to
time with his load of jet lag and fettucini, then snapping
awake with a start to blink wonderingly at the bright, deep,
gaudy country around them. The trackers giggled. The
big fat bwana snored like a gut-shot *fisi.* Yet when he
worked the sleep from his eyes, they noticed that he had a
good grasp of game.

    "*N'giri,*" Blackrod said, pointing to a family of
warthogs scuttling buglike up a distant brush-choked
draw.

    "*N'dio,* Bwana," they chuckled.

    "*N'dofu?*" he asked, pointing to a huge mound of
droppings on a game trail nearly a mile up the mountain
road ahead of them.

    "*Hapana,* Bwana," they said, denying that it was
elephant dung. "*Mafi ya kifaru.*" Rhino.

    "*Kubwa sana,*" said Bucky. "Very big."

    "'*Dio,* hah, hah." Their laughter indicated that
everything in this country was very big. The trackers liked
Blackrod already. Not only did he have good eyes and a
willingness to speak Swahili, but he smelled good, too. It
was a strange odor to the boys. The *tumbaco* they could
identify from his cigarettes, but the sickly sweat of too
much whiskey was alien to their subtle noses. They knew

the smell of *pombe,* the native beer, but not of spirits. At any rate, the total effect of Blackrod, nasally at least, was strong, and of that the trackers approved. Any man who smelled weak was not a man, and those men who smelled of flowers and spice were doubtless women.

Blackrod concurred. In the course of more than twenty years' travel through the more remote corners of the planet, he had developed a deep affection for wild places and wilder men. The killing grounds were his favorite haunts—any deer camp, any grouse cover, any battlefield. He loved the stink of gunpowder and the sweet smell of blood, even the harsh, puke-provoking whiff of opened guts. He enjoyed the way men and other animals smelled when they had been long in the woods: smoky, acrid, sharp with the reek of grease and sweat and rotting leaves. By contrast the clean airs constantly moving through open country tasted infinitely sweeter. It was the extremes of sensation, he mused as he inhaled the odors of rancid fat, unwashed human hide, dust, running water, crushed thorn, exhaust fumes, stale snuff, sun, and rhino shit, that justified, finally, the entire, moderate midrange in which men lived most of their lives. At first, though, Africa came on very strong indeed. His own introduction to the continent, a decade earlier, had been so upsetting that he spent the first two days sprawled in a bathtub at the New Stanley Hotel in Nairobi, keeping the water unconsciously but precisely at the temperature of amniotic fluid, afraid to be born into the reality of Africa. Finally he had emerged, a huge wrinkled washerwoman's finger, to poke at the rot and the sun.

Africa was different. It bestrode the equator, a suntanned Colossus. The sun pounded down on this huge landmass, the second largest on the planet, and the sun made changes. The vast weight of its energy, more powerful in a single instant than all the hydrogen bombs in the human arsenal, worked constantly—altering life-forms even as it altered landforms. It scorched the world's largest desert, the Sahara, and fed the world's strongest jungles. It melted the ice from the peaks of the Ruwenzori and Kilimanjaro and sent it coursing down the great rivers—the Congo, the Nile, the Zambesi. It spawned the rain that fed the Niger, the Tana, the Senegal. It made Africa the Bright Continent—not the Dark one they used to write about, before they knew how great and horrible and wonderful it was.

And now I'm hooked, he thought happily. What a marvelous addiction. Why in the hell should I ever go back? I'm sick of that world back there—a world of failed marriages, eroding values, bucks and bosses. I've probably earned half a million dollars in my working career, and I'm worth about the price of a ticket to the Knicks game. Taxes, alimony, booze sucked up the rest. I haven't owned a car in five years, a house in fifteen. My only really close companion is the Guinea worm. He peeked at his leg surreptitiously, hoping that perhaps the worm had its head out. It would probably enjoy the scenery, if it had eyes. Which he doubted.

Anyway, Africa was his Holy Land—his Golden Fleece, his Grail, his Land of Milk and Honey—and Blood and Smoke and Fiery Sun. Here, he knew, he could find the redemption that had eluded him in the civilized world, even if that redemption was death. He felt the Guinea worm writhe pleasurably in his thigh under the scratch of light and heat and anticipation.

The G.T. had wound along the northern lip of the Kansdu Range, heading east toward a pass that crossed the mountains just below the Great Tirika Swamp. Mount Baikie loomed to the left, fully twelve thousand feet tall, its icy skullcap haloed with turbulent, purple-black clouds, its shoulders humped with bamboo and glinting with runoff. Gerenuk browsed on the thorn in the dry river edges, giraffelike antelopes with huge dark eyes, the males with their short backward-curved horns looking as vulnerable as the hornless females—standing erect in the spiny foliage, forefeet braced against the trunk, munching mouthfuls of needle-sharp wood and bitter leaves. *Lithocranius walleri,* Blackrod thought. They drink no water.

He slammed his hand hard on the roof of the G.T.'s cab.

"Yes, Bwana," said Winjah, halting the truck and leaning out with a cherubic smile.

"How about that *swala twiga* back there?"

"He was good enough. We'll see better farther on, but we need meat for the *kampi*."

"I'll take him," said Buck. He might as well get over the first bloodletting as soon as possible. It was always a baptism. The trackers twitched and quivered like gun dogs as they leaped from the truck bed. Blackrod fell in behind the leader, a tall, almost frail-appearing Dorobo named Lambat, who carried the 7-mm. magnum Schultz & Larson. They walked in single file, crouched, shuffling along stiff-legged for speed and bent-backed for cover, to within two hundred yards of the gerenuk buck singled out for slaughter. Groucho Marx on a murder mission, thought Blackrod. He almost laughed, but the lads would not approve. He could feel the seriousness of the stalk vibrating off them in great wicked waves. This was death they intended. It always excites.

At the edge of a tall gray boulder he dropped to his haunches, then to a sitting position. Lambat handed him the rifle. The gerenuk was alert now, standing foursquare beneath the tree on which it had been feeding. Its large eyes studied the rock face for movement. Blackrod waited until it turned its head to search for its does, then brought the rifle to his shoulder. He wound the sling around his forearm and placed his elbows slowly, ever so slowly, on his knees. The image through the four-power Redfield scope was flat but clear at this range: The big black eyes focused bulbously in their direction, the ruddy brown hide of the antelope grainy on the field. Blackrod laid the tip of the post on the gerenuk's shoulder and began his squeeze.

At the shot, Dawn thrust her pelvis forward involuntarily. Her box slapped once, lightly, against Winjah's wrist. He turned and smiled.

"Nice shot," he said. "We'll have meat for the pot tonight."

Bucky felt something tickle the back of his knee. Looking down, he saw the Guinea worm. He smiled at it.

b
BUCKY'S UNDERPANTS

"*Seku yake na kwisha,*" said Lambat. "His day has come."

The gerenuk lay on its side, its inky eyes taking the glaze of death, one leg still kicking feebly. Blackrod reached for the .22 magnum rifle to finish it, but then decided not to waste the bullet: The animal was done, all right.

"I wonder what he sees," said Donn. He had come up from behind with his Nikon to film the death scene. "It must be frightening, these skinny upright figures on two legs coming toward him. Probably never seen men this close before." He leaned in close on the unfocused eyes and clicked the shutter. "His last sight on earth: a man taking his picture." Donn's voice was doleful.

Lambat grabbed the buck by a horn and slit its throat with his hunting knife. The halal. There were Moslems on the staff, and unless the animal was bled before it died they could not eat of the flesh. Blackrod cupped his hand and filled it with some of the slackly flowing blood, then lapped up a mouthful.

"Could be dangerous, Bwana," warned Winjah. "They carry a lot of parasites."

"You have to taste the first blood," said Bucky. "At least we always do back home. Anyway, I've got plenty of tetracycline."

The first blood was very important to Blackrod. At the age of twelve, his father had taken him deer hunting in northern Wisconsin. They stood in the tamaracks beside a confluence of trails until a young spike buck happened by. With his father whispering encouragement and calm into his ear, young Bucky had dropped the spike with one shot from his 30-30 Winchester, dropped it kicking and eye-rolling at a range of nearly a hundred yards. Then his father had opened the deer's gut, cut loose the bladder, and spilled the blood and urine all over Bucky's beardless face.

"I don't know why we do this," his father said, "but we've always done it this way with the first deer a man kills. I suspect it's a reminder of some sort. That you don't kill lightly. That what you've killed was alive and hot and full of piss, just like you, the hunter. I hope you'll remember this all your life."

Standing there in the freezing woods, with the stink of cooling deer piss in his nostrils, tasting it on his lips, shaking with the letdown of the kill and the shock of the baptism, Bucky figured he never would. He could do without the urine, but from that day on he always tasted the blood of the first animal he killed in any hunting season, or on any long hunting trip. The mysticism of it no longer reached him in the form of the shakes, but rather in a warm memory of his father, and of all those other fathers down through time who had taught their sons what it was to kill. A sadness that tasted of blood.

Back at the truck, Dawn was giggling on the edge of hysteria. She pointed to Blackrod's bush shorts. He had pulled them on over a pair of white boxer underpants, and with the crouching required by the stalk the outer shorts had hiked up, so that now the wrinkled legs of his undershorts were showing.

"You looked so silly," laughed Dawn. "So serious, so stealthy, and so silly with your little white flags showing. 'I see London, I see France, I see Bucky's underpants.' "

"I guess you should go bare ass from now on, Bwana," said Winjah, laughing along with the rest of them. "Selous hunted that way, with just a long-tailed shirt and a pair of veldschoens. The looser you hang, the tighter you shoot."

The echoes of the shot that had slain the gerenuk rolled out over the mountains, reverberating from bamboo slopes and lichen-clad cliffs, spreading and diminishing as it climbed, filling the quiet air with—finally—just a shiver of noise, a hollow, fading thump. The backwash of the shot rolled down, finally, like waning surf at the far side of a sandbar, into the Great Tirika Swamp.

Butterflies roused to the echo. They lifted from the piles of buffalo dung on which they had fed and rested, swirling briefly in a spin of purples, golds, and reds. Not a breath of air stirred in the glade. Bees hummed busily through the piles of dung, sucking up sustenance and looking for color. A swarm of bees hovered over a bright spot hidden in the tall, saw-edged grass at the far end of the glade—a brightness that changed color slowly, as the sun moved across its faceted face. As the dim thump passed through the glade, passed over and under and whirled its way through the glade, the bright spot grew suddenly agitated. A pair of ears, hung with ticks as juicy as grapes, perked to the sound. A pair of piggy bloodshot eyes blinked under the gleaming boss. The Diamond Bogo, his hide bald beneath its coating of swamp mud, rose to a kneeling position. His shiny nostrils flexed to suck the air. The faintest molecule of gunpowder tickled its way up his nose. His tiny brain read the message.

He rose to his great, splayed, two-toed feet.

He moaned once, and the sharp black horns quivered.

7
CLICKRASP

Clickrasp. The sound, bent by the wind, attenuated over those long thorny hills, their backs broken by the eons, reached the merest hair atop the pointed ears of the listener. The ears peaked.

Q'lueq . . .

He rose from his haunches. His lips widened in a smile. His eyes, aquamarine in color, brightened and crinkled.

Wide eyes, heavily lashed, an extreme intelligence. *Grassp'h.*

Clickrasp the Tok had awakened.

8
WHITE LEGS

"The Big Rockcandy Mountain," said Winjah, halting the G.T. at the top of the ridge. "How do you like it?"

Below them the country fell away and opened out into a broad savanna, framed on the north and west by the mountains over which they had passed. Jebels rose from the plain, the stubs of older, long-since-eroded mountains, poking through the decomposed lava of the basin like the calcified fingers of a giant. At the base of the tallest jebel lay their camp, convenient to one of the few springs that watered this semiarid land. Herds of zebra, impala, kongoni, and wildebeest circulated through the yellow grass. The western edge of the plain was cut by the River Kan, a fast, strong, mottled python of a stream that drained the slopes of Mount Baikie and spilled, finally, into Lake Tok far to the south. Across the river rose the scarps—three thousand feet high—that protected the Tok Plateau. Seen in this late afternoon light, the plateau itself was a haze of dark green, blotched by clouds and swirling with backlit mists.

"It's a grand country," said Donn. "How long will we stay here?"

"A week at least," said Winjah. "Long enough to get toughened up for the Tok Plateau. We'll have to walk in. No track for the poor G.T."

"Who lives here?"

"There's a Samburu *manyatta* tucked away in the northern end of the plain, just below the Tirika Swamp. And up on the plateau, of course, there are the Tok."

"The what?" asked Dawn.

"We'll get around to them later," said Winjah. "Right now let's get down to our lovely little kampi. I'm feeling a bit peckish, and I'm sure the memsahib could use a hot shower and a bit of the old kip."

The jebel under which the camp was pitched rose a full thousand feet above the surrounding plain. Its name, in Samburu, was Naibor Keju, which meant "White Legs." As they drove down toward it, they speculated as to the derivation.

"It isn't remotely white," said Winjah, "more of a dirty gray at best."

"And there's only the one shaft of rock," added Donn. "Why 'Legs'?"

"Maybe if you look at it from another angle," suggested Dawn.

"I'd much prefer to study the white legs of the fair Dawn woman," said Winjah. "Never much for geology, I must say."

Dawn blushed and Donn gritted his teeth. He'd read about white hunters and their ways with female clients. Donn was used to men bird-dogging his wife—she was, after all, quite beautiful—but as far as he knew she had never succumbed to their advances. Still, Winjah was more man than any of the others. Rattling along in the Green Turd, rolling his eyes and singing "North to Alaska" in a perfect Johnny Horton drawl, Winjah nonetheless conveyed a sense of murderous, grave purpose—he was a killer and a cocksman, no doubt about it. And who the hell were the Tok?

The green tents of the camp were pitched in such a way as to look out over the game plain to the River Kan and the Tok Plateau. Africans in freshly starched green uniforms bustled about as the G.T. pulled in, uttering their shy "Jambos" and offering their limp calloused paws in friendly handshakes as Winjah made the introductions. Bucky lurched out of the back of the truck, his nose glowing red with sunburn, and begged for a beer.

In the mess tent, tea was already laid. Joseph, the majordomo, was a grave and grizzled Waziri who had been in Winjah's service for nearly a quarter of a century. His demeanor would have befitted a maitre d' at the Plaza or the George V or the Villa d'Este. He was far kindlier than anyone at Brown's Hotel. Or so Donn thought: Had he the magical wherewithal to wade through any given week of Joseph's early manhood, he would have drowned in blood. Dawn excused herself and went to the shower tent.

"Our own little nightclub," sighed Winjah as he sipped a steaming mug of Earl Grey tea thick with milk and unrefined sugar. "I call it the M'Bogo a Go Go. *Regardez!*" For the first time Donn noticed the buffalo skull mounted against the tent pole supporting the far wall of the cubicle. The boss of the horns swept out and downward to either side of a bone-white "part" like some sinister parody of a 1920s hairdo, then curved outward and upward, thinning to black gleaming points. The nose bone and skull were bleached beneath the horns, while the empty eye sockets—big around as cannon holes—glared balefully into the tent. Small spiders, metallic green and bronze, hung in their webs, spun from the craggy ridges of the eye sockets. The spiders were sitting off center in the sockets, and their glint—as Donn's eyes grew accustomed to the aquatic gloom of the tent's interior—gave the buffalo a mad, slightly cockeyed look.

"Kee-ripes!" exclaimed Bucky, blowing the foam from his third mug of Tusker's. "How big does he go?"

"Fifty-five inches measured across the outermost

curve of the horns," said Winjah, "by eighteen across the thickest reach of the boss. And he was a young'un."

"Where did you take him?"

"Up there." Winjah gestured carelessly through the mosquito netting toward the Tok Plateau, over which the late afternoon sky had now begun to boil with rain clouds under the thrust of a reddening sun. "That was fifteen years ago. I believe that I was the last white hunter in there. At least, there have been no safaris to return from the plateau since then."

"So we'll find buff at least this big up there still?" asked Bucky.

"I should imagine so."

"And just who are these Tok?" asked Donn.

"In the fullness of time, Bwana Donn. In the fullness of time." Winjah rose and finished his tea. "Right now I must see to the kampi, make sure my loyal lads have met with their harsh but evenhanded Bwana's every demand—like remembering to bring along the cookstove, etc. After the fair mem is finished with her *bathi,* just give Joseph a holler and he'll have the hot-water bucket replenished."

While Blackrod showered—Donn had insisted as subtly as possible that perhaps the Big Bucko would enjoy a wash far more than he—Donn walked out behind the camp and studied the jebel called White Legs. Brush-clad for the first third of its height, the ancient rock then bared itself to the waning light—a browning red, like dried blood, veined darkly with crevices filled with small shrubs and rubble. Eagles and a few vultures, drawn by the gerenuk which the boys were butchering just now at the skinner's tent, turned on the ground wave high overhead. He heard a faint barking from the upper reaches of the jebel and, peering closely, spotted a half dozen scuttling black figures leaping from knob to knob. Baboons. He fetched his Orvis 7x40 binoculars and a copy of Dorst and Dandelot's *Field Guide to the Larger Mammals of Africa* from his pack, then focused on the apes. Judging from size and the diagnostic "broken" tails, they were anubis baboons—the largest and most widely distributed of these strong and sociable primates. Up to ninety pounds in weight and nearly four feet long, they were fierce fighters, capable of a highly effective group defense against their most common enemy, the leopard. Or so it said in the book.

Donn, leaning back against a termite hill, watched them through the glass. This was evidently a "play group" of youngsters, watched over by their mothers. They gamboled and frolicked like kindergartners, squabbling in high-pitched yelping voices, retreating when the going got too rough to the shaggy dugs of their mothers, then venturing forth again to pinch and poke and gnaw on their pals. Donn felt his heart jump as one or another of the young primates came dangerously close to falling—it would be a hundred yards straight down, a high price for a misstep. But the baboons always kept their balance, and gradually he grew bored with their cliff-hanging excesses.

A faint familiar odor now reached his nostrils from the direction of the skinner's tent. He sniffed. Dope. Well, I'll be darned! Sauntering down that way, he noted that the smell grew stronger as the voices of the Africans grew jollier and more agitated. Sure enough, when he turned the corner of the tent they were hunkered down around the pile of red meat, toking heartily on a banana-sized joint wrapped in newspaper. Donn sniffed as they looked up at him, then smiled broadly and rolled his eyes in the universal sign of hungry approbation. Otiego, the lean Turkana tracker, grinned back and, pretending he didn't know what Donn wanted, handed him a slab of gerenuk meat, raw and dripping. When Donn recoiled in mock horror, the lads all laughed. Otiego passed the joint, and Donn, suppressing a faint revulsion at the saliva-slippery business end of the rolled newspaper, took a deep hit. How do you say "Don't Bogart that joint" in Kiswahili? he wondered. The smoke hit him hard, spreading his already travel-weary head back over the entire route they had followed, and on out to the Tok Plateau. Otiego rolled another and they smoked, giggling.

"*Bhangi,*" said the African, his blocky white teeth flashing within those thin purple lips. "*Muzuri sana.*" Between hits, he wolfed down strips of raw meat, the blood oozing down his chin, onto his scarred and naked chest. Donn looked away, waiting for the bomber to come around again.

The Tok Plateau now lay dark under the shadow of distant mountains. Strange shapes seemed to move along its lumpy silhouette. Donn felt a chill up his backbone. The rest of the boys had drifted away to the cookfire. Otiego lay back against a peeled thorn log, stoned to the eyeballs. Donn could hear Winjah and Bucky talking over the strains of a Merle Haggard tape in the M'Bogo à Go Go, their voices faint and falsely vivacious, it seemed to him, over the dark mood the bhangi had inspired. Then, suddenly, a piteous scream ricocheted down from the jebel. Whirling around, Donn raised the binoculars and scanned the rock face. Was it Dawn?

High atop the jebel, bathed in a final plasmic light, a large dark figure held a smaller, squirming one at arm's length before it. The large figure stood erect. It had pointed ears. Light flashed on polished stone. The scream, rising to urgency, died short. Focusing the glasses with fumbling fingers, Donn zeroed in. He watched in horror as the pointy-eared creature spooned brains from the open skull of the baby baboon, then hurled the limp carcass into the darkness below. Just as the line of dying sunlight rose above the murderer, it caught a wink of bright green eyes, huge eyes that seemed to bulge their way down the lenses of the binoculars and burn deep into Donn's own. He shook uncontrollably—wracked by dope and weariness and horror—and the scene shivered out of focus. The killer had white legs and a hard-on.

9
KING OF THE DEADWOOD STAGE

For the next five days they hunted out from White Legs, toughening up for the difficult trek to the high plateau across the Kan. The horses and donkeys that would pack the party and its gear into the high country would not be brought up from Palmerville until the last possible moment, to avoid the risk of tsetse fly infection. They saw few of the swift, ugly little cross-winged killers, but those that appeared were vicious. This was the southern reach of their local range, Winjah explained. Up in the Tirika Swamp they were thick as midges. Indeed, the word "Tirika" in the Tok dialect meant "Crap in Your Hand"—whenever a man squatted to defecate the flies zoomed in to bite, and the resultant slaps produced the native name.

The early morning hours were devoted to bird shooting, over one or another of the springs in the vicinity. Rising in the predawn gloom, awakened by the yammering baboon colony which served as a natural alarm clock, they gulped quick cups of steaming tea in the dew-dank mess tent and then piled into the G.T. for the bouncing, shivering ride to the birds. The best spot was the Maji Moto, a hot spring just twenty minutes from camp. Thick mists cloaked the ground at that early hour. The tufted tops of doum palms reached up from a faintly sulfurous shroud like clenched fists. Walking in one morning through the hot fog, they jumped a rhino cow and her calf on one of the many broad, well-trampled game trails that served as spokes to the Maji Moto's life-giving hub. Through the distorting mist, the rhinos loomed like saurian holdovers from the Jurassic Age.

"Faro!" hissed Lambat, who was in the lead, carrying one of the twenty-gauge Beretta over-and-unders. He raised it to his shoulder. They all crouched.

The mother rhino loomed ahead of them through the mist. They could see her horns casting sideways as her nostrils sucked at the fog. She moaned and chuffed. The baby, a giant piglet, butted at her teats. Whiffs of barn smell reached their noses.

"Look for the nearest tree," whispered Winjah. "That popgun will only tickle her the wrong way."

"I couldn't see a tree if it was growing out my nose," hissed Bucky.

"Then pray," said Winjah.

Donn concentrated on his third eye, hoping perhaps it could penetrate the fog.

But the rhinos went away, finally, splashing off through the hot water and clattering up a ridge to disappear into the gray miasma, which itself quickly evaporated under the hot hand of the rising sun. Then came the birds—sand grouse and ring-necked doves by the tens of thousands, skimming in low from the surrounding deserts in clusters of as many as a hundred at a time. Some actually landed at the edges of the spring to drink; others merely hovered on backed wings, sipping downward from the air, and filling their neck feathers with water, then flashing away again into the wasteland.

"The males soak their throat feathers to give drink to the nestlings," Winjah explained.

The shooting was fast and chaotic at first. Standing under widely separated thorn trees, which served as partial blinds, Donn and Bucky flailed frantically at the sky with their charges of No. 8 shot, hitting only perhaps one bird in every five shots. Neither of them had shot at flighted birds in quite these numbers before. Growing up on ruffed grouse and woodcock, pheasant and mourning dove, they were used to singles and doubles, jumped up and away from them, or else passing swift and solitary in the cold American air. Here the very abundance of birds served as a defense. That and the heat, the exotic circumstances. Finally the futile pounding of the gun butts taught a lesson: Concentrate on one bird at a time, swing with him and through him, slap the trigger, then pick another target. Soon the sand grouse were puffing and breaking to the patterns, corkscrewing down or spilling tip over tail to thud on the sodden earth, all awry-eyed and dead.

"Behind you, Bwana!" yelled Winjah.

Bucky wheeled and saw a pair of sand grouse skimming in low over the filigree of spikes, mounted the gun as he tracked and hit the trigger. Nothing. The safety was on. He cleared it, still tracking, and folded the first bird with the gun nearly overhead, then kept following the second, bending backward, backward—*pow!* The bird crumpled and fell. Bucky too—flat on his back.

"The classic high passing shot!" whooped Winjah. "The Classic Safety On At First High Passing Fall On Your Arse Double! Oh, Bwana, I love it!"

Prowling the White Legs country, Donn and Bucky took turns riding shotgun on the Deadwood Stage. That's what they called the G.T. when they came on guinea fowl or francolin or yellow-necked spur fowl and the man up behind the cab of the truck got to shoot them on the run. These were frantic chases, particularly after the guineas which scuttled like scatbacks, weaving slate black through the bush, leading the truck through kidney-squashing

leaps and slides around the ubiquitous ant bear and
warthog holes, down rock-filled nullahs and over sand
washes that bogged the tires and slammed the gunner
gut-first onto the hot metal of the roof. At first Donn
would not shoot until the birds flushed from their run, an
event that occurred only rarely since the truck usually fell
far behind after the first ten minutes. It was his sense of
sportsmanship. But then he realized that the chase itself
was sporting, that his chances—from a bucking truck bed
at thirty miles an hour—of hitting a bird that dodged and
cut behind rocks and brush were slimmer than if it flew.
Once he accepted that fact, he felt the quick-draw instincts
return, the ability to align gun and target in a blurred
microsecond that suddenly came to focus, so quickly that
the image was gone before it reached his consciousness,
but not before he had hit the trigger and the bird had
tumbled dead to the shot. After that, Donn was Top Gun
of the Deadwood Stage.

At night, though, he wasn't so certain. Sitting around
the campfire over whiskey and port, with the jackals
yipping in the dark beyond the yellow tongues and the
smell of stale blood drifting up from the skinner's tent, he
felt quite small in this vastness. The adrenaline had
retreated to its cave in the bottom of his stomach. Dim
shapes moved in his mind, memories of baboon death on
the cliff face. He had not mentioned the incident to
Winjah and the others, not even to Dawn. Just another
hallucination, like so many he had experienced in his drug
years. But at night, waking for a pee, walking to the door
of the tent, he had seen things out there—things that bore
no resemblance to the creatures of the day. Probably just
hyenas like those that ripped each night at the carcass of
the zebra Blackrod had killed the first day, a pin-striped
Grévy's stallion blasted flat in its nobility by the heavy .375
solid at three hundred yards. Winjah had hung the
skinned carcass to draw lions, and a few had appeared, but
mainly hyenas that squalled and farted and drowned out
Bucky's snoring—a welcome thing. Probably just hyenas
that couldn't get to the meat. But still . . .

He walked out and peed into the starlight. When he came back to the tent, Dawn was awake.

"What is it?" she asked.

"Nothing," he said, sliding into the wide cot beside her. "Just hyenas working that zebra carcass. I wish Winjah would cut it down and then maybe we could get some sleep."

"It scared me at first," she said, "hearing them snarl and rip out there. But now it doesn't bother me anymore."

"It bothers me," he said after a while. "Intimations of mortality, to paraphrase Wordsworth." She laughed and snuggled against him.

"He killed that zebra for its hide," Donn continued. "I couldn't kill a zebra to save my life. It's too much like a horse. Hell, I couldn't kill anything. It's mean, it's wrong, it's cruel."

"You kill the birds well enough," Dawn said.

"That's different. It's like skeet, back at the club. And anyway they're good eating."

"Well, you can kill me anytime you want to," she said. "In your own particular way. The little death, isn't that what they call it?"

He gave her a taste of the little death.

10
THE ROPE OF GOD

To the west, the country gradually descended, drying as it fell. Dongas choked with whistling thorn wound down from the height of land. Salt flats and soda lakes shimmered, pink and white, in the midday mirage. No tire tracks marred this deep sink, just the ancient troughs of game trails, filled with a powdery dust that filled the sinuses and tickled the eyes. A few small herds of Beisa oryx trotted off ahead of the truck, stopping only at a safe distance to look back.

"There," said Winjah, braking the G.T. "You see before you the source of the unicorn myth." On a low rise to their right, outlined against a milky backdrop, an oryx bull posed amidst his *hareem*. The *dume* was immediately distinguishable by his greater bulk, his thick horselike neck and shoulders. He had only one horn, a yard long at least and nearly straight, curved just a bit like a black saber. His mulish ears twitched and peaked as he studied them. "The males frequently lose a horn in the mating battles," said Winjah. "As they are almost always seen at too great a distance for proper observation, it's easy to imagine that the horn grows from the center of the skull." He opened and then slammed the door of the truck. At the sound, the bull turned and galloped away with a bucketing gait. His hareem followed sedately.

"I've got one on my license, don't I?" asked Bucky.

"Yes," said Winjah, "but we'll take him later. The deeper we penetrate the desert, the larger the oryx." He grinned at Dawn. "We'll stake out the fair beldame here as bait. The unicorn is said to go weak-kneed in the presence of a virgin."

In the midst of the desert, toward sunset, they came on a lone jebel rising like a rotten fang beside a soda lake. Donn, who was riding in back with the trackers, thumped on the roof of the cab, their signal that he wanted to stop for a photograph.

"Let's give it a few minutes," he said. "We'll have some dynamite light pretty soon. What the hell is that thing?"

Winjah wheeled up to the jebel, which rose nearly a hundred feet above the flat desert floor, pink now in the waning light and bloodred near its peak.

"Actually it's the stub of an old mountain," Winjah said. "But I'm sure the Samburu have some mystical explanation for it. See all the graffiti scribbled on the shaft?" Stick figures, crude stylizations of game animals (among them an elephant, or perhaps a mammoth), and wavy squiggles, all done in ocher, adorned the granite pillar. Winjah asked Machyana what they meant. The young Samburu told the story shyly, ducking his head from time to time as if everyone knew the tale to begin with. The other Africans listened and nodded wisely.

"He says this used to be the Rope of God," Winjah translated. "The sky was much lower then than it is in these evil times, and God—Ngai as they call Him—was quite close to the earth in those days, much closer to man. The Samburu, Masai, and Wandorobo were one people back then, and they all grazed their cattle here. The country was greener, too, and there was much game. Now and then, though, the lions and hyenas would grow too numerous for the people to protect their cattle, or else the Tok would come down from Kansdu, drive the cattle away, and eat the people. That was when the Rope of God came in handy.

"From it flowed milk and blood in quantities as rich and copious as the people extracted from their own herds. In bad times, the Rope of God kept them alive. Ngai had made it clear, however, that this was only an emergency service, offered out of friendship, and not to be abused. One day, though, a Dorobo who had lost his cattle to the Tok got to thinking. If all that milk and blood flowed through the Rope of God, then there must be plenty of cattle up in the sky. He climbed the rope and found great herds grazing amongst the clouds. They were beautiful cattle, red and white, and the clouds were spun of milk and blood. And the whole of heaven smelled of it. He went to Ngai and asked him for the loan of some of these heavenly cattle, promising that he would replace them once they had calved and replenished his own herd. Ngai said sorry, he couldn't help the Dorobo. The cattle must remain in the sky, else there could be no clouds or sunset. The Dorobo must make his own way on the earth.

"Angered, the Dorobo climbed back down the rope, took his simi, and cut the Rope of God. Great floods of blood and milk cascaded over the land, and the Rope itself, severed now, flailed like a beheaded python, thrashing away the grass and the cattle and the game. Then the Rope shriveled up, rising into the sky and taking the sky along with it. Contact with God was lost forever, and the Dorobo and his kinfolk from that time on were forbidden to keep cattle. God allowed them only to herd bees. Bees, he says, are their only cattle."

Machyana laughed and nodded shyly as the hunter finished his translation. Lambat, the Dorobo, smiled proudly as Donn posed him, spear and sword in hand, beside the stub that was once the Rope of God. Off in the distance, a single saddle-billed stork padded slowly through the mud puddle—all that remained of that cataclysmic flood.

"A beautiful story," said Donn.

"Yes," Winjah replied, "but don't get carried away too easily by African romance. This spot, in more recent years, was a way station on the slaving route from the interior to Mombasa. I once met an old man, a true Swahili, who had been through here many times. The Tok would come down from the hills to buy slaves to eat. The slavers had them chained to the base of the Rope of God—there, see the rusty bolts protruding? The slavers marked the choicer cuts with chalk, so much for a tender buttock, so much for a juicy arm. The head, though, was the most expensive, as the Tok like brains better than lean meat. This old Swahili slaver waxed quite nostalgic as he recalled the good old days. 'Plenty food, plenty women,' he said. 'Beautiful.' "

They camped that night beside the Rope of God, and after dinner they sipped brandy around the campfire and admired the play of firelight on the ochered stone. Donn worked on his notes. "Paradise Lost," he wrote. "I can see now the source of Bucky's fascination with Africa. It lies in the contrast of sheer ugliness with unbearable beauty, of real death with undying legend. I didn't think he was that poetic, but he still has a lot to learn about the niceties. This is no Lindblad Tour." He paused. "Though it certainly is comfortable."

That night, Bucky woke with the fever. Shivering and sweating in alternate waves, he managed to light the candle beside his bed. Outside he could hear the African night scratching and tearing in time to the chattering of his teeth. He threw back the covers and listened while the ache spread down his neck and spinal column. When it reached his lower legs, he felt the Guinea worm move. He waited.

The Guinea worm emerged below his left ankle. It waved its pointy head at the candle flame and slithered farther, farther into the open air. Bucky could see it shiver to the exposure, or perhaps it was merely reverberating in time to his own shakes. Just before its tail cleared his skin, the Guinea worm rose to its full length—two feet at least—and swayed its cobra dance one last time. Bucky was too weak to grab it. It seemed to him in his fever that the Guinea worm was waving good-bye. He wanted to shake its hand.

Then the Guinea worm fell away and Bucky dropped into a sleep full of horror.

11
THE ORPHANED COLT

In the fever dream, Buck and his buddies were stalking
the giant Abyssinian forest impala. It moved ahead of
them through a dingle that darkened to their every step.
Now and then they caught glimpses of its roan back,
bulging and warped as the muscles flowed red in the
scattered light, like some huge deflating medicine ball that
rolled ahead of them through the jungle. Once it stood
looking back over its shoulder. Its neck, twisted at
attention, seemed far too slim for the massive body
beneath it, or the massive head above, the eyes too large
for the foxy face. Between its lyrelike horns grew a smaller
rack—resembling that of a starved Virginia
whitetail—spread like a poor man's Christmas tree.
   "Quick," said Winjah. "Take him."
   At the shot, the guard hairs on the ram's neck puffed
and flew, but he did not go down. Instead he lurched off
into the dim wood. They followed, slowly, their feet leaden

with the gumbo of Buck's nightmare. Then the thorn forest thinned and they came to the edge of a lumberyard.

The trail led through the fence, past tall piles of fresh-sawed cedar as bright as the blood itself, almost as sweet.

"You'll have to track him out on your own," Winjah said. He looked at his watch. "I have to go. Another client is waiting."

Blink.

Gone.

Bucky ran into the lumberyard office to get permission, but no one in the maze of cool marble corridors seemed to know where the boss was. Saws buzzed hollowly in the distance, a humming counterpoint to the clack of typewriters. Otiego ran up to report that the giant Abyssinian forest impala had left the lumberyard at the far end. Bucky could not find his rifle. Perhaps he had left it in the anteroom of the main office. A secretary, cool and brusque, could not help him. Had it been stolen? Then he found it, leaning against a water cooler, and he ran through the corridors, fumbling in his pockets for tokens to work the subway turnstiles that blocked every turning of the labyrinth.

At the far end of the lumberyard, beyond the slat fence, out in the eye of the sun again, he saw that the land dropped away into a deep industrial valley. A freeway ran past, and down below he could see factories spinning smoke into a yellow sky. The giant Abyssinian forest impala lay dead beneath the freeway overpass. Three figures crouched over it, knives winking in the smog. Spears stood stacked against the solemn, lopped-off head.

As Bucky trotted up, working a round into the chamber, the butchers turned to face him. Short, broad, their green eyes set deep in boulder-sized skulls, they began to click. . . .

It was hot in the tent, hot and apple green with the smell of old canvas and the hard midafternoon sun slapping down between rainclouds. Part of it was the fever. Winjah was right, Bucky thought. I shouldn't have tasted

that blood. But it was a low-grade fever and Buck had
hunted despite it. The combination of fires—sun on the
outside, the slow peat bog smoldering in his veins—had
tried the fat from him swiftly: A good twenty pounds now,
he exulted. Fever-bright and giddy, he felt so slim that he
was sure he could run the veldt with the easy speed of the
trackers. Whatever weakness his fever had caused was
more than compensated by the weight loss. Except for his
shooting and the nightmares, he felt terrific. He had been
shooting miserably.

First the impala—four easy standing shots in a row,
each within two hundred yards, following a slow,
crouched, energy-conserving stalk behind the cautious
eyes of Lambat the Dorobo. And each shot had fallen short
to the left, kicking dust from the brick-hard plain, the ram
and his hareem pronking off at first in fear, then on the
last shot merely cantering away, bored, bored at the
persistent recurrence of this loud inept fly that always bit
the earth before it reached them. "Let's give him best,"
said Winjah when he returned disgusted to the truck.
"We'll go on back to White Legs and have some lunch and
a bit of a lie-down. You feeling all right, Bwana? You'll
have to shoot a lot better than that when we get up in the
bogo country."

But that was nothing compared to the humiliation of
the following evening. Walking a dry watercourse toward
dusk, they had spotted three eland bulls grazing in a
mixed herd of impala and Burchell's zebra. The eland
stood mountainous and gray among the lesser animals, the
largest of them half again the size of the others. Even at
half a mile, Bucky thought, I couldn't miss that big a
target. But he did—and worse.

After pussyfooting up to the cover of a termite
mound, Winjah had erected a bamboo tripod for Buck to
use as a rest. The eland's shoulder filled the scope, gray
and grainy, so close that Bucky felt he could count the ticks
crawling on the animal's belly. He looked up from the
scope to ask Winjah about shot placement: He meant this
one to be perfect. "On the point of the shoulder," Winjah
said. "Break him down. That's the .375 you're

shooting—should do the job." Buck brought his eye back to the scope and concentrated on the cross hairs. When he had them steady on the gray field, just where the bulge of the shoulder blade turned, he began his squeeze: slow, smooth, gradual, so that when the rifle slammed back into his shoulder it came as much as a surprise to him as to the others.

"My God!" yelled Winjah. "You've shot a zebra!"

Buck cleared his eyes and stared. A striped heap lay still in the short grass. The rest of the herd pounded off, tails high, with the three unscathed eland bringing up the rear.

When they walked over they saw it was a zebra mare, taken cleanly through the shoulder.

"She's still in milk," said Winjah. He pressed a boot toe against the teats and a bluish trickle seeped out. "Maybe you should drink some of that, Bwana. It might ease your fever."

"Well," said Donn. "At least she didn't suffer. The shot was right on the money."

As they walked up the thorny rise after the fleeing eland, Buck heard a shrill, almost hysterical moaning echoing back toward them. It was the colt, Winjah explained disgustedly. Calling for its mother. They followed on for another mile before coming up to the eland again. This time the shot was longer. Buck put a round into the big bull, but after lying down for a minute it got up and walked off into a grove of fever trees. Gut-shot. They followed again. Lambat and Otiego circled upwind of the thorn thicket, casting for sign, while Winjah, Donn, and Bucky made their way slowly along the blood trail, which was spotty at best, the crushed dry earth soaking it up as quickly as it dropped. They heard Lambat and Otiego yelling and then the wounded bull emerged from a patch of cover to their left, angling away from them. Bucky raised the .375 and snap-shot, swinging on the shoulder at a scant seventy-five yards. He heard the bullet smack and saw the bull stagger, but it kept on going and before he could jack another round into the chamber had disappeared into thicker thorn along the dry riverbed.

"We'll let him lie down for a while," said Winjah. "That's what he was doing when the trackers jumped him. Once the adrenaline is up in these larger animals, they can go forever even when they're dead." He shook his head. "That's why the first shot is so important." There was a bite to the words more bitter than the bark.

Buck smoked a cigarette. He could hear the colt crying in the distance. It was starting to cloud over and he could smell rain on the light southeasterly breeze that had sprung up. Down the rise to the right, he saw a figure approaching them—tall and skinny, wrapped in a dirty red blanket and carrying a spear.

"A Samburu," said Winjah. "Heard the shot and hopes to collect a bit of meat for the old manyatta." When the man came up to them, Winjah spoke to him in Swahili and the Samburu smiled. He had a long bony face with only a few yellow teeth remaining in his jaws, but he was very friendly. Lambat and Otiego took him with them as they set off to track out the wounded eland. Soon they heard a whistle.

"They've found him," said Winjah. "Let's go."

The eland lay at the edge of a thick thorn copse, still alive. Its head swayed, large as a Volkswagen it seemed in the fading lemon light. The eyes were already glazed, sick, and the tongue lolled. Buck took the .22 magnum Anschutz rifle and walked around behind the bull, then put a bullet into the base of its skull. Still it would not die. He put in another. And another. At each shot, the bull flinched, then resumed its metronomic head-swaying. Finally Winjah took the .22 and on his second shot the bull slumped, dead at last. It began to rain.

Buck stood in the rain, thinking about botched bullfights he had seen years ago in Mexico. He felt sick. The truck came up with Dawn and the driver. It was nearly dark now. The Samburu was inside the eland, working at guts as thick as firehoses. An ankle-deep pool of blood, black in this light, covered his broad splayed feet. He sliced small chunks of fat with his simi and wolfed them down surreptitiously, eyes flashing incandescent in the sweet darkness for fear that he might be caught at his thievery. Buck walked over to the G.T. and got in next to Dawn. She smelled crisp and fresh in her starched khakis, and her long pale hair shone in the gunmetal dark. He put his head on her shoulder.

"You're burning up," she said, stroking his forehead.

The colt cried again in the darkness, and Bucky wept for the Guinea worm.

12
NIGHTWATCH

"In this best of all possible worlds
Rousseau's father repaired watches
in a Turkish harem
which brings up the question of time
and why so much trouble with watches
when there's nowhere to go

"No moon
and the light of all these stars
collecting in me
as some sniperscopes collect the light
of stars for killing

"Killed by the starlight
to be made infinite
drilled by the light of a star
dead for a century

to be loved by a woman
known as legend to my grandfather

"We are drawn to that space between stars
the insatiable blackness
consumes us

"I couldn't sleep
so I got up and changed my name
with no excuse
anything's possible

"Clocks were made to imitate the stars
till we found a time
to be bound by

"Tomorrow and tomorrow and tomorrow
and tomorrow
and tomorrow and tomorrow
and tomorrow and tomorrow and tomorrow
and tomorrow

"At the bottom of the Marianas Trench
there's a creature that resembles me
No one has ever seen it
or ever will."

Donn's voice trailed off into the night. They were sitting under the fly of the mess tent with the stars bright overhead in a sky washed clean by the rain. The fire glowed and flared but gave off little heat. Donn had read them one of his newer poems, in what Bucky considered his "plummy" voice. Dawn sat back uneasily during the reading, humming and twitching her cheek muscles, while Winjah grunted and aha-ed. Bucky—drunk—merely sneered.

"Tomorrow and tomorrow," he said. "A creature like you in Mariana's trench. Yeah, I can see it. *Letti* whiskey, Joseph! *Con leche,* if you got it." He smiled apologetically at Winjah. "My gut's going sour."

"You really oughtn't to drink so much with the fever on you," Winjah said. "It blocks the effects of the antibiotic."

"Don't worry," Buck said. "Joseph tells me that the milk comes from the bag of that zebra mare I shot this afternoon. I'm sure it'll cure me of what really ails me."

" 'The lonely child who drinks the hot fresh milk,' " Donn quoted.

"Yeah, Buddhism," Buck said. "I don't know how you can go for that shit, Young Gavern. Accept the world with all its warts, love it even when it fucks you and breaks your wife's feet and grows a hump on your daughter's back and bites your son's balls off. Don't eat meat, though. It might be your dead uncle. Sit with your heels in your asshole all day long while the wind blows sleet down your neck. Grin at the avalanche even as it engulfeth thee. Deadpan the muggings and the TEN-DEAD-IN-FIERY-FREEWAY-CRASH. Be like unto the milch cow, making no judgments, taking no action. After all, everything that happens is merely . . . what's the word?"

"Karma," said Donn solemnly. He paused, searching for further words.

"Yeah, I met him once," Bucky interjected. "That runty Karmic IRA man who perfected the motor bombs." He laughed, bitter and self-pitying. "The Car Mick."

"Enough, Bwana," said Winjah. He stood suddenly and flung his glass of whiskey into the fire. "You're getting sickeningly drunk—drunk on some kind of disgusting need to feel sorry for yourself. And I won't *have it in my camp!*"

They all looked at him. Winjah enraged was something to see: His normally pleasant face contorted with swollen veins, the fair hair fairly bristling with electric anger, the calm blue eyes spitting something close to death at them. Bucky sobered immediately.

"I'm sorry, I'm sorry," he said, his own voice lowering to a husky whisper even as Winjah's had risen in rage. "It's just—my shooting was so bad, I fucked up so awfully. I hate it that way, hate myself for it. So I take it out on the lot of you." He hung his head and flipped his own whiskey glass into the fire after Winjah's. A smell of boiled milk drifted up with the mimosa smoke.

"No," said Winjah finally, sitting down again. "The bad shooting is beside the point. I know you can shoot well when you have to. But you were letting yourself get carried away on a wave of self-pity. That just can't be permitted here. This country we're going into simply eats up softies." He looked over his shoulder through the fire glare, toward the west—the Tok Plateau. "The country itself is tough enough, cold and trackless, except for the game trails. It's steep, even where it's flat. All dongas and karongas, full of rotten lava that will snap your ankles at the first bad step. Hunks of it as big as a rugger field break out from under you and drop away into God knows what kind of dismal slough. The lions up there all have black manes and eat white hunters for breakfast. Snakes up the arse, some as big as drainpipes. Leopards come into your camp at night and breathe in your face, unless they bite it off first. And we have no vehicles—nothing to get us out if something goes wrong. If one of us gets hurt, all of us must care for him, be slowed by him, suffer with him, because that is the only condition under which I will take you up there. It could be any one of us, of course, but since I am the hunter, the leader, that makes it all the more likely that I will be the one who gets hurt. The leader takes the chances. *Must* take chances. Do you understand?"

They nodded. Buck wanted to call Joseph for another whiskey, but decided against it. Dawn felt a chill in her stomach—Winjah had never sounded this serious before. Donn thought further on karma.

"I think we should tell them about the Diamond Bogo," Winjah said to Bucky. "And about the Tok."

Bucky nodded agreement, his head still down. Out beyond the campfire, they heard a lion cough. Kind of a hiccup, but deeper. Then they heard teeth and claws working the rotten zebra flesh. They listened for quite a while, as Winjah let the effect sink in.

"Yes," he said. "The Diamond Bogo. Buck and I chose not to tell you about him until we were about to go after him. I'd written Buck about it shortly before he asked you along on the safari. Actually, we needed 'rich' clients to bring this off, to provide our cover, and that's why you were chosen. My own European richies would never have worked—too unreliable, too ready to trade adventure for profit. Neither of you"—he stared at Donn and Dawn, eyes hard blue still in the off-light—"would ever do that.

"Thus, the Adventure of the Diamond Bogo." His voice was lighter now, a touch flippant but still serious. "It's a huge Cape buffalo we're after, perhaps the biggest in Africa. But its horns will never be seen by Rowland Ward's. A mad Russian named Rokoff, a diamond prospector, has managed to mount a huge diamond—a twelve-million-dollar diamond—between the bogo's horns. Don't ask me how, I'm still not sure, though it has something to do with one of your silly American products called Krazy Glue. It's there at any rate, the stone. And the bogo is mean. He's killed plenty of hunters already, earlier this year, and then given the rest of them the slip. He's up on the Tok Plateau; I learned that from Machyana, the Samburu tracker. Machyana saw him kill a few men just last month. We're going up there after him, and if we can kill him we'll get the diamond out of here safely, split the profit three ways." He paused, waiting for objections. None came.

"I need the money to get out of Africa," Winjah continued. "My time is just about up. I've been here since 1954, when the white man was still not only welcome but necessary to the country. Now he is unwelcome, at any rate. I have no choice but to leave. The hunting is about finished here—not due to any lack of game, but to the understandable desire of Africans to 'Africanize.' To these people, the game is an embarrassment. A symptom of their inability to dominate the land. They encourage the expansion of tribes into regions unfit for men, or at least for men in the state of agricultural and cattle-driving ineptitude that now prevails. They will poach the edible game, drive off the inedible, burn out the grasslands, unsettle the landscape, and then die themselves of starvation and plague. A node of numskulls will remain, of course, and from them will grow the New Africa. Ah, but I wax philosophical, like Donny Boy here."

Winjah grinned. His humor was intact again. He cleared his throat theatrically—symptom of an impending limerick:

> "*There once was a poet named Donny*
> "*Who thought it would be very fonny . . .*"

They pondered a bit, then Bucky looked up:

> "*To visit Afrique*
> "*While acting quite chic*
> "*And crying out: 'Hey, nonny, nonny!' *"

Nobody laughed. Then Donn asked: "What about the Tok?"

Bucky laughed.

"The Tok are a strange people," said Winjah, "who dominate the plateau we'll be visiting. They are quite fierce. I've talked to various anthropologists about them, and as best anyone can determine they are not quite human. They may be subhuman, but from my experience of them they are superhuman." He paused to let that sink in.

"How?" asked Dawn.

"Tremendous cranial capacity—fully two liters," said Winjah, turning to smile at her. "We *Homo sapiens* measure a brain capacity of one and a half liters, fifteen hundred cubic centimeters. The Tok, judging from the few skulls that have been recovered, measure two thousand cc.'s. Maybe a touch more. That, however, is mere science, and I intend to tell you about things far graver." He looked toward the mess tent. "Joseph," he yelled, "letti whiskey."

"The Tok," he said, smiling fully now, "are very strange indeed. They are short, but immensely strong. They walk erect, the males even more so. If I may be so indelicate in the presence of a lady, the men are always, shall we say, sexually prepared. What's more, like the Hottentots of southern Africa, and the rare Bushmen, they are steatopygic, which means that they store their body fat in their buttocks, rather than around their middles and thighs and jowls, as we do. When game is available they get immensely tail-heavy, but that development of the derrière doesn't put them off their stride whilst on the chase. When game is scarce, they grow even fleeter of foot. A wonderful physiological development. Another strange factor of the Tok is that they are white-skinned and green-eyed, to a man (or woman). In ancient times they inhabited most of the country around here, but in the past half century they have been driven ever deeper into the high plateau of Kansdu. The limiting of territory has only intensified their ferocity, and those few of us who have seen them up close and emerged alive can testify that they are far more dangerous, far less easily killed, than, say, the Mau Mau of the past or the Somali shifta of the present day." He took a whiskey from Joseph, who had padded up in bare feet and black tie, dead quiet, from the mess tent. "*Asante sana,* Joseph."

"*Do itashi mashite,*" answered the Waziri in Japanese. He winked and eased back into the gloom.

"Yes," continued Winjah, "the Tok are tough. They speak the click language, though even a Bushman cannot make hide nor hair of it. And if hide or hair is around, a Bushman will find it. As to their dietary habits, the Tok are primarily meat-eaters, devouring everything from termites to elephants, and like most African hunting peoples they augment the weakness of their weaponry with poisons. Snares, pitfalls full of poisoned bamboo stakes, drop-log traps studded with poisoned spikes, that's their style." He paused and smiled grimly. "I save the best for last. Their favorite dish is human brains, cooked if they have the leisure to do so, otherwise scooped raw from a hole chipped in the base of the skull. Interestingly, this is the same technique used by an earlier variety of man. You may recall that the thirty-odd skulls of *Sinanthropus,* or

Peking man, found in China earlier in this century, were all victims of brain-eaters who had holed the skulls at the base. While I was recuperating from my visit to the Tok Plateau some fifteen years ago, I had the opportunity to mention this phenomenon to Derek Weakley, the anthropologist, and he found it fascinating indeed. He was very sorry that I hadn't brought a few Tok skulls out with me, but of course my condition had precluded the toting of any extra luggage."

Darkness, wet, mysterious disappearance, Donn thought. Brain-eating superhumans. A buffalo wearing a diamond as big as the Ritz. Where the fuck am I?

"Right, then," snapped Winjah in his best sergeant major's voice. "It's tough country, full of tough critters. We must all be at our best if we are to go up there and hope to come out alive. I know you are capable of such a journey, but you yourselves must be certain. Else we can simply turn about right now and hunt our way out on lesser species, through lesser country. Are you game for it?"

"I sure as hell am," said Bucky. "It's what I came here for. I need the money."

"Good show, old Buckeroo," smiled Winjah. "And you, young Bwana Donn? I realize that the plight of the Fair Dawn Lady must give you pause—yes, she gives me paws, too, don't you know?—but what the hell, we can take care of her. How do you vote?"

Donn looked at Dawn. Dawn looked at Donn. It was, after all, Adventure.

"Let me put it this way," Donn said finally. He stood and cleared his throat, then in his most plummy voice recited:

> *"There was a young poet named Donny*
> *"Who thought it would be rather fonny*
> *"To stalk a bright bogo*
> *"And carve his own logo*
> *"On the place where he found it most brawny."*

He smiled, bowed stiffly from the waist, and resumed his seat.

"Which logo?" asked Bucky, smiling warmly once again, the self-pity all gone now, all better.

"Why, my brand, of course, the brand from my ranch," said Donn. *"The Wondering Why."*

PART TWO

THE LAND OF THE TOK

13
NIGHT FRIGHT

The packhorses—six of them—came up from Palmerville during the night, accompanied by a trio of frightened Africans. There had been eight horses when the men set out from town nearly a week earlier, but two had been taken by lions, along with one of the men. The African drovers related this tragedy with much weeping and shivering. They were detribalized Waziri and Samburu who had surrendered the security of their people's manyattas for the brighter lures of the city. Skinny and scabbed, they wore torn, faded khakis—cast-off bush shirts and shorts—and sandals cut from old truck tires. Two of them carried rusty World War I German Mauser rifles, the split stocks wired with coils of ill-twisted battery cable. They cried like children as they told their tale of woe, hopping about from foot to foot, eyes red and streaming as the trackers listened, deadpan.

"A huge lioness, *kubwa sana,* took the first horse just a

few miles out of town," Winjah translated. "In the heat of the day. Just marched up to them bold as brass in the middle of the track, like a woman out shopping for a roast as they tell it." He fired a quick question at them in Samburu. They babbled and wept some more.

"No, their rifles would not shoot. Try as they might. Some evil shaman must have put bad *dawa* on the bullets. Knowing these beggars, the shaman is doubtless nicknamed 'Rusty.' "

More weeping and gnashing of teeth.

"During the night, the simba came back. This time she took one of the boys, a chap named Lomitu. Young chap. Barely a moran. (See how our boys sniggered when they said 'moran'? As if these city scum could pretend to being moran.) Lomitu had fallen asleep on watch and the lioness took him by the shoulder, carried him off aways and began playing with him. They could hear him crying out to them for help. He said, 'It hurts.' (Oh, I can bet it did!)"

Another quick question. More cries.

"But what could they do for poor Lomitu? The bundooks were bad, would not shoot. They listened to Lomitu scream until they heard the crunch when the simba bit his head. Then they built up the fire and went back to sleep. *Shauri ya mungu,* they say. It was the will of God. Bloody cowards."

Another question.

Another snivel.

"They lost the second horse last night, just up there at the mouth of the pass. They think it was the lioness again, but this time they did not hear her. They heard a whistling. Just a moment . . ."

More quick questions, harsher this time, more detailed. The men answered less hysterically now, puzzling, scratching their dusty heads.

"Yes, it might have been bone whistles. Bloody hell!" Winjah cursed and shook his curly hair, staring up into the mountains. "The bloody Tok use bone whistles to communicate within their hunting parties. Could have been the bloody Tok took the horse." Now, though, the men were laughing, shaking their heads. "Oh, no," Winjah mimicked, translating in a silly falsetto, "there are no Tok, no Tok anymore. *Na kwisha.* They are finished." He grabbed one of the rifles the drovers had stacked beside the tent and tried to work the bolt. It was frozen with rust. He spoke sharply to the men and their laughter died. "Told them they'd bloody well better look after their bundooks or they'd be as finished as the Tok. Told them where to find the gun oil. Oh, well, the loss of the horses doesn't really hurt. I figured we'd lose a couple in the early going, either to flies or predators. But that business of the whistles ain't so nice. Let's get packing."

By midmorning the horses were laden and they set forth for the land of the Tok, belly bands creaking, horses still fractious and kicking, the blacks in the party loud with a jolly marching song. In addition to the three trackers—Lambat, Otiego, and Machyana—there were Joseph the majordomo, Kiparu the skinner—an elderly, leathery Wakamba with only three teeth left in his head, always smiling—and Red Blanket, the Samburu who had adopted them during the day of the botched eland hunt. Winjah had hired Red Blanket as an apprentice tracker. Red Blanket claimed to speak a bit of Tok. ("There's no way to tell if he's lying, since no one in the world can rightfully claim expertise in the Tok tongue," Winjah said, "but these backcountry Africans are usually truthful. Anyway he's strong and relatively bright.") The rest of the staff remained at White Legs, awaiting the safari's return. Looking back, Dawn saw them standing in tall, lean ranks, neat in their freshly starched green uniforms, waving that limp-wristed African farewell that seemed so poignant, coming as it did from such tough men. The three drovers from Palmerville were busy oiling their rifles and did not even look up. She felt like crying.

Indeed, back in the tent last night, after the revelations about the Diamond Bogo and the Tok, she *had* wept. But not loudly enough to awaken Donn, who had written for an hour—a whole hour—in his journal before turning down the gas lamp. Bucky's snores—hollow and erratic—echoed from the neighboring tent as she lay awake.

It wasn't fair. They hadn't warned her that the safari would be so perilous. Nobody but the stars, and Donn didn't believe in the stars anymore, if he ever had. *She* was the one in danger, not Donn or Winjah or Buck. *She* was the one the Tok would seek out for rape and sacrifice. Dawn had a sudden image of herself, lashed spraddle-legged against some grotesque rack of peeled saplings, her Abercrombie & Fitch safari outfit ripped and soiled, one breast protruding, its pale pink nipple erect in fear, her long blonde hair streaming and flying to the push of a throbbing wind, a wind from the Tok drums as the hairy, toad-headed little creatures advanced on her, their misshapen cocks pulsing to the drumbeat. . . .

Sacri—fiss. . . .

Just then, from afar, Bucky let out a snore so strange and awful that she lost the reverie. The snore began like the sound of a strangling horse, then elevated itself into the roar of a subway train at three in the morning, broke into a high ululating chortle, the kind of sound you'd expect from a turkey-duck or a madman. Sympathetic magic. She burst into laughter. Bucky was a snore-triloquist, she thought. He propelled his snores across whole veldts, shot them into tents miles away. God, what a talent! If only vaudeville hadn't died . . .

Now she had to pee. Rising from the camp bed, glad that her giggles hadn't awakened Donn, she walked in her nightie to the front of the tent. Black clouds blew like lady hair across the face of the moon. The fire had died to white-crusted coals, a gentle red in the near distance. She could not find the flashlight, but there seemed to be no hyenas outside, no lions. The moon cast enough light. Walking toward the loo tent, she saw the moonlight on Naibor Keju—for the last time, perhaps, she suddenly realized—and saw, at once, why it was so named. In the night, with the white light on it, a crease up the middle, not obvious during the harder light of day, fell into shadow. The jebel became a Jezebel—long-legged, comely, with a woman's hips, yes, even the shadowy wedge of a silken-haired pudendum. . . .

White Legs fell into darkness. A cloud across the moon. Dawn froze where she stood, panic icy between her legs. A sound came from the dark ahead of her, to her right, then was obscured by the rapid thudding of her heart. A splatter of rain hit her face from the cloud high above, rattling on the tent flies, shivering through the thorns.

Darkness. Water. Mysterious disappearance . . . A figure emerged, darker than the shadows.

"Just a momentary blackout, Fair Dawn Lady."

The moon leaped from the cloud cover and she saw Winjah standing under a thorn tree just ahead of her. A rifle was cradled in his arm. He smiled, movie-star bright in the moonlight. She wanted to rush into his arms with her relief.

"I had to visit the ladies' room, don't you know?" she said. "Powder my nose."

"I'll keep watch over you, my love," he answered, hoisting the rifle in a mock-heroic pose. Then he was gone, back into the darkness.

Later, in the tent, she had crawled in with Donn. He woke, smiled, and made love to her. Then finally she slept.

But now she marched—they all marched. Down from Naibor Keju, which shrunk in the northeast until it was merely a thumb-tip over the spiked blur of the thornscrub, past the Rope of God, itself blurring and shimmering in mirage as they approached it behind the horses, past the soda lake that once was a sea of blood and milk, and then, through the hard hot afternoon, through *real* desert. The alkaline soil crunched; dust blew into their mouths. They stopped often for water, until Winjah began to impose discipline.

"We've got plenty of water," he lectured them, "but you'll notice that the lads"—he gestured at the Africans—"aren't drinking a tenth as much as we are. They can live on less of it. So can we. If we don't show some fortitude right now, we could be in for trouble later.

Not through lack of water necessarily, but through lack of respect for the harshness of the country. When I first took Lambat on as a tracker—he was just a skinny Dorobo who had a good nose for game—we were up in the northern frontier of Kenya after beisa oryx. Up in the Chalbi Desert, by contrast with which this piece of dirt"—he kicked the crust—"is a bloody Eden. One afternoon I came out of the tent and saw Lambat splashing water on a rock. Just pouring water down it, then standing back to watch it shine. Flew into a bloody rage, I did. What the bloody hell was he up to? 'It's funny, Bwana,' he told me. 'Looks pretty on the rock, doesn't it?' " Winjah sighed and grimaced. "They'll do that, you know. They never think ahead. Go out into the bush forgetting to fill the petrol tanks. Forget the water. Forget the bloody ammo, even, if you don't keep close watch on them. And if you all die out there, themselves included, well, it's bloody *Shauri ya mungu.* Will of bloody God."

Toward evening the weather cooled and the horses began to prance again, smelling water in the low hills ahead. The pace quickened. The Africans began singing and two of them—Lambat and Otiego—ran ahead to set up camp in the green rise that marked the margins of the River Kan. Secretary birds watched from afar, peering studiously down long sharp bills. One had a snake dangling from its beak, a snake that still writhed in pain despite the bird's ponderous solemnity. Bucky burst out laughing at the sight, and Dawn joined in when she saw it.

"Christ," said Bucky. "Africa."

Up ahead they caught a flash of metal. Winjah stiffened. But it was only Lambat, waving a spear to attract them to the campsite.

"Kampi," Winjah said. "We'll need meat." He scanned the grass ahead, where a mixed herd of gazelles and hartebeest fed. "Take that tommy ram there, Bucko. The one all the way to the right, with the longest horns."

Buck took the 7-mm. magnum and stalked out toward the tommies while the others stood and watched. It's a test, he thought. To see if that sermon last night straightened me out. Well, I'll straighten the tommy to show him. Right now, at four hundred yards.

Buck sat and wrapped the sling around his forearm. Elbows on his knees, he leaned into the butt plate and brought the post up onto the gazelle's shoulder. At the grainy edge of the sight picture, he saw the black and white tail flirt nervously. The rifle exploded without his being aware of the squeeze. The tommy dropped without a quiver.

"*Asante sana*," said Otiego, coming up with a warm limp handshake. "Before you were Bwana Risasi Ini—Bwana Four Bullets. Now you are Bwana Risasi Moja—Bwana One Bullet."

Donn sat on the rocks while the others went over to butcher the gazelle. How can they praise him for something so easy, he wondered. If a slob like Bucky could kill a tommy at four hundred yards with one shot, Donn knew he could kill one at eight hundred. He hadn't shot a rifle since his cowboy camp days—and that was only a .22 at a hundred yards. But he'd been the best shot in camp. The instructor called him Ol' Dead Eye. That was one skill Donn knew he would never hone.

The world had too many marksmen in it already, too many Dead Eyes, young and ol' alike. What's more, it wasn't fashionable to own guns in his set. Oh, maybe a shotgun for the skeet range, or for a pheasant shoot on a private preserve. But certainly not a rifle, and certainly not for big-game hunting. The ranchers—the old-time studs and their slack-jawed sons—carried rifles in the window racks of their pickup trucks. It was crude.

Bucky walked back, grinning unbearably.

14
THE SKULL CAVE

"I call it EDB," said Winjah. "Elephant Dung Beach. When I was here last, the lads had literally to shovel the elephant droppings away before we could pitch the tents."

No such problem presented itself this time. The reddish hard-packed sand on the banks of the River Kan was stippled only with hummocks of wiry grass and the smooth gray trunks of river-washed trees. While Joseph supervised the household chores, Winjah and the others walked the beach, looking for sign.

"There," said Winjah. "Simbas, six of them. One big male for sure." He pointed the pug marks with the toe of his camel-hide boot. "They'll be back tonight, you can be sure, when they smell the horses. You'd better take a jerrican into the tent tonight, Fair Dawn Lady, rather than essay any more evening strolls to the loo."

Farther downstream, under the bank but still well above the tan swirling waters, they came on a mountain of bones. A buffalo, Winjah said, maybe two or three. Yes, two. Smallish cows. He examined the bones carefully for the scars of man-made weapons but found none. "Must have drowned upstream during a freshet. Et up by crocodiles down here—see the tooth marks?"

Across the river, a quarter-mile wide at this point, half a dozen of the reptilian diners lay quiet in the water near the reentry of a game trail. Crocodiles, one of them fully fifteen feet long. Their eyes, the tips of their noses, and the ridges of their serrated spines protruded above the flood. It took Dawn a while to make them out, but when she did she shuddered.

"Ugly brute, the bloody corkindrill," said Winjah. "Funny thing about them, though, is that they have a very phlegmatic stomach. Don't digest things fast at all. One of your Peace Corpsmen got gobbled by a big croc up on the Omo River in Ethiopia awhile back and when they finally shot the culprit two days later the Yank's legs and arms—about all they found in the stomach—were still fairly fresh. Hair on them and all. Generally they'll store a body underwater, under a ledge you know, for a few days before polishing it off. Let it get good and high, like an English pheasant. You've got a croc on your license, Buck. Want to take that chappie there? He's a good'un."

"Naw," said Buck. "Then we'd have the hide to drag along with us uphill and through the bogo country. On the way back." If and when, he added to himself.

"As you wish."

Knobs of reddish wind-worn rock rose along the riverbank, studded irregularly like the fang-stumps of some long-extinct saurian. Below one of these—the tallest in the immediate vicinity—they found what Winjah said was day-old buffalo sign. The twin-toed, cattlelike hoofprints had pulped the hardening mud and a barnyard reek still sweetened the air. Donn was back in his cowboy days, riding a Chisholm Trail of the nose down into his boyhood. He had spent three fine tough summers riding with the wranglers of the Bar None Ranch in northern Arizona, up in the rimrock country above Prescott. What was it they said? "Cowboying is what you do when you cain't do nothing else." But it was hard work—the sort that requires close study of seemingly casual techniques, cinching belly bands just so to prevent a fatal fall from a slipped saddle, learning the precise angle at which to approach a red-eyed range Hereford without causing it to bolt once more, even the best technique for boiling coffee when the wind is blowing flat and full of dirt. It wasn't like hunting, where the rifle did all the work and you just sat there on your ass and pointed it. And cowboying was productive, not murderous. You were doing things for people, putting meat on the table, not heads on the wall.

"Let's scamper up on this rock pile and see what we can see," Winjah suggested. "Just be careful where you put your hands. Snakes and scorpions, you know, but they'll get out of our way if we make enough noise." He sang "Rule, Britannia" as he climbed, belting it out manfully in a music hall baritone.

From the top of the knob, the view was vast. The River Kan wound away to the north, beige and brawny where it could be glimpsed through the stands of doum palm that marked the watercourse. Snow and ice flashed from the peak of Mount Baikie to the northwest, while a roseate light filled the lowlands along the river and the game plain stretching back toward White Legs. Across the Kan, the three-thousand-foot lava-lipped scarp that guarded the Tok Plateau stood black in the backlight. Winjah and Bucky leaned their rifles against a rock while Donn pulled a bhangi bomber from the flap pocket of his khaki shirt.

"Anybody care to join me in some Upcountry Tumbaco?"

"Sure," said Bucky. "Dis is de place, sho nuff."

While Bucky and Donn smoked, Winjah prowled around the boulder-strewn top of the knob. From time to time they could hear him, chortling over this find, exclaiming in a Colonel Blimpish "Egad!" over that. The rock was warm and smooth and the cannabinols powerful. Buck felt the tensions of the earlier bad-shooting days ease out of him entirely now, unknot themselves and slide away through his nostrils, like the sweet tendrils of bhangi smoke, floating out over the strong-backed river into a vague benign distance. It was good to smoke grass now and then, though he still preferred the madness of hooch for a real high. Booze tapped the anger in a man's gut; pot brought out the pussy in him. But when you were really wound down tight so that the springs squeaked, a healthy gurgle of grass was doubtless the best medicine.

From upstream a great dark winged figure appeared high above them. As the light caught it, the white breast, pocked sparsely with brown dots, flared to their eyes. As it neared, it peered down at them and barked—a short, half-swallowed, gulping bark.

"You ought to add that to your snore-triloquism routine, Buck," laughed Dawn.

Donn took the J. G. Williams Field Guide from his camera bag.

"It's a martial eagle," Donn said. *"Polemaetus bellicosus.* The largest eagle in Africa, except for the crowned hawk eagle, which is only a touch bigger. Hey, wait! Look at that!"

Downstream, a group of small dark figures—monkeys or baboons, it was too dark to tell—trooped along through the close-grown hardwoods. The martial eagle stooped and barked again while the primates scattered, yelping and scuttling in terror. The huge wings flashed black against the lesser blackness, braking, and a scream rose with the soaring bird. A monkey, clear now as the eagle again caught the light, squirmed in the trailing claws.

The eagle flapped off into the shadow of the scarp, pinions hissing even after it had disappeared in the high dark. The thin screams of the captured monkey continued, echoing back and forth now out of the darkness, then ceased abruptly.

"Egad!" came Winjah's voice from the far side of the knob. "Ahah!"

Then a long pause.

"Oh, shit." A deep and dying fall. "You better come around here, boys and girls."

Winjah stood crouched in the low mouth of a cave on

the shadowed side of the rock. In either hand were what looked like round dark-red boulders. On closer examination, they proved to be skulls. Human skulls.

"It's a Tok eating-cave," the hunter said, unsmiling. "At first I thought maybe it was a leopard's lair, full of baboon skulls. But these are definitely human heads. There are paintings on the wall in there, and signs of a fire. Stick paintings by the Samburu, I thought. But they're too well done. Take a look."

They crawled one at a time through the narrow opening, nostrils flinching to the faint, moldy smell of old ash and rotting bones that met them as the cave widened. Winjah flicked on his belt flashlight. The beam followed around the wall: figures in the round, bulb-headed, white, outlined in orange ocher that still shone thick and wet against the dry dull sandstone. Scenes of a feast, the smaller, white figures hacking the long dark-brown bodies of their victims, holding dark heads aloft, ugly tools cracking the backs of severed skulls, a fire full of blackened lumps. The diners were all green-eyed in the wavering light. The diners all had enormous penises, writhing with smaller, wormlike ocherous projections.

"And then there's that," Winjah said, his voice hollow in the darkness. The flashlight beam flicked into the far corner. A pile of moldering skulls stared out at them, fire-blackened except for the few white teeth that still hung from the jaws. "God knows how long they've been eating here. The skulls at the bottom of the heap are nearly decomposed. In a climate dry as this, they might have been here for a century, for centuries. Fortunately, the ones near the top are pretty well gone, too, so it looks like the Tok haven't been here for a while. Maybe five or ten years. Let's get the hell back out into the air."

On the way back to camp, Winjah let Donn and Dawn move out ahead and then dropped back with Bucky.

"Really?" Buck asked. "Five or ten years?"

"I didn't want to get their wind up," Winjah answered. "Much more recently. Only a few months at best. But D. and D. are getting a bit spooky. Not that I'm precisely a tower of unconcern myself."

"But we could handle them if they come, couldn't we? With all our firepower?"

"You haven't seen them yet, Bucko me boy. I have. They're tough little sods, and far more persistent than any Africans I've dealt with. It's like I said yesterday. The Tok are superhuman—not in physical strength, no. You or I or any of the blacks could handle a Tok, one on one, without too much trouble. But they have an uncanny sense of teamwork. They're like bloody *safari* ants—always coming at you. They don't seem to mind dying."

"Well, Donn and Dawn can handle the fear part all right," Bucky said after a pause. "They wouldn't have come along if they couldn't."

"They haven't seen *that* yet," Winjah said, gesturing over his shoulder to the high plateau.

The dinner of broiled tommy tenderloin was excellent, as was the Margaux served with it. The last of the fresh peas and potatoes rounded out the main course. Then Joseph, resplendent as usual in his tuxedo and black tie, shoes spit-polished to a gleam that matched his cheekbones, brought forth a huge round cheddar cheese. The candles guttered under the fly of the mess tent. Moths the size of game birds fluttered against the propane lamps. Beyond the netting, the fire flared as Kibaru threw on another log of driftwood.

"We'll make ourselves a Warrior," said Winjah as the cheese arrived. "Joseph, bring me a bottle of port." Winjah had been solemn all through the meal, but now his spirits revived. With his knife, he scooped a deep dimple in the top of the cheddar, mashed the scooped portion, and poured a hearty dollop of port wine into it. "The Warrior," he proclaimed, stabbing the point of the hunting knife deep into the top of the cheese. "As the wine soaks in, it flavors the cheese, turns it red as the enemy's blood. It will hearten us on our outward trek, sustain us on our triumphant journey home. The Warrior grows better and better as the campaign progresses. Now then"—he spread a dollop of the wine-softened cheddar on a tinned cracker—"eat hearty, lads and lassie. Gain strength from blood as does The Warrior!"

Rising, Winjah crunched the tidbit in his strong white teeth, then chased the cheese with a glass of port.

"The Diamond Bogo!" he cried, the mock-theatricality of his voice barely masking a deeper, harsher tone. He gulped the rest of the wine.

"Hear, hear!" yelled Bucky, rising also, crunching and gulping in kind.

Donn rose and ate and swallowed but said nothing. His eyes could not stay away from the two skulls Winjah had brought back from the knob. Charred and grinning, they stared back at him, the hollows of the eye sockets highlighted by the dancing candle flame. The wine had gone bad in his belly, bad with paranoia.

Dawn took a jerrican into the tent with her that night. Donn took a shotgun.

"What are you going to do with that?" Dawn asked.

"In case the Tok come."

"But it's only a double-barrel. Only two shots. What if there's more than two of them?"

"When I splatter two of them, the others will run away."

"Winjah says they aren't afraid to die, they keep coming."

Donn was silent. He knew what he would do with the two shotgun rounds, but he couldn't bring himself to tell her.

"Would you?" she asked.

"What?"

"On us."

"I don't know."

They sat on the edge of the cot, the candle winking in the green dark.

"I'd want you to," Dawn said at last. "I'd rather have you do it than them. I've been afraid of that sort of thing all my life."

"I don't know if I could," Donn said.

"If you love me," she answered, "you could."

Donn blew out the candle and eased into bed beside her.

15
OXTAIL SOUP?

Winjah's plan was to quarter upstream in search of buffalo sign, hoping at least to get a rough indication of the Diamond Bogo's whereabouts, or at best to bag him without having to make the climb into Tok country. They might just get lucky. Stranger things had happened in the annals of African hunting.

"What's more," he added to Bucky, "I want to see you shoot at least one bogo before we go up against the real thing. You've got three buff on your license. We can pop one down here and have the lads dry some biltong—what you call jerky. Also, I'm getting a mite peckish for a bowl of good oxtail soup, and bogo makes the best I've ever tasted."

Dawn came back from the shower tent, pale and worried.

"Something strange is happening," she said. "There's toilet paper looped and pulled out all around the loo tent. And no tracks going in or out."

They walked over to see. Just as Dawn had reported, the trees around the lavatory tent were festooned with strips of toilet paper. Not a pug mark showed on the carefully raked sand around the tent. Winjah peered into the sky and rubbed his chin.

"Hmm," he pondered. "It must be the Pterodactyl of the Ptoilet. Thought I heard something strange last night. The Pterodactyl of the Ptoilet, ptearfully ptearing ptissues." He smiled. "Actually it was done by weaverbirds. Take a look up there." High in the acacias, families of weaverbirds were busily mending their nests with sheets of toilet tissue. Mystery solved.

They set out after breakfast, walking upstream on the margin of palm and underbush that flanked the river, the sun casting intricate webs of light and dancing shadow through the foliage overhead. Brilliantly feathered starlings flapped and scrawed like stiff hinges, flushing ahead of them, and a family of Sykes monkeys—perhaps the very troop raided by the martial eagle the previous evening—scampered in outrage, the males hanging back to hoot and bellow from the swaying treetops. Winjah carried the .458 Remington, Bucky the .375.

"In cover like this it's best to carry your own piece," Winjah said. "These lads are not likely to bolt, but still it's safer this way. Feel a bit of an ass if a bogo or rhino came out and you reached back for the old thunderstick only to find it up a tree with your faithful bearer. I've sent Otiego on ahead to look for that herd whose sign we saw last night near the Skull Cave. But still you never know what's likely to come crashing out of this riparian bush. Keeps the old testes in tone, what?"

All morning they walked, cool enough in the bankside shade and bothered only rarely by tsetse flies. But when the flies were there, they knew it. They stung fast and hard, zooming in low to come up on the back of a knee or elbow, then the searing nip like a red-hot nail slammed home by a master carpenter. Dawn nursed a welt on her thigh as large and hard as a golf ball. Sign was plentiful in the damp sand—serval cat, dik-dik, duiker, guinea fowl, elephant, sitatunga. Winjah read short zoology lessons over each set of tracks or scatter of dung. At one point, four lions slunk out of the bush ahead and then sprinted, bellies down, into the tall grass east of the river.

"A lioness and her cubs," said Winjah. "The little chap bringing up the rear will be a beauty one day. Did you notice the beginnings of the dark mane? I can't kill them anymore. Glad you don't have one on your license, Bwana. Lions are easy. Thin-skinned and weak in the lungs. Mean enough when they're hurt, but not like bogos. Nothing like bogos."

Toward noon they came on a spring flowing out from another of the sandstone mounds that rose beside the river. The water was ice-cold and clear. They lunched on cold tommy cutlets and potato salad made from the last of the potatoes, and Tusker beer chilled in the icy spring. Mounds of buffalo dung studded the glade, some of it less than a day old. Squadrons of blue-and-yellow swallow-tailed butterflies clustered on the droppings, disguising them at first. Then a flight would lift off and the brightly colored lump, which might have been some strange, quivering new ore, was revealed as nothing but dung. Buck thought it revelatory—a symbol of Africa.

"I believe I'll lambaste the Lepidoptera," said Winjah, rising from his lunch. He hefted a lump of dried buffalo dung in his hand as if he were a shot-putter and lofted it at the butterflies below. When the lump hit, the butterflies flushed in panic though none had been hit.

"Wait," said Donn. "Let me get the camera." He screwed on a wide-angle lens and shot as Winjah and Bucky lambasted. "Dynamite stuff!" he said. "Just dynamite!" The game ended, though, when Bucky dropped an outsized buffalo flop directly on the headquarters of the Butterfly Air Force, killing two dozen with a single bogo-bomb.

"Dreadful," Winjah said. "The Dresden of the Butterfly War. You're a murderer, Bwana."

Perhaps, Bucky thought later as he dozed in the shade, but more accurate with a piece of shit than with a rifle bullet. Still, his shooting was coming back. With the tommy yesterday he'd at least gotten out of the lumberyard of his nightmare. He suddenly realized, half dreaming again now, where that lumberyard actually was, in the real world. It stood on the banks of the Menomonee River near the outskirts of the village of Wauwatosa, Wisconsin, where he had grown up. In those days the river and the woods along its banks had been his playground. During the war years, he and his few friends—he never had many, always a bit of a loner—had shot imaginary Jap snipers out of the riverside trees, fought pitched battles with imaginary but no less monstrous Nazi storm troopers, killing with every shot and never receiving anything more painful than a cleanly perforated shoulder wound in return. Buck had been too young for World War II and could hardly bear it. Once, early in the war, his father had come home from work with the "news" that the U.S. Army was accepting enlistments for drummer boys, *à la mode de'* Civil War. Buck (then barely eight years old) was ecstatic. He begged his dad's permission to volunteer—who could tell, perhaps he might be promoted to rifleman, or get caught in an ambush and have to cast his drums aside in favor of a . . . yes, a machine pistol! A clattering, wasp-snouted Schmeisser he'd take from the corpse of a dead SS sergeant, storm a machine-gun nest all by himself . . . Then his father had ended the joke. He could see the boy was serious.

Too young for World War II, too young still for Korea (though he could have enlisted, toward the end there, could have if college hadn't been "more important"). Then too old for Vietnam. Just as well, perhaps, but Bucky had always missed it, missed the fact of war. For me it's still a fiction, he thought. Perhaps it always will be.

But the Menomonee River had been more than a battleground, mocking though it might have been. During the summer it was his Africa, the woods along the banks turned by a squint of the eyelids into the realm of Tantor the elephant and Numa the lion, himself the young Tarzan, lolling on the swaying limb of some giant forest

monarch as he waited the stealthy approach on the game
trail below of Bara the deer, a quick bit of luncheon meat.
He would drop from the limb onto the unsuspecting
animal's back, sink his strong white teeth into its jugular,
and plunge his hunting knife— "the blade of his father,"
as Burroughs called it—deep into Bara's heart. Then tear
the bloody sweet flesh from its loins to sate his savage
appetite. Since his own father never offered him a hunting
knife, Buck once saved $1.25 from lawn-mowing jobs and
hiked into town to buy his own. When he got home with it,
his mother—always fearful of weapons—made him take it
back.

So his depredations along the Menomonee River were
limited, in those years at least, to catching crayfish out of
the rocks, using a hunk of liver tied to the end of a string,
and boiling them in a coffee can. Some Bara. Or else
raiding Victory gardens and munching raw kohlrabi—still
a favorite snack after all these years. Later, older and wiser
in the ways of mothers, he had actually hunted and
trapped along the river, but he kept his knives, his traps,
his shotgun, and his hunting bow at a friend's house. The
fantasy was never the same.

But perhaps now it was retrievable. This country
along the River Kan, open and parklike in places, no
hotter really than a southern Wisconsin summer, and full
of more game, more peril, than anything he could have
imagined in even those early, most imaginative years, yes,
this country *could* be the Africa of his boyhood dreams.
And with the Tok around, it might finally be his war.

Bucky slept. His snores shook the woods for miles
around. Monkeys scrambled higher in their trees;
crocodiles awakened, yawned, and sank into the silence of
the deeper waters; the quadrumvirate of lions spooked
earlier in the day pricked their ears, the cubs cuddling
closer to their mother; even Tantor the elephant, swaying
in half-sleep far up the river in a cool, shady glade, flapped
his huge ears and opened his red, piglike, but nonetheless
intelligent eyes in response to the strange echoing sound.

And high atop the plateau, Clickrasp the Tok smiled
as he peered downward.

16
NO OXTAIL SOUP TONIGHT

"*M'bogo mingi sana,*" said Otiego. He squatted in the sand of the grotto, sketching a map of the country just ahead, smiling his cynical Turkana grin. Nothing ever surprised Otiego, not even many, many buffaloes. "*Thelatini, hamsini.*"

"He says it's a herd of about thirty, maybe fifty bogos," Winjah translated. "Lying up along the riverbank about two miles ahead. No big bulls in the main body of the herd, but one big one—*kubwa sana*—and three askari just beyond them, up on the edge of a draw. Askari, in case you're wondering, are 'soldiers,' the younger bulls, in this case, that stick with an older, superior bull and protect him, warn him of danger, fight his battles while he escapes. Well, what say you? Shall we see what the Good Lord hath provided?"

"It'll be tricky getting past the main herd, won't it?" asked Bucky.

"Perhaps. But trickier still if we get a shot and the herd decides to panic and run over us on their way out. We'll have to case it thoroughly."

Otiego led the way, staying close to the river, using the low sandstone ridges and intervening bush to mask their approach. Winjah and Buck followed in order, with Dawn in the middle and Donn, Lambat, and Machyana at the rear. Red Blanket had been dispatched back to camp to bring up some horses, in case they killed a bogo. It would help to pack out the meat.

The grassland beyond the sandstone outcroppings was high, the grass itself sere and noisy underfoot. They moved slowly. A covey of button quail—dark tiny replicas of their bobwhite cousins across the seas—flushed from under Winjah's foot, buzzing out through the dry grass like a machine-gun burst. Winjah shook his head and mouthed a silent obscenity. They froze, listening for any rumble of hoofs ahead that would indicate the buffalo herd in flight. Nothing. Crouched now, they moved forward even more cautiously. Something huge and thick and mottled slithered away through the grass, far more silent than the button quail. Winjah looked back and grinned. He mouthed the word "python."

Bellies down, they eased their way up a sandstone slope. At the top, Winjah took his 4x35 birding glasses from a shirt pocket. Cupping his hands to mask any reflective flash—they were looking now into an afternoon sun, sinking slowly toward the scarp—he studied the near-bank cover. Then he turned and nodded.

"A big bull all right," he whispered as he slid back down to them. "Just to the north of the main herd. Lying up next to a dadblasted thicket so I can't see his head just yet. But he's big, big. *Kubwa sana.* Could be our boy. Come on up here, Bucko, and see for yourself."

Bucky eased up to the lip of the ridge, the sand grating his kneecaps, and focused the glasses. He could see the herd, a lumpy mass of black shapes with now and then a head swinging up and clear—the shiny black horn tips contrasting sharply with the rough, barklike bosses and the nearly hairless mud-caked bodies. A few calves frisked and flicked their tails at the flies. He swung the glasses and saw the thicket. Then the big bogo came clear. Just his ass-end showing, Bucky thought. But look at the size of him! He hissed approval to Winjah.

"Big bleeding sod," whispered Winjah. "Ain't he? Can you see his head?"

"No. What's the range?"

"Bit over two hundred. We'll have to move in closer if we're to take a shot, but I'd rather not shoot until we see the head. Could be sticky if we go down in there and the herd comes out over us. We'll wait a bit."

He slid back down the slope to tell the others. Buck kept his eyes on the big bull. He could see it swing its head now and then, but he couldn't see the horn tips. Then he saw them—far wider off the head than he'd been looking. They were enormous. Fifty inches easy, he thought. Maybe fifty-five. Oh, Christ, it could be the Diamond Bogo, couldn't it? He could feel his scrotum tighten.

Winjah was beside him again and Buck passed the glasses.

"Christ, yes," Winjah sighed. "A good head, Bwana. Even if he's not the D.B., let's bloody take him." He turned and smiled, his eyes alight. After all these years, Bucky thought, after all the animals he'd killed. God, once it's in you it never goes away. He could feel Winjah's joy pinging through to him, pervasive, like some psychic electromotive force.

Lambat led the way this time, very slowly, very low in the grass. He carried a puffball in his left hand, squeezing it every now and then and watching the cloud of greenish spores filter on the wind, seeing to it that the wind didn't back around on them and carry their scent to the herd, and especially not to the big bogo. In his right hand, two spears. One foot at a time. One foot at a time.

Finally they reached the low scrub-grown knoll, rested a minute, then eased to the crest. Looking back, Bucky could just make out Donn and Dawn on the sandstone ridge they had left. Their yellow hair clashed with the reddish stone. But they kept their heads still. He could see that Donn had the Nikon up beside him, the long lens covered with his hand. Good boy, he thought.

"Okay," Winjah breathed. "He's still looking away from us, but you've a nice angle on his left shoulder blade. Take a peek."

The bull seemed to be right at the base of the knoll. Huge and black with scabs of dried mud flaking on a whalelike back. Through the scope, Bucky could actually see flies moving through the sparse black hair. His heart was hammering now, shaking the scope so that the cross hairs danced across the bull's shoulders. Seventy-five yards. No farther. He was shaking clear down to his bowels.

"Easy, Bwana, very easy," came Winjah's whisper, faint as the hint of a breeze. "I'm backing you with the four-five-eight. Don't take the shot unless you're sure you can make it. We've loads of time, now, loads of time."

Buck could see the muzzle of Winjah's .458 Remington poke out beside him, out of the corner of his eye. The hunter's words had calmed him. The shakes were gone. The hairs lay steady now on the buffalo's shoulder. Bucky eased the safety forward and began the trigger pull, slow, steady, slow, slow . . .

Up on the sandstone slope, Donn sighted the Nikon. He too was breathless, steady. Dawn's mouth was open. She could see Winjah and Bucky below, and just the dark shadow of a shape were the bogo lay, its head up now, starting to swing back to look at the hunters. Bucky's buns were clenching and relaxing, like a fat man chewing tobacco. Bruxism of the butt, she thought, giggling to herself. . . .

At the explosion, the big bogo leaped to his feet—erupted to his feet, it seemed, so quick was the upward, forward movement—and dove into the thicket. The askari bulls lying nearby sprang up and stared for one wild-eyed instant, then bolted after their leader. The herd, some hundred yards away, arose almost as one animal and charged—directly toward the low knoll where Winjah and Bucky lay.

And then, in a single blinding instant, they saw it—they all saw it. From a patch of thin brush to the far side of the thicket, perhaps fifty yards farther on, an enormous black mountain of an animal ascended. It came to its feet in one powerful, steady movement, its horns seeming to span half the horizon, its shoulders basalt boulders, its head a squared, thick black wedge as big as a truck. Between its horns flashed a prism of blinding light—purple, white, red, gold. The Diamond Bogo turned as the dust from the stampeding herd of lesser buffaloes obscured him, obscured the whole scene.

"My God!" Dawn said, "they're trampled!"

"Did you see him?" Donn asked. "Did you see him?"

"My God, yes, how could you miss him?"

"Miss him, did he miss him?"

"Who?"

"Bucky."

"Where? Oh, is Winjah all right?"

"I don't know, do you see them?"

"Who?"

Then, as the dust began to settle, they heard a single, long, agonized groan echo up from the draw down below. And they saw Bucky and Winjah, waving at them, grinning from the knoll. They ran down.

"He's finished," said Winjah, grinning hugely. "The bull Buck shot, I mean. But did you see the Diamond Bogo? Did you see that great sodding beast? Oh, sweet Jesus, what an animal he is. Biggest bloody buff I've ever seen."

"Yeah, we saw him," Donn said. "But I was frozen at the switch. Never got a single picture off."

Bucky was pale under his tan, shaking again with the letdown that comes after a concentrated shot.

"You're sure the bull I shot at is dead?" he asked.

"Yes. That groan you heard. When they groan like that, they're finished. But Christ, if we'd had a clue that the D.B. was there . . . *I* even froze at the switch when he came out. I'd been planning to shoot right after Bucky's shot, but I knew he'd placed it well and held back. So there

I lay, with a bullet up the pipe, and when that bloody great creature stood up with that headlight blazing between his eyes, I just gawped at him like a bloody snotnose kid with buck fever. Er, no offense, Bucko me lad, you shot bloody well." He grabbed Bucky's hand and pumped it. "Now let's go collect us our baby bogo." He grinned again.

"How did you miss getting trampled by the herd?" Dawn asked as they walked down to the edge of the donga where the dead buffalo had fallen. "It looked to us up there that they charged straight over you."

"They split either side of the knoll," Winjah said. "It was thick and loud in there, I'll tell you. Rather like an earthquake. But not a one of 'em came within five yards of us. We just lay belly down and prayed."

Lambat had run ahead and now signaled to them from the trees at the edge of the donga. He was smiling seraphically. Dead bogo, all right. Pushing in, they saw it at the very lip of the ravine, a thick piglike body hanging head down, one horn tip hooked into the dirt just over the edge. Ticks crawled on the bulging scrotum.

"Two more jumps and he would have been down there," said Winjah, pointing into the tangle of vines, thorns, and scrub that choked the donga. "Had you only wounded him, Bwana Buck, we'd have been going down there right now with a knot in our arseholes. Now aren't you glad you know how to shoot?"

Bucky nodded, still weak and giddy after the shot. This buffalo, though smaller by far than the Diamond Bogo, was still quite an animal. The boss of the horns looked thick and broad, the points themselves widespread and unmarred by chips or cracks.

"He'll go fifty inches," Winjah observed. "A fine bull, Bwana. I say, would you care for a drop of the old S.W.?" He pulled a silver flask from the patch pocket of his corduroy shorts. "Scottish wine, don't you know? Thought it might be in order in the event we bagged something extollable, or even tolerably extollable."

They walked back up to the ridge while the trackers butchered the buffalo and sipped Scotch while they waited for Red Blanket to arrive with the horses. From time to time the Africans trudged up the hill with slabs of red meat over their shoulders, grinning happily, not minding the load. It was, after all, meat. Otiego carried a buffalo hoof in one hand, while with the other he dipped a chewed twig into the marrow of the ankle bone, slurping the gooey green liquid with glee. Looks just like guacamole, Dawn thought. Then Lambat, with the bogo's head across his back, arms hooked over the horns, the bull's glazed eyes staring sadly over the Dorobo's wiry shoulders. Tongue hanging loose. Flies in the cannon-mouth nostrils. Sad.

"Well," said Winjah, "we know the D.B.'s down here along the river, hanging on the edges of this herd. He's probably not an accepted member of the herd, what with that doodad between his horns, but they tolerate him at a short distance, so he'll stick with them. That's just dandy for us. Looks like we won't have to go up there, after all." He pointed to the scarp, and the gray smokelike tendrils of fog that blew off its lip, gold-edged with the falling sun. "Dammit, I wonder what's keeping that bloody Red Blanket? Getting late."

Ten minutes later, Red Blanket appeared from the edge of the forest, running, slowly, almost falling. He labored up the hill. His eyes were wild in his bearded face, his ribs thumped in his chest.

"Tok," he said, falling to his knees. *"Kampi na kwisha.* Camp finished. Tok."

They sat for a long, loud, awful minute. The clouds worked out over the edge of the scarp, tentacles grappling with the dry wind of the plains. A small rain began to fall. Red Blanket's gasps slowed, the harshness easing from his chest. Winjah looked up. His face was wet, and Dawn wondered if it was the rain.

"Bloody 'ell," the hunter said at last. "No oxtail soup tonight."

17

"THE SIMI, S'IL VOUS PLAIT."

Winjah loped the game trails in the waning dusk, Otiego doglike at his heels, both of them running easily and quietly, never talking but communicating all the while: where to place a foot to avoid a thorn, where to skirt the inside of the corner and with it the snake—a puff adder this time—that had coiled back in terror at their swift approach. They had run like this so many times, Winjah thought. Back in the police days, when we went out with just the water bottle on the hip and the old .38 Webley slapping against the thigh, and Otiego with his Turkana spears swinging along right behind. Yes, a good lad, never could learn English, never cared to, but the Turks are so bloody tough, so bloody good. Never heard him bitch once.

Glad I left Lambat back with the Bwanas and the Fair Dawn Lady, though. Lambat's Western clever. He'll understand them. A bit rough just yet, but old Lambat's a good'un too. Never trust a Dorobo. Too bloody wild. We'll curb him yet, though. He'll take care of 'em. I hope I hope I hope I hope . . .

But if they've killed Joseph, those bastards. Bloody Tok . . .

It was Joseph and the question, unanswerable by Red Blanket, that had brought Winjah back this dying day. Two hours of daylight left, but a good moon tonight. With Red Blanket's report that the camp had been destroyed by the Tok during their absence, Winjah's first worry had been for the Waziri who had been with him now, he reckoned, for years beyond reckoning. Red Blanket had seen only the flames, and the gnomish figures of the Tok leaping and flashing their spears in the smoke. Horses were crying, yes, but no human voices. A figure on the ground, through the smoke, quiet, bigger than the Tok. Kiparu perhaps. Joseph perhaps.

Funny, it had been at the end of a run rather like this one that he first met Joseph. Back in the police days. A band of Waziri had made off with some Samburu cattle. Winjah, Otiego, and two other askari went after them. Up in the mountains above the Guaso Nyiro, up in the bamboo, they had lost the sign. They squatted there in the cool green dark of midday, pondering, and then they heard a sound from a short way off. *Tink.* "A bellbird," said Otiego. *Tink.* But wait a minute, Winjah had suddenly thought. There are no bellbirds at this altitude. It was the sound of a jerrican hitting rock. The rustlers were refilling their water jugs from a well. They quickly closed in on the sound and found the cattle and the thieves resting in a glade beside the well. Otiego and the others were for cutting loose right away with their .303s, gun 'em down and have done with it, but Winjah believed in fair play. He stepped out into the open and demanded the rustlers' surrender. The Waziri answered with their spears.

So we gunned 'em down, Winjah remembered. Only one left alive after the fusillade. Big man, gut-shot, smiled at me as I came up to him. Asked for his simi so he could kill himself. Don't worry, he said. It was a fair fight. I would have done the same to you, Bwana, had our positions been reversed. Now, the simi, please. But I didn't believe in that sort of thing, not back then anyway. We carried him out, using my shirt between two poles as a stretcher. At night. Bloody bogos on the trail ahead of us coming out. Bloody elephants too. But we got him down to Merti, to the police barracks there. Why did you save him, Bwana? Well, that was Joseph. Bloody good investment it was, too.

And now these bloody Tok!

As they entered the camp, sour smoke wafting through the doum palms, Winjah slowed and took the .458 from Otiego, then sent the Turkana to circle out behind the fires. He carried only the two spears, but at close range—fifty yards or less—they were as accurate and deadly as any rifle. Going in once on a wounded leopard, Winjah had seen how deadly. The leopard came out of heavy cover, quite close, and as Winjah shouldered his weapon (a twelve-gauge shotgun loaded with 00 buck) he saw Otiego's arm flash past his ear. After the recoil, after the smoke cleared, the leopard lay dead just twenty feet ahead of them, a spear through his chest. "Good," Winjah had said. "One spear." Otiego smiled and shook his head, held up two fingers. And by God yes, there *were* two spears in the cat, two spears in the time it had taken Winjah to get off one shot. Accurate and deadly and fast.

Winjah entered the burned-out camp with his rifle at high port. The tents still smoldered, green canvas charred, orange-edged where the mild breeze brushed the coals to life. He counted the bodies of four horses in the picket yard. A marabou stork already strutted contemptuously on the bloating belly of one. The horses were headless. The stork rattled its bill, then leaned forward, its raw pink air pouch swaying obscenely at the front of its naked throat as it secured a grip on a hunk of windpipe. It tugged, sawing sideways with the heavy beak. A strip tore loose and the bird swallowed, then looked back at Winjah through the heat haze and rattled its bill once more. *Leptoptilos crumeniferus,* Winjah thought, that's pretty crummy of you.

He could see no human bodies in the wreckage. His

ammunition box, though, hulked big beneath the ashes of his tent, blankened but apparently not exploded. A bit of good luck, that. The fire must have burned past so quickly that the ammo didn't cook off. It'll be a bit touchy, I expect, but it'll shoot all right. Good. It'll shoot a few Tok for me. He wrapped a rag of unburned canvas around his hand and dragged the safe clear of the coals to cool. Then he heard Otiego whistle.

Otiego was standing beside the ashes of the toilet tent. He smiled sardonically and shook his head. The lower half of a human being protruded from the honey hole, legs slashed deep, to the bone, with spear cuts. Shoeless. Splayed feet, thick with callus. Green shorts. Kiparu the skinner. They each grabbed a leg and pulled the body out. It too was headless. A streamer of soiled toilet paper blew from the neck stump.

"Oh, yes," said Otiego in Turkana. "Let no one say that the Tok lack a sense of humor."

Winjah spun on his heel and shouldered the .458. At the explosion of the big cartridge, the marabou atop the dead horse erupted in a cloud of dirty gray feathers. That's one pterodactyl that won't feed at this ptoilet, Winjah said to himself. Otiego laughed and laughed. The Bwana was even funnier than the Tok.

They pushed Kiparu's body back into the hole, then covered it over with dirt and rocks. As good a grave as any, far better than the vultures and storks and jackals would do as undertakers. They dragged the ammunition safe back into the thornscrub and buried it, after filling two bandoleers. Then they set out on the trail of the raiders.

An hour of light left, Winjah thought peering up at the glare above the scarp. Clouds still blew over the lip, but the sunlight behind them was darker now, brassy, and rainbows danced through the ragged edges. The Tok trail was easy to follow—the short, broad, long-toed feet apparently contemptuous of pursuit, sign thick in even the damp and muddy places that a man fearful of followers would instinctively have avoided. Joseph's tracks were readily distinguishable from the others. A long narrow foot with a deep instep. A Waziri foot. So he's still alive, but for how long?

They forded the river well downstream of camp, wading armpit-deep in the brown water, the weapons held high overhead, Winjah waiting resignedly as usual for a bite of the corkindrill which had not come yet, after thousands of crossings, but could come at any moment on rivers like this one. It was a trick of some tribes, in war, to kill a captive and sink his body at the edge of a ford, thus attracting crocodiles which would then wreak havoc among the pursuers. Maybe Joseph was down there right now, belly wide open, stones tied to neck and ankles, baiting up saurians to eat his master. But the bite did not come.

Yes, Joseph's tracks resumed in the mud of the far bank and on through the alluvial bush to the edge of the scarp. There, in deep shadow, the trail became harder to follow. Great slabs of rotting lava that had broken off over the eons turned the scarp into a maze. Smaller rocks and rubble clotted the trail. They worked their way upward, slowly, Otiego with his keener eye in the lead, looking for recently turned rocks, faint scrapes of skin against the sides of boulders, the odd impression of a heel in gravel, a toe in the sand. It grew darker. Once, a clattering in the rocks above caused Winjah to throw the rifle to his shoulder, but it was only a klipspringer—a small rock-dwelling antelope—spooking off before them. Then, halfway up the face with the light rapidly fading, they heard yells just ahead of them. They ran, scrambling and kicking, steeply uphill. Screams and the clatter of iron.

Silhouetted on a shelf not fifty yards away, Winjah saw a tall figure swinging a spear at many shorter ones. A figure in evening dress. Joseph had his back to the wall, the spear darting and parrying as the Tok screamed and howled at his ankles. Running, Winjah snapped a shot at the outermost Tok and saw the figure smash backward into the dark. Good shooting on the run! He worked the bolt but missed the next shot. The Tok were aware of him now. He saw Otiego's spear arm cock and unleash. A grunt from above. Spears and knobkerries now rattled all around them as they climbed. Winjah slammed another round home and fired from the hip—distraction was as important as hits. The roar of the .458 echoed off the rotten lava, starting small avalanches all along the face of the scarp. The Tok backed off, broke, and fled uphill. One of them—the last—stopped in a gap between the boulders and cocked his spear arm. Winjah raised the rifle. Otiego raised his last spear.

The Tok threw.

Winjah shot.

Otiego uncoiled.

Joseph grunted.

The Tok died instantly, head shredded by the heavy soft-pointed bullet, chest skewered by the laurel-leaf spearhead, but Joseph was not so fortunate. He stood pinned against the crumbling lava by the Tok spear. Blood slid slowly over the ruffled white dress shirt. The spear had taken him through the chest. Winjah pushed the haft through the wound as gently as he could manage, then lay the Waziri down on the rocky shelf. He took off his own shirt, wadded it under the dying man's head. He unknotted the neat black tie. Joseph smiled up at him, a crooked smile.

"Ah, Bwana," he said in Waziri. "I think we have been here before. A long time ago. But this time I mean it: the simi, *s'il vous plait.*"

From far below, far upstream, came the faint pop of a rifle. Then another and another. Winjah caught the wink of gunfire, single shots, back in the direction of the buffalo kill. Oh, Christ! he thought. They suckered me. Suckered me. Joseph, too, heard the sound. Still smiling, he offered his empty hand. Winjah pulled the hunting knife from its sheath and passed it to the Waziri. He stood and looked down the hill. Otiego had collected his spears and was trotting toward him, alert and eager as a gundog after the flush. When Winjah turned back, Joseph was dead. Winjah kissed him before he resheathed the knife.

They headed back down the scarp.

18
KIDNAPED!

"Gone," said Donn. "Both of them." He rubbed a lump on the side of his head, bitterness just now beginning to enliven the stunned tone of his voice. "Bucky tried to stand them off for a while, dropped three or four of them, but they were all around us, dancing through the weeds, hopping and ducking and flipping those damned spears at us. These guys weren't much help." He gestured contemptuously over his shoulder at Lambat, Machyana, and Red Blanket, who sat heads down just at the edge of the firelight. "They threw their spears and ran with the rest of the guns back into those rocks up there. Where we watched you shoot the buffalo."

Winjah chewed on a piece of broiled bogo. It wasn't much, but it was meat, and they'd need it. He wished Donn would eat, but with the clout on the head he'd received from one of the Tok knobkerries he was understandably short of appetite. That and the loss of his wife.

111

"What happened then? It's important for me to know precisely, so we can figure out if they merely wanted prisoners, or if . . ." Winjah let the last part of the sentence trail off into the dark. "Or if the bodies are lying out there in the night without their heads," he almost said.

"When Buck started to reload, they rushed him," Donn continued. "We should have had two rifles, dammit. Then we could have spelled each other while we reloaded. Shit, I've thought of all the possibilities. All of them." He wiped his eyes. "The main one is, we shouldn't have been here."

"Karma," said Winjah, after a suitable pause. Donn pulled himself together again.

"Yes," he said. "Well, Buck saw they were about to take him and he threw the rifle and the box of ammo over to me. I was lying up, with Dawn next to me, under that acacia back there. One of the Tok clobbered him with a knotted hunk of stick, what you call a rungu, and I managed to get off a couple of shots. I don't know if I hit any of them, but it seemed to keep them down. The next thing I knew, I was out cold. One of them must have snuck around behind me and hit me with a club. When I came to, they were gone. Bucky and Dawn. Both of them."

"But the Tok left the rifle?"

"Yes. Damned if I know why. They seemed pretty primitive"—he laughed bitterly—"so maybe they don't know what it is."

"Well, that's a plus, anyway," Winjah said. Businesslike. That's the tone, he thought. "Our ammunition is intact. When they burned the kampi, they failed to destroy my ammo safe. We've plenty of rounds, and the rifles, and we've got the lads here. We'll follow them on out and rescue Dawn and Bucky, that's what we'll do. What say, young Gavern?"

Donn groaned and stuck his head between his knees.

"I say I'm going to be sick." He got up and staggered out of the firelight. Winjah heard the sound of retching. A knock on the head, he said to himself. Do it every time.

But Donn wasn't sick over the club blow. He had not

told Winjah the truth. After Buck threw him the rifle, Donn had panicked. Dawn was screaming beside him. He could not close the bolt—a cartridge had jammed, coming up cockeyed from the receiver, bending against the bore. He had grabbed Dawn's wrist and run for the donga. Just as they neared the edge, a Tok club caught her on the knee and she fell, pulling loose from his grasp. He turned and worked the bolt once more. Still jammed. The Tok were coming through the grass, short lumpy men, bounding high and scuttling low, spears slashing the brush, glinting in the light, their wide green eyes gleeful at the impending kill. Stones from their slings whistled and cracked overhead. Dawn, looking up at him, her face a mask of horror.

He had thrown down the rifle, plunged into the ravine, over the lip where the bogo had hung, down, down into the vines and thorns and brush. And then, only then, momentary unconsciousness when his head smacked a rock.

But that was not the worst of it.

Creeping up to the top of the donga—how long? Twenty minutes later perhaps—he had seen the Tok exulting over his wife. They had her trussed like a deer, wrists and ankles bound to a bamboo pole, her head twisting and turning, her hair uncoiled now, hanging blonde in the dying light, writhing like pale fire. Bucky limp, unconscious, on another pole. And the rifle, unaccountably, still where Donn had thrown it. He snaked an arm out to recover the weapon, cleared the bore of the bent cartridge, eased another home, and then climbed over the edge of the ravine. The Tok spotted him instantly, his wife a moment later.

"Donn!" she had screamed. "Shoot me! Please, please, please!"

And he had tried. With the last Tok stones whistling past him, with the Tok running off now, carrying Buck and Dawn with them on the poles, he had held for her head, seeing her face huge through the scope, bouncing, concentrating his eyes through the glass as he had through

so many camera lenses, knowing that this would be better
than what she feared—the rain coming down harder now,
the darkness falling, the scarp and the land of the Tok
ahead—but when he shot, he missed. As he knew he would.

Her face, the last glimpse he had of it, was empty,
fallen in resignation.

Winjah was talking with Lambat and the others, no
doubt getting their side of the story. Donn saw the hunter
look over at him now and then in the course of the
gesticulate narrative, his face somber. He didn't care what
they thought. He was desolate, desperate—no, too wiped
out for desperation. Maybe later.

"Bwana." It was Otiego, hunkering down beside him,
his face thoughtful, quiet, perhaps even compassionate.
Cruel as they could be to outsiders, Donn realized, these
people understood loss within the group, felt it deeply.
Otiego fumbled at his shirt pocket and came out with a
plastic bag of bhangi. He smiled and gestured back in the
direction of the burned-out camp. Must have salvaged it,
thank God and Otiego. His Zig Zags were in the bag, too.
Donn rolled a bomber and lit up, offering Otiego the first
heavy toke. The Turkana smiled and smoked. They
finished that one and then did another. Donn would have
rolled a third, spreading as he was now on the night surf of
euphoria, but a sudden pang of paranoia hit him: He'd
better start conserving this stuff. They might be up there
on the plateau for quite a while.

"Two of the horses survived the massacre," Winjah
said, walking up to the fire. "If the lions don't get them
tonight, we'll round them up in the morning. Then you
can ride back to White Legs with Red Blanket. Take one of
the trucks and make for Palmerville. You can ask the
police chief there for army help. Perhaps they'll have a
helicopter in working order. Meanwhile, the boys and I
will head up top and see what we can do."

"Hunh?" said Donn. Winjah stared down at him.
More gone than he'd thought.

"Oh, please," said the hunter. "Well, I'll explain it all
in the morning."

"But I want to go up there with you," Donn said,

suddenly awake again. "I've got to go up there."

"No," Winjah said flatly. "Look, we'll be moving fast and very quietly, and in no great comfort. Cold camps. No tents. Sleeping under hides. Eating biltong if anything at all. Not your style, Bwana. Not a bit of it."

"Waddaya mean? Waddaya mean?" Donn was fighting the spin of the grass. "I've camped cold in the Absaroka, in the Bitterroots. I've packed in and gone for days on beans and fried trout, berries and snowmelt. I'm . . . I'm *fit,* Bwana. And I have to go up there with you."

"Look, Donn. I'm trained to this sort of thing. This is my profession. And more than that, my responsibility." Once more the rage at having been suckered by the Tok, suckered into leaving what they clearly were after all along, unprotected save by one rifle in the hands of a besotted journalist—the rage swept through Winjah like a grass fire. "And anyway, you can't shoot."

"I *can* shoot!"

"The boys told me." He stuck that one into Donn, with his eyes, and turned the handle.

"But I couldn't shoot her, Bwana. Not my wife. Not even with her pleading that way. And I was shook, shocked, knocked back on my haunches by the way they came at us. I'm over that now." He saw them again behind his eyelids, squat and quick, the spears and the swaying erections. "I just . . . I just . . ."

"We'll talk about it in the morning," Winjah said, rising. "Right now I've got to get the lads to work drying out some biltong. You catch some sleep. I'll send Red Blanket with half the bogo hide, once he's scraped the hair and the dried shit off of it."

Donn lay back with his boots under his head as a pillow, his right side toasted by the fire, his left wet with the dew. The rain clouds had piled higher now over the scarp, black mounds that shifted and rumbled against the stars, lit occasionally from deep within by green lightning. He dozed and dreamed of Tok. Then he heard Red Blanket come, felt the heavy limp hide fall over his chest, and fell finally to sleep with the smell of raw meat in his nostrils.

19
PRIAPIC PIPSQUEAK

Some shvantzes, thought Buck. So that's where all the legends of Priapus come from. They're an old, old people, sure enough, but they just as sure ain't us. Bucky had regained consciousness halfway up the scarp, his head split with pain from the knobkerrie blow, gagging with the hurt of it, feeling the rawhide thongs cutting into his wrists and ankles with every lurching step of his bearers. One of the Tok had stuffed a wad of bitter herbs into his mouth and aped a chewing motion. Buck chewed—what the hell, he thought—and felt the pain ease quickly. Even the bonds no longer hurt.

Hanging head backward, he saw Dawn, trussed as he was, bouncing along just ahead of him, head uphill, her pert, pear-shaped butt swaying to the pole ride. At least she wasn't screaming. At the top of the scarp, the Tok had unbound them, then resecured their wrists and ankles with loose hobbles that permitted a reasonable walking stride and hand movement, but precluded any attempt at escape or attack. With the herb still at work in him, Buck felt pretty good, back on his pins, headache gone, enjoying the cool beat of the rain, the sweeter, greener smell of the high plain. It was dark now, but the ground underfoot seemed smooth and well worn, a wide game trail no doubt. The Tok trudged along all around them, straight-walking little men, their huge heads wobbling, top-heavy, as they plugged along. The tallest of them only came to Dawn's shoulder, yet they were all heavily muscled, deep of chest and broad of shoulder, with narrow hips and melonlike, protuberant buttocks. Most of them had leather slings wrapped around their foreheads and waists. Some wore animal hides—bushbuck, serval cat, what looked like lesser kudu—over their shoulders, but otherwise were stone naked. Yeah, Buck thought, stone naked—with those weird dinguses of theirs waving in the breeze. Strange damned phenomenon. But that's the source of the legends, I'll bet.

"Priapus," he said aloud. Dawn, stumbling ahead of him, turned her head and stared back. He explained his theory, but she was beyond hearing. Her eyes were dull, her steps automatic.

"Did they give you any of that weed to eat?" Buck asked her. She shook her head, then tripped over her hobbles and almost fell. Bucky whistled and two of the Tok looked over at him. He mimicked eating and pointed to the skin pouches on their hip belts, then at Dawn. One of them nodded and took a handful of the weed from his pouch.

"Chew it up and swallow the juice," Bucky told her. "It's bitter, but it will take away the weariness. They gave me some on the way up the hill and I feel like I had twelve hours' sleep. Come on, try it."

She chewed as they walked, choking once on the bitter leaves and stems but getting most of it down. The Tok who had given her the weed smiled—a wide, thin-lipped, even-toothed smile, not a Dracula fang in the mouthful, Bucky thought—then patted her on the shoulder and clicked. Yes, Bucky thought, the click language. We're going to have a hell of a time communicating with them.

"What was that you said about Priapus?" the Tok asked. "I couldn't help overhearing you and the young lady." He nodded deferentially, with a shy smile. "As I understand it, the Priapic myth concerned the Greco-Roman god of gardens and vineyards. We're essentially a hunting people, though we practice some rather intensive horticulture, yet I suppose it's possible that the early Hellenes had dim racial memories of the days when our species dominated Eurasia and merely transposed the myth."

"What?" said Bucky.

The Tok began to repeat what he had said in simpler language. Buck gawped.

"No, no," he said, interrupting. "It's . . . You speak English?"

"Yes," said the Tok. "Me spik English good, no?" He grinned impishly and punched Buckly lightly on the shoulder. Then he winked. "We'll continue the conversation later. Right now I have to go to the head of the column and look for a campsite." He trotted ahead into the dark.

Buck looked at Dawn. Dawn looked at Buck. "Did you hear what I heard?" he asked her. She nodded.

They marched for what felt like another hour, cutting off from the main game trail to the right, into a maze of lesser tracks and paths, walking now through high wet grass that slashed at their arms and legs and soaked their clothes. Yet they felt neither the cuts nor the cold. Dawn had revived, thanks to the drug, and walked smoothly, steadily, her eyes still grave but not as deadly glazed as they had been earlier. The cloud cover had blown over and the sky was clear, a fragmentary moon straight overhead, stars blazing in many colors. Ahead Buck saw a fringe of forest and a low rise of rock. Some of the Tok shook out into a skirmish line and moved into the trees, spearpoints forward, while the rest of them waited. After a short while, a bone whistle shrilled from the woods and the main body moved in.

A small fire was already popping in the shadow of the rocks. Bucky and Dawn sat backs to a boulder, feeling the yellow warmth pound against them. Now that he was finally sitting, Buck realized how tired he actually was. His thigh muscles fluttered uncontrollably, and one of his feet had cramped. Dawn pulled off his desert boots and massaged his feet. Tok ran in from all sides, carrying more firewood, and soon the blaze illuminated the entire scene. They were in a natural bowl of rocks at the top of a low hillock, surrounded on all sides by forest. Guards stood at the top of the hill, watching their back trail for pursuit.

After the fire had burned for a while, a Tok came up with a green branch and raked coals into a shallow depression in the rock to one side of the main blaze. Then another came out of the darkness lugging something big and oblong and shiny. As he came into the light, Bucky saw that it was a horse's head, coated thickly with mud and green leaves. Strands of the mane bristled through the mud in places, and the coating had flaked clear of one eye, which stared bulbous and wet in the firelight. The Tok laid the mud-coated head in the coals, and another Tok threw green, leafy branches on top of it. Then the third Tok scraped more red-hot coals over the already-steaming mound. A smell of singed hair and cooking meat wafted outward on the smoke.

"Yes," came a voice from beside them, "a bit of dinner would be in order about now." It was the Tok who had spoken to them earlier. He rubbed his hands and squatted down. "Horse, or *punda* as they call it in Kiswahili, isn't actually the tastiest of meats, but then soldiers can't be choosers, can they?" He smiled affably. Bucky noticed now in the firelight that his shoulder-length, lank hair was shot with gray, as was the wispy moustache on his long upper lip. His eyes, wide, slightly Oriental in cast, were a lively dark green. A shiny scar ran down his face from ear to chin on the right side. The hide over his shoulders,

poncho-style, was of leopard skin, as was the strip of hide
that held his hair back.

"How is it you speak such perfect English?" Bucky
asked, ignoring the horsemeat pleasantry. He wasn't all
that hungry now, anyway.

"We've had other prisoners over the years," the Tok
replied. "We get lonely up here in the clouds, and since so
few people from the outside world come up here willingly,
we have to procure our company betimes by radical
means. Actually, we're all quite good at languages. The
click tongue, I hope you realize, is the most elaborate
language on earth. Your simpler sounds are child's play to
us—ah, but I wax boastful. Forgive me." Again he ducked
his head deferentially.

"Oh, no," said Buck. "That's quite all right." What in
the hell is this? he thought wildly. Am I going nuts? Or is it
that weed they made me eat—a hallucinogen?

Two of the younger Tok snaked the horse head out of
the coals and kicked the fire-hardened mud from it with
their horny heels. Then they bowed to the older man and
withdrew. He in turn took from its hide sheath at his side a
long thornwood club and prepared to split the cooked
head open. From the knob of the club projected a large,
clear, gleaming stone—a diamond, Bucky thought. And a
huge one! The Tok tapped the horse head smartly
between the eye sockets, from which tendrils of sweet
steam wisped away, and the skull split neatly lengthwise,
exposing a pink lobed, smoking mass of cooked brain. He
cleaned and sheathed the club, then withdrew a wooden
spoon from his belt pouch.

"I say," he began, "I've completely forgotten my
manners. Let me introduce myself. My name is . . ." and
he rattled off a long string of clicks and rasps, smiling
amusedly the while, "but you may call me Clickrasp. I'm
chief of the Tok and your humble servant." He bowed
from the waist.

"I'm Bucky Blackrod, American journalist, and this is
Mrs. Dawn McGavern, housewife," said Buck. He offered
his hand. Clickrasp took it. His hand was wide and strong,

though short-fingered. The shake was dry and firm. They smiled at one another. Dawn dropped a curtsy and blushed.

"All right," said Clickrasp, "dinner is served. Sorry I can't offer you better cutlery, but after all . . ."

"Yes," said Bucky. "We're quite used to roughing it."

"Of course," Clickrasp agreed. "Mrs. McGavern, would you care to begin?" He offered her the wooden spoon.

"Is there perhaps a place where I might, well, powder my nose?" Dawn asked. Clickrasp said there was a spring behind the boulder. She excused herself.

"I don't think she cares for horse brains," Bucky whispered. "She's an avid equestrienne back home."

"I understand," said Clickrasp. "The excitement and all. It's not every day that one so beautiful gets kidnaped by Stone Age savages." He seemed a bit miffed.

"Well," said Bucky, "it's just the brains. We don't eat them regularly in our culture. Oh, you still see calves' brains in the butcher shops now and then, and in the French restaurants. However, I'm a brain-picker from way back. If you don't mind, I'll dig in." He picked up the spoon and scooped a steaming mouthful. "Yum, yum," he mumbled as he chewed, rubbing his tummy and rolling his eyeballs in mock joy. Actually, the brains tasted sweet, a bit soft, but not at all gluey, as most horsemeat did. He passed the spoon to Clickrasp, who shoveled a mountainous scoop into his mouth. They finished off the brains and then Clickrasp stuck a thumb into the horse's eye socket. He pulled out a steaming eyeball, big as a pear. He crunched on it, the hot aqueous humor running down the sides of his mouth, swallowed, then spat out the lens.

"Looks good," said Buck, grubbing in the opposite eye socket. He ate and swallowed, but forgot about the lens.

"It won't hurt you," said Clickrasp. "Roughage, you know." With a short knife, bladed in diamond, he sawed at the horse's cheeks, extracting lumps of firm pink flesh, which he and Buck shared. Dawn was still behind the rock.

"I say, Mrs. McGavern, are you all right?" called

Clickrasp. "Shall I save you the tongue? It's quite good, you know."

"No, thank you . . ."

"She'll probably feel better in the morning," Clickrasp said. He sliced chunks of tongue and popped them back into the coals to crisp. "It always amazes me," he added, reclining again beside the fire, "how different cultures react to different foods. Over along the Nile River and the Great Lakes, the locals won't eat a fish until it's running with rot, yet they think us beasts for eating brains."

"But of course, you eat other brains than horse brains," Bucky said, as gently as possible.

"Brains are brains," yelled Clickrasp, suddenly angry. "They're good for you! All kinds of brains. Horse brains, eland brains, elephant brains, people brains. I couldn't help but notice, Mr. Blackrod, that you and your party were engaged in a bit of headhunting of your own down below. Yes, you slay those animals and actually save their heads. You stick them on your walls at home for the amusement of your guests and the elevation of your own egos. Yet you throw away the best part of the head. The brains!" He leaped to his feet and began dancing madly around the fire, his shaggy erect phallus flailing in the smoke. Then he peered at the rock where Dawn's dim shape could be discerned. "I'll be back in a minute," said Clickrasp.

Buck didn't dare to look. He heard a muffled scream from Dawn, then a scuffling sound. Christ, he had to do something. Donn would never forgive him. He'd never forgive himself. He got to his feet, and four Tok emerged from the shadows, spears at the ready. Then, from the darkness by the rock, came a slap, a thump, and a rasping moan. A figure staggered back into the light.

It was Clickrasp, clutching his phallus, which was buckled like plant stem after the hail. Dawn followed after him, cheeks and eyes blazing. "You Priapic Pipsqueak!" she shrilled. "Leave me alone!"

The four spearmen advanced. . . .

20
DONN'S SHOOTING LESSON

"The point of the shoulder," Winjah whispered. "Right where it bulges there, where the sun shines on it. Lay the top of the vertical post directly on that spot. The horizontal hairs should parallel the backbone, like a butcher's ink mark on a side of mutton."

They lay behind a termite hill in the early morning. Some three hundred yards upwind, hock-deep in the fresh green grass, an impala ram watched from the edge of a bachelor band. The impala was a plump young spike, good eating if Donn could down him. The trackers were out seeking the fate of the two surviving packhorses, and Winjah had decided to see if Donn could shoot.

"He's getting nervous," Winjah sighed. "Squeeze, squeeze . . ."

But Donn could not seem to make it happen. He was squeezing, all right, but his own nervousness at a possible miss had frozen his finger, sensitized it so that he could move the trigger only a micromillifraction a minute. The spike ram suddenly snorted and pronked, bouncing off deeper into the plain with his bachelor buddies in close pursuit. Winjah stood up and brushed the termites from his legs.

"You don't have forever, Bwana," he said caustically. "It's all well and good to make sure of a steady trigger squeeze, but at some point or other the sear must break, the pin must fall, the primer must ignite the main charge, the bullet must spin its way out through the rifling of the barrel, exit the muzzle, follow its ballistic trajectory through the atmosphere, and then you will know if you have killed what you're aiming at. Then and only then. It can't all happen in your head."

Donn nodded, mute with embarrassment, and stood up. They started out again, across the plain, after the small impala herd. This was the third time in an hour that Donn had been unable to shoot. He felt sick. When Bucky had shot, hit or miss, Donn had viewed the whole procedure with a disdain that bordered on contempt. Anyone could kill a large animal with a modern telescopically sighted rifle. It was so easy that even to try it was beneath a modern enlightened human being's dignity. It sullied a man to kill this way. Besides, it was bad for the ecology. All of Donn't arty friends hated big-game hunters. They were brutes, neofascists, closet leather boys. Donn had seen the deer hunters: fat men, drunk at sunrise, who sat around the woods in Santa Claus suits and waited for the chance to kill something—anything that moved. Oh, bird shooting was all right, and killing the odd trout now and then (but only if taken on a dry fly). Indeed, Terry O'Shane, the far-out doper novelist and Hollywood nonsquare, decried even the killing of fish. He told Donn that he had not killed a fish in five years, though he fished almost daily when he was in residence at Key West, and had once set a world saltwater fly-fishing record for snaffled grunt, or some such flats-dwelling game fish. Yes, killing was too easy.

And now I can't even get a fucking shot off, Donn cursed to himself. If he couldn't shoot, couldn't overcome this impotence of the trigger finger, Winjah would send him back with the ponies to Palmerville and rescue Dawn all by himself. And Donn could just imagine what would happen next. The way Dawn had looked at him as she was being carried off, that gaze of utter loss, total disappointment, complete conviction that he had somehow unconsciously created this dreadful karma for her . . . Winjah would have her in the sack before they got halfway back to the escarpment. I have to go along, Donn cried to himself. If Bucky can shoot straight, I can shoot a hundred times straighter.

"There's grease on the scope," he said suddenly to Winjah. "From Bucky's thumb! I can tell his thumbprint." The hunter took the rifle from Donn's shoulder and studied the lens. He tore a strip of tissue from the wad in his breast pocket and scoured both ends of the sight. He shook his head and handed the rifle back.

"At this rate," he said, "those impala will be halfway back to White Legs before we drop one. It'll be a long carry back to camp, Bwana."

"I'll do the carrying," Donn said. "I can handle it. I'm fit."

This time the impala were in a shallow rocky depression beyond the edge of the grass, alert to danger, their ears flicking at every sound. Donn and Winjah lay in the edge of the grass, feeling the hot wind of the desert drying their faces. The herd was easily four hundred yards away.

"Allow about an inch of daylight between the backbone and the horizontal cross hairs," Winjah warned. "At this range, that should drop the bullet directly into him. This seven-mil magnum shoots very flat to two hundred, and then falls gradually out to five or six. After that it drops like a stone. With the breeze directly in our faces, you don't have to allow for cross-windage. Just pick your ram and, please, shoot."

Donn set his elbows in the sandy soil and wound the sling tight on his forearm. He picked a ram to the left of the main herd, another spike, perhaps the same one as before, and laid the sights. The cross hairs leaped and danced. He readjusted the sling, sliding his hand in closer to the trigger guard.

"Your head's coming up," Winjah cautioned with a whisper. "Don't get too far up or they'll see you."

The cross hairs continued their dance, finer now but still too funky for accuracy.

"Take a deep breath, hold it a moment, and then let it out very, very easily. When you're almost down to flat lungs, you'll steady up. And the shot should go right then."

Donn inhaled, feeling the blood pound in his temples, and then sighed out. The cross hairs steadied as they fell into line. His squeeze was coming along nicely. As the last of his breath slid away he felt the gun slam. For an instant the recoiling barrel blotted out the target, then fell back.

Nothing was down.

A puff of dust drifted toward them on the wind from just beyond the point where the ram had stood.

The impala herd leaped farther into the desert, rumps wiggling an obscene farewell.

"Let's give them best, Bwana," said Winjah, choking back his disgust. "We're too far out into the desert now. There's game much closer to camp."

Donn tried to think of an excuse. An ant crawling across the scope picture. A sneezing fit that he'd had to stifle. A sudden fart in a distant cathedral. Nothing worked. And that should have. It was perfect—sight picture, squeeze, exhalation. Maybe he simply couldn't shoot.

"Before we head in," said Winjah, "why don't you just pop off six or eight more rounds, get better acquainted with the trigger pull. We've plenty of ammo, and we've spooked all the game out of the immediate vicinity." He emptied the last few shells out of a box of Remington 7-mm. magnum bullets and walked off two hundred paces, then stuck the box on the branch of a bush. A mound of sand served as the backstop.

Donn shot eight rounds. All but one perforated the

target. Winjah scratched his head. "I don't know," he said.

As they hiked back toward the river, Lambat came running across the plain toward them, smiling happily. The horses had been recovered. A large simba had been in the vicinity, but it was lying up on an eland kill. Machyana and Red Blanket had taken the horses back to kampi. And there was a band of tommies just over the next rise.

"You're shooting well now, Bwana," said Winjah as they bellied up to view the Thomson's gazelles. "This time you'll drop him in his tracks, just watch."

Once again the adjustments, the lineup of the sights, the deep breath, the slow exhalation and squeeze. Once again a miss.

"I can't do it!" Donn yelled as the tommies bounced away. "It's their eyes. Those big wet brown eyes. They're too beautiful. I just can't kill such beauty."

Winjah translated for the astounded Lambat, who could not believe that even a blind man could miss a tommie broadside at 150 yards. Lambat sneered as Winjah spoke. His bloodshot eyes bored into Donn.

"Why don't you go back to America with your cameras," he said, "and make pretty pictures?"

"But they're too beautiful," Donn snapped back. "You wouldn't understand that."

"Beautiful or ugly," said Lambat, "the heart is the same."

Donn seethed as they marched back to camp. Where did this bloodthirsty savage get off telling him what was beautiful or ugly? This man couldn't even write his name until Winjah took him out of the bush; Donn wrote poems. He'd even had some published in *The New Yorker.* He wished Lambat would run out two hundred yards and then he'd see how soft Donn could be. Yes, then he'd see. . . .

Out of the deep grass ahead, a bushbuck sprinted, from left to right, angling away. Chestnut red with marks like a white harness down its back and rump, it ran with an ugly hunched determination. Equally determined, Donn swung the rifle to his shoulder, felt the recoil of the shot even as he realized the sight picture—on the shoulder, slightly ahead. A dull crack echoed back to them as the bushbuck toppled rump over head and lay still in the grass.

"*Pongo!*" exulted Lambat, leaping high on his toes and clapping his hands like a kid at a parade. "*Muzuri sana!* Very good, Bwana Donn. Very good shot!" He grabbed Donn's right hand in the two of his and smiled ecstatically into his face. "Now you are like us. Now you are a killer!"

They paced it off: 250 yards. The bullet had broken the bushbuck's neck. Donn gutted it himself, still grim-faced but warm inside, almost enjoying the hot blood on his arms, the strong smell of blood and raw meat. Then he wiped his hands and forearms in the grass.

"Can I come with you?" he asked Winjah.

"We'll leave in the morning," the hunter replied.

Back in camp, Otiego had rigged the buffalo hide on poles to form awnings. A slow fire burned under a greenwood rack draped with long strips of buffalo meat. The biltong was drying nicely. Over a separate fire bubbled a pot salvaged from the burned-out camp, and the smell of oxtail soup filled the still midday air. After they had eaten, Donn took his notebook and walked down to the riverbank shade for a lie-down. He took the 7-mm. rifle with him.

Birds hopped and chattered in the cool brush. The river hissed through its slippery channels, roiling over rocks in some places but for the most part strong and quiet, opaque. A pied crow, one of dozens drawn to the camp by the drying meat, croaked overhead in a doum palm. The afternoon shadow was just beginning its slow crawl up the escarpment. Donn pulled a fountain pen from his breast pocket and opened the notebook:

> *There will be no going back*
> *No feeding that longing for a former self*
> *No returning*
> *to patterns or nature or loves*
> *Spiraling outward in a web of my own*
> *Shadow on the mountain*
> *and a noon bird singing like a rusty swing.*

21
SURE CURE FOR SNAKEBITE

"Oh my, look at this!" chirped Dawn.

Bucky sat up and instantly wished he hadn't. His head felt as if it had been used for practice by the New York Cosmos. The effects of the narcotic weed given him by Clickrasp had worn off, and the club-blow of yesterday came back in spades. He and Dawn lay under a leopard-skin blanket, with cushions of grass-stuffed hides under their heads as pillows. At Dawn's feet lay a basket, woven of reeds, full of jungle fruits and flowers. Another strip of leopard skin was tied around the basket in a neat, ornamental bow, and attached to it fluttered a square of parchment. Dawn untied the bow and read the note, penned neatly in something that looked like red ink.

" 'Darling Dawn,' " she read aloud, " 'My humblest apologies for my rude behavior of the evening just past. Those horse brains must have gone to my head, hah hah. I hope this poor offering of the fruits of my land may in some small way compensate for the inexcusable conduct of

Your Devoted Servant, Clicky. P.S. The red ones are best!"
She chuckled to herself and rubbed the cutting edge of her
right hand. "Maybe I shouldn't have given him such a
sharp karate chop," she mused to Bucky. "I hope I didn't,
well, *ruin* him!"

Bucky groaned and staggered to his feet. In the jungle
beyond the rocky bowl in which they had camped, early
morning monkeys chattered. A dull-red ball of sun
climbed through the triple-canopied forest to the east,
mocking the ache in his head. Two Tok approached with
steaming bowls in their hands. They bowed to Bucky and
Dawn, placed the bowls at their feet, bowed again, and
withdrew. Down below, Buck could see other Tok busying
themselves around a cookfire. The smell of cooking horse
heads rose to his nostrils, to be obscured a moment later by
the odor of—could it be? Tea!

He picked up the bowl of hot dark liquid and sniffed.
Then sipped. Yes, tea sweetened by wild honey. And
flavored, subtly, with another, darker taste. Sure. More of
that magical herb that had cleared up his headache
yesterday. He gulped the boiling liquid and in moments
felt the sick ache slide away from him.

"Well, whatever you did to dear Clicky," he told
Dawn, "you ought to try more of it today. He's turned into
a most gracious host."

They broke their fasts on the fruit, which proved
sweet and slightly citric though it resembled nothing that
Buck had ever seen or tasted in his experience as a
globe-girdling journalist. Must be peculiar to the region,
he thought. A large red seed-filled globe the size of an
indoor softball vaguely resembled pomegranate but
contained far more meat, of a far more delicate flavor,
than any he'd ever tasted. Another, purple as an eggplant,
and half again the size, smacked of a cross between
Concord grape and cantaloupe. The tea-bearing Tok
appeared once again to refill their bowls—beautifully
engraved and painted ceramics that bore on their sides
delicate, slightly abstracted depictions of oryx and impala,
jolly crocodiles and glowering buffalo. When they had

finished both the tea and their morning ablutions, the two Tok reappeared once more, collected the utensils, and gestured toward the main body of their captors. "We march," said one of the Tok, and then giggled at his linguistic temerity.

"They're charming people," said Dawn as they resumed the march, this time without the hobbles of yesterday.

"If you treat them with a firm hand," laughed Buck. "I thought we were finished for sure when you socked old Clicky on the pecker that way. All I could see was you with your eyes blazing, him with his manhood in his hands, and those four spearpoints moving in on us. Clickrasp clicked them away from us in the nick of time—no pun intended."

"I wonder what they have in mind for us?" Dawn said.

They marched all day through the rain forest, the going fast and easy on the leafmold, spongy floor. A green underwater light filled the woods, and the only sounds apart from their footfalls was the hollow natter of birds and apes in the triple canopy high overhead. The boles of the trees, some of them ten feet through by Bucky's guess, were gray beneath their hoary black veins of liana and elephant ivy. From time to time Buck caught glimpses—mere flashes—of the sun through the foliage above, and judging by the time and the unwavering line of their travel, estimated that they were heading almost due north, with just a bit of westering thrown in now and then. It would be important to know the route well if they were to make a successful escape. He figured they were paralleling the flow of the River Kan, well west of it perhaps, but thus avoiding the impenetrable swamps and the scarp itself. Ahead must lie Mount Baikie, though it wasn't visible through the heavy forest cover.

Clickrasp stayed at the front of the column, never looking back at them. Occasionally, though, he would call a halt, order a couple of younger Tok up a particular tree to pluck fruit from its distant limbs, and then send the gleaning by runner back to Bucky and Dawn, who were marching in the middle of the troop. Eager to please, Buck did his best with the fruit, but eventually he felt a desperate need to crap. When he tried to pull out of the column, the Tok behind him growled fiercely and prodded him with his spear. Buck mimed the need to defecate, but the man didn't understand.

"All right, you bastard," Buck said. "You asked for it." He dropped his shorts and squatted in the middle of the trail. The Tok recoiled in horror, then covered his eyes with shame and embarrassment. He ran clicking and clattering to the head of the parade with his news. I wonder what *they* have for bowels, Bucky thought as he plucked some dry leaves from the ground. Garbage grinders, no doubt.

They marched on through the afternoon, with no rest, but both of the captives felt strong. The rain forest was cool and the pace quite easy, thanks to the shorter legs of the Tok. Bucky studied the wildlife, rarer here of course than in the game plains or the river edges, but all the more fascinating for its rarity. Gigantic butterflies flapped batlike through the lower canopy, sipping on the flowers—red, orange, mauve, yellow, blue—that seemed perennial in those leafy heights. Orchids, some of them as big as cook pots, bloomed from creases in the tree trunks. Gaudy parrots clacked and climbed the trees, using their hooked, heavy bills as levers. Flying squirrels coasted through the bottom branches, or glided down across their path to alight on the bole of some forest monarch, then scramble chittering to the top and another flight. Once the column halted and Clickrasp dispatched three spearsmen into a bamboo thicket ahead and to the right of their line of march. The hunters advanced in a crouch, spears cocked and quivering slightly in their throwing hands. As they neared the copse, a large giraffelike animal burst out the other side and fled untouched into the green gloom. A giraffe with a wry neck, thought Bucky. It must have been an okapi. Striped haunches and forelegs with a purplish-red back. By God, the rarest of African game animals! Where's my rifle?

He enjoyed watching the Tok move. They were

well-knit little men, few of them much taller than four and a half feet, he reckoned, though with their relatively heavy bone and musculature they probably weighed about 120 or 130 pounds. Their skin was not exactly white, as Winjah had said, but more of a lustrous tan, with a touch of gold in it, like some Southeast Asians or perhaps the Central American Indians. Apart from the grotesquerie of their genitalia, which reminded him of medieval jesters who sometimes wore fake phalluses as part of their costume, they were a handsome people. The big eyes helped a lot, as did the excellent dentition. There was nothing really "primitive" about their features, nothing on the order of those ghastly museum re-creations of Java man or *Sinanthropus* or *Homo neanderthalensis*—flat noses, brutal eyebrows, slack jaws, unseemly slouches—yet Buck, who had studied anthropology in college, suspected they derived from an earlier species of the genus *Homo.* Perhaps they were living survivors of such a species. Yes, he thought, it's apt. *Homo erectus.*

"That's gross," said Dawn when he explained his theory to her. She giggled nonetheless. Perhaps it was too early to tell, but Bucky felt that their relations had improved considerably over the past few days. Not just the capture, but everything that had happened since the group decision to go up after the Diamond Bogo. Perhaps since the fever. That must be it, he thought. I've lost a lot of weight, gotten a good tan, and taken a shower every day. Yes, it's the cosmetic virtues that she values most. What more could you expect from a woman who'd been pampered all her life, desired only for her beauty, who'd been a goddamn cheerleader in high school? Too dumb, too introverted to see that a man might choose slobhood as a sort of costume, just as Donn so carefully selects his faded French jeans and his Abercrombie-casual safari clothes to create an effect. I know the "right" costume as far as these people are concerned, he thought, but I'm damned if I'll wear it. I gave up uniforms of all kinds long ago. Fuck the Beautiful People!

Yeah, and sometimes you wish you could.

Up ahead there was a flurry of activity. The column halted. Tok ran clicking and husking up to a knot of men in the front. Bucky and Dawn ran up to join them. One Tok lay on the ground, writhing in agony while the others chattered around him, looking woebegone and desperate. Another Tok held a dying snake on the end of a spear. Its head was pinned to the ground, but a definite hood spread and closed under the spearpoint. The snake suddenly shot a double stream of yellowish fluid a full four feet into the air.

"A spitting cobra!" said Bucky.

"Yes," answered Clickrasp, at his shoulder. "It hit poor Xolz in the eyes. These reptiles have uncanny accuracy. The snake must have been at least ten feet away on the edge of the trail. I'm afraid there's nothing we can do. Xolz will be blind."

"No," said Bucky. "I remember reading somewhere, maybe in Meinertzhagen, or was it John Hunter, about a remedy. Here—let me in there."

Clickrasp sibilated an order and the men stood aside.

"Have two of them hold him by his shoulders, firmly, face up," said Buck. He unzipped his fly, prayed for rain, and then urinated in the snake-struck Tok's eyes. The surrounding Tok gasped and muttered in outrage. A few raised their spears.

"Tell them not to be upset," Bucky said, zipping up again. "I don't know if it's the uric acid or the ammonia, but something in the wee-wee neutralizes the venom. The pygmies of the Ituri Forest, over in the Congo, do precisely this when one of their hunters gets hit by a spitting cobra. Tell them no insult was intended, merely help."

Clickrasp spoke to his men, more harshly this time, and they quieted. Already the victim's eyes—bloodshot and spouting with tears just a minute ago—were clearing. He blinked and sat up, no longer twitching with pain. Bucky soaked his bandana in a pool of water from a rotting tree stump nearby and washed the man's face.

They camped in the jungle that night, not wanting to

move the injured man unnecessarily. Clickrasp explained that the City of the Tok was still a four-hour march away, up in the foothills of the mountain range. The Tok quickly set up camp, clambering up the trees to crack down dead branches for firewood, clacking and chirping when one of them fell in the process (though showing great concern for the poor fellow when he finally stood up); stringing hammocks between the lower limbs (some fifty to seventy-five feet above the ground, Buck guessed); building a huge blaze on the ground, well away from the hammock sites; and then awaiting the return of a three-man hunting party that had been dispatched earlier. Clicky was the leader of the hunting group.

They came back just at dusk, their bone whistles tootling at first in the distance—a happy tootle, Bucky thought, unlike the more ominous, longer-lunged and higher-pitched piping that had accompanied the attack yesterday. Then they appeared through the ghostlike boles of the trees, trotting excitedly, capering and chittering like so many playful children. The bag was surely a mixed one: a clutch of monkeys, brightly furred and gape-mouthed, their eyes rolling loosely, dull in the sockets, the fangs shining in the evening gloom; a scrut of parrots, their feathers already fading in death; a creep of small, loose-skinned, ratlike creatures, plus one truly gigantic rat, with a two-toned black and white tail and huge cheek pouches that flabbered as its body jostled on the Tok's back; and a mound of bulging scales, fat-sided, shiny, like a medieval pig clad in armor.

"Yes, we've slain two giants," Clickrasp announced to Dawn and Bucky as the pile of dead was stacked. "At least in the Linnaean sense. The outsized rodent there is the giant rat, *Cricetomys emini,* largest of the true rats. West of us, I'm told, they grow only to about eighteen inches long and two pounds weight. This one will go five pounds easily. Note the large forward-pointing ears, the naked tail black at the base and white toward the tip, the short, sleek, brown fur of the back, shading to vineaceous at the sides and white on the underparts. An eater of fruits, bulbs, and vegetation, it is prized as food throughout its range. Normally found only near human habitation, here it occurs in the wilder reaches as well. Ah, but I grow tedious. Must sound like a bloody zoology professor." He sighed, rather wistfully, and Bucky thought: Of course, that is precisely what he'd like to be. "The reptilian-seeming creature is a giant pangolin, *Manis (Smutsia) gigantea* Illiger, called by the Germans *das Schuppentier.* The Manidae, of course, are an order all their own, with but one family and one genus. Very ancient indeed, but related to the anteaters. Dine the same way. Some visitors to these parts erroneously call them armadillos, but the true armadillos—Edentata and Dasypodidae—are found only in tropical America. Hard to kill, these pangies. You have to get the spear in just right, under the overlapping plates of dermic armor. They're also quite difficult to clean." He issued orders and the pangolin was dragged off for butchering. "The smaller rodentlike creatures are red-backed flying squirrels, *Anomaluridae erythronatus,* common in this neck of the woods. We throw rocks at them."

He escorted Buck and Dawn toward the fire, leading the way like a diminutive English lord, suffering perhaps from satyriasis but nonetheless determined to exercise good manners. "Yes, the African flying squirrels. They're not true flying squirrels, you know, not even remotely related to squirrels of any sort. The Anomaluridae are the only survivors of a family now extinct everywhere on earth, save in tropical Africa." They paused at the fire and Clickrasp smiled up at them. "The same could be said of the Tok. As soon as we have finished dinner, I'll tell you about us. And about"—he chuckled in a mock-nasty manner—"the lurid anomaly of your Fate!"

That night Buck dreamed his Fate. He saw his head being served, in the manner of John the Baptist, to a horde of ravenous Tok. Firelight played on the Tok huts—hovels built of dung and straw, teeming with vermin—and ugly, huge-headed children sawed at his headless body with dull diamond-bladed knives. Clickrasp stuck a thumb in one of his steaming eyeballs and popped it loose. . . . He whimpered in his sleep.

"It's all right," soothed Dawn, warm beside him under the hide. "It's all right."

But she knew it wasn't.

PART THREE

THE GRIP OF THE NYIKA

22
THE BOGUS HUNTERS

Winjah had seen the dust cloud the evening before but dismissed it as a stampeding herd of game—zebra or hartebeest fleeing a pack of wild dogs, perhaps. Now in the early morning, just as they were about to ford the Kan and begin their ascent of the scarp, they heard the motors. A whining of torque, gritting of gears, faint at first, then increasing in volume, sometimes lost completely as the vehicles—at least three of them, Winjah estimated—disappeared into a donga or behind a jebel.

"Trucks," he said. "But they're not ours."

"Whose, then?" Donn asked.

"We'll know in a minute," the hunter answered, pointing to the dust cloud that now rose ragged over the doum palms close at hand. "They sound like military vehicles." He reached his hand back to Lambat, who stood just behind him, for the .458. It had better not be troops, he thought. That could be very bad. Give an African a machine gun and he'll kill before asking any questions, just to see the bodies flop. Even the bloody officers, when they're out in the bush and there's no one around but vultures.

The first truck rumbled into view, others bouncing behind it, and Winjah saw that it was an ex-U.S. Army two and a half ton with the yellow crossed-scimitars insigne of the Kansduvian Armed Forces on the sloping green hood. Black faces under fatigue caps peered at him over the cab, black arms in olive drab and camouflage pointed. A great flashing of teeth in the dusk, and the glint of weapons. Winjah spat. The saliva was sparse, all right. Then he saw a white face peering through the windscreen.

"It'll be all right," he said. "There's a bwana with 'em."

The truck stopped, three others rolling to a halt behind it, and the white man stepped out. He was tall and big-bellied, with a florid, beefy face only partly hidden by a patchy graying beard. An Aussie-style, flop-brimmed hat with a fake leopard skin sweatband perched atop his minuscule pate. On one hip hung a holstered, pearl-handled revolver, on the other a large bowie knife. He tucked his sweat-soaked khaki shirt into the top of his capacious safari shorts and glowered with tiny black eyes behind a pair of rimless glasses as Winjah walked forward, a polite smile on the hunter's face.

"Who the hell are you," the man yelled, "and what are you doing in *my* hunting bloc?"

"I beg your pardon?" Winjah said, stopping short.

"I said this is *my* bloc. There's not supposed to be anyone hunting here but me and my boys." He gestured behind him toward three teen-agers, tall and vacant-eyed, who had just dismounted from the following trucks. "The general said so himself. God knows I paid enough for the privilege."

"Well, I'm sorry but I also have papers permitting sole hunting rights in this bloc, until the end of August," Winjah said. "Unfortunately, the papers were burned by raiders who destroyed our camp two days ago. But duplicates are on file in Palmerville." He eyed the intruder coldly, the big elephant gun cradled easily, Indian-fashion, in the crook of his left arm. "Where's your hunter? I'm sure he and I can work out a mutual understanding."

"*I'm* my hunter," the man said. "I don't need none of you professional parasites to show me how to kill animals. The general said I didn't. Now you guys just better pack up and get to hell out of here." His sons stood beside the man, grinning eagerly. One of them scratched his crotch with the muzzle of an Israeli Uzi machine pistol. Winjah noticed that the troops, some thirty of them, were similarly armed. They stood in a loose semicircle, hard-eyed and eager, watching the confrontation.

"Now wait a minute," Donn interrupted. "Those raiders that burned our camp also kidnaped my wife, along with a friend of mine. I'm not getting out of here for you or anyone, generals included, until I get her back."

"Lemme take him, Pa," leered one of the boys. "He's easy pickin's."

"Shut up, Stroth," the man said. "Just who the shit are you, sonny?" he asked Donn. Donn told him. The man pondered the name for a moment, scratching his beard. Then he suddenly smiled.

"The millionaire race-car driver? Sure. I thought you looked familiar. Why, the boys and me are all racing fans. Go to Indy every Memorial Day, and the sporty car races too. You drove for Shelby in the early days. Donny McGavern, King of the Cobras." He stepped forward and offered his hand. "I'm Tex Nordquist from Big D, oil and fast foods, and these here is my boys. Strother, Heber, and Fernando." Donn shook hands all around. "Why didn't you tell us right off that the coons had nabbed your lady?" the elder Nordquist asked. "We'd be glad to help you get her back, wouldn't we, boys?"

They retired to the shade of the trucks where one of the boys wrestled down an ice chest full of beer. Coors and Pearl, though Nordquist allowed as how he preferred the Texas brew. He chugged one in three gulps, crushed the can, belched, and went to work on another as Donn explained how the Tok had effected the kidnaping. Winjah listened in silence.

"Yes," Nordquist said. "The general told us about

them little bastards. The Dorks, ain't that what they're called? Well, we got plenty of firepower. The general loaned me a whole platoon of his palace guard, automatic weapons, bazookas and all. Plus we got our own secret weapons. Show 'em, boys."

Heber, Strother, and Fernando ran back to the rearmost truck and dropped the tailgate. Grunting, clanking, cussing. Then the sound of motorcycle engines. They came barreling back to their father, mounted gleefully astride a trio of ugly little three-wheeled cycles with fat, knobby-studded tires. Heber tried to cut a doughnut and spilled on his face in the dust. The other brothers laughed and tried to run over his arms.

"ATCs," said Nordquist. "Honda All-Terrain Cycles. Ninety cubes, plenty of power to get us anywhere we want up on that plateau. Got another one back in the truck for the old Boss Honcho to ride." He slapped himself on the chest and grinned proudly.

"They'll climb the scarp all right," Winjah said. "But how do you propose getting them across the river? It's quite deep all along here. The nearest ford is some thirty miles upstream, in the heart of the swamp."

"We also got us a Zodiac raft with a forty-horse Evinrude," Nordquist answered. "Ol' Tex always comes prepared. Like I got me a half a truck of beer along with us, so's we don't run dry, and lots of good hot homemade chili." He cut an echoing fart. "Keeps the bowels a-movin'."

"Hey Pa," yelled Strother. "We wanna go hunting on the cycles." He brandished his Uzi. "Down by the river."

"Well, don't wander too far. I'm gonna start the nig-nogs packin' our gear up the mountain so be back by dinnertime—no later'n noon."

The boys roared off toward the Kan, whooping and looping, and for the next two hours the rattle of machine-gun fire rolled back from the walls of the scarp, punctuated occasionally by the scream of dying monkeys. Nordquist stalked back and forth from trucks to riverbank, bellowing Texican curses at the blacks who lugged gas drums, cases of beers, cartons of ammo, crates of food, tents, and a Porta-Potty down to the Kan. Donn and Winjah watched from the shade, their own lads gathered quietly around them. Only Otiego was grinning, but then he was always happy.

"Should we go with them?" Donn asked.

"It wouldn't hurt," Winjah said after a while. "Not for the first few days at least. They've plenty of firepower, as Ol' Supertex said, which could come in helpful if the Tok have arranged an ambush for us at the top of the scarp."

"But Christ," Donn said, "they're so dreadful."

"Texican bluster," Winjah replied. "I've had plenty of them as clients over the years. They're a pain in the arse, all right, but most of them are plenty brave. And they all shoot well. I just wonder if they know about our friend with the stone in his brow." Winjah sent Lambat and Otiego to talk with the officer in charge of the Kansduvian platoon, telling them to say nothing about the Diamond Bogo but to sound the man out as to whether or not the Texans were aware of the beast's existence.

The trackers returned with a folded newspaper clipping. Winjah read it and cursed.

"Listen to this. 'High in the mountain fastnesses of Kansdu, a tiny African republic that only recently achieved independence, a fortune is on the hoof.' *The News of the* Bloody *World*. It must be on all the news wires by now." The byline read "Tony Treacle."

Nordquist confirmed their fears as they stood beside the river, watching the long line of bearers snaking up the scarp, while the Nordquist heirs—returned from their monkey shoot only after they'd expended all their ammo—cavorted on the far shore with their cycles. Huey, Louie, and Dewey, thought Donn. At play.

"Yeah," said Nordquist, "it was in all the papers back home. *Newsweek* had a piece on it that said they doubted the story, but *Time* believed it. That's why we came. Shee-it, when we left Palmerville the other day, the airport was jammed with hunters. Like openin' day in the Big Bend Country. Krauts, Frog-eaters, Eye-ties, but mainly

Amurricans like us. All come to hunt the great embogus. Ain't that what you call a buffalo in nigger? The Diamond Bogus. But the general give me the sole hunting rights to this plateau, and promised he'd steer the other bogus hunters down to the south, around Lake Tok and thereabouts."

He stared at Winjah and Donn, then spat between his hand-tooled cowboy boots.

"Didn't reckon on finding you boys here, but since we're all together we might as well get one thing clear right off the bat. I paid the general $250,000—cash—for the chance to take this bogus. Promised him a helluva lot more, for the future, and you can bet your ass it warn't no chain of taco stands, neither. These nigs want oil and I got it. So if we connect with the Diamond Bogus, just remember. He's mine."

"All I want is my wife back," said Donn.

"And Bucky," Winjah added. "If he's still alive."

23
TOKSVILLE

Set against a backdrop of somber mountains, the City of the Tok gleamed like an icefall in the midmorning light. No, thought Bucky, that's too weak a word for it. It blazes. Scintillates. Beams. Fulgurates. At this distance, the very shapes of the buildings were obscured by spicules of light that leaped and danced from the city. Beside him, Dawn breathed shallowly, holding his hand.

"My God," Buck said. "Is it built of diamonds?"

"Not entirely," said Clickrasp. "Mainly daub and wattle, but every house has a diamond or two set in the walls. It creates rather a pleasing effect, don't you think? Particularly in this light."

"Rather," Buck answered sourly.

"Yes, the stones are fairly common in this vicinity. Not much utility to them, but my people have a deep aesthetic sense, and our craftsmen are expert at cutting and polishing. We use them for urban decoration, and in some

147

of our weapons. But apart from that they are of little value in our economy, which as I explained is still basically on the hunting and gathering level. Well, shall we get on? I'm sure the damsels of Tok are eagerly awaiting your arrival, Bwana Buck." He smiled mischievously and stepped out.

Yes, the damsels of Tok, Bucky thought. After a dinner last evening of broiled pangolin and stewed monkey brains, Clickrasp had explained to them the reason for their capture. They were reclining around the fire, Bucky and Dawn wrapped under the leopard-skin rug, Clickrasp playing a casual game of mumblety-peg with his diamond-bladed knife. His phallus was still in a splint, though he claimed it felt much better this evening than last.

"As you may have surmised," he began, "we Tok are not of the same species as you *Homo sapiens.* I've studied as many anthropological texts as I could procure, during various raids, and have concluded that we are the last of the line called *Homo erectus.* No puns, please. The only true test of specific difference between animals of the same genus, of course, is whether or not members of the opposite species can 'breed true.' That is to say, Dawn and I might well be able to produce a child between us, but would that child then be able to reproduce itself? If so, we are of the same species, regardless of any apparent difference in physiology, such as size, color of skin, amount of body hair, even so striking a difference in kind as this." He slapped his cock, then winced. "But if the child proved sterile, then we are definitely of different species. The mule, as you well know, is the classic example of this natural law. Product of the horse, *Equus caballus,* and the donkey, *Equus asinus,* the poor chap is larger than both its parents, a trait known commonly as 'hybrid vigor,' but unfortunately is doomed to a childless life. Sterile as a surgeon's gloves." He smiled sadly and shook his head in lamentation for the miserable mule.

"A long time ago," he continued, "up until the days of my great-grandfather's rule, we routinely mated with our captives of your species. Yes, and we produced offspring.

But those offspring were sterile. So sad. You see, we Tok revere children far more than we do, say, diamonds. Yet the 'mules' that dropped from these couplings were colossal creatures. Larger even than the Watutsi of Rwanda and Burundi. But muscled like Tok. Very strong indeed. And smart? You wouldn't believe it. One of them, a young lady named Ygrxx, once memorized the entire first volume of the Britannica between breakfast and lunch.

"You may have noticed that our heads are larger, proportionally and in true displacement, than yours. My measurements show that the average Tok brain displaces two thousand cubic centimeters, while the average *Homo sapiens* cranium contains only fifteen hundred. Our musculature is also superior to yours, despite our smaller size. In my youth, if you'll pardon the boast, I could bench-press four hundred and fifty pounds. And I stand only four foot eight. So you can imagine what the hybrid vigor of these *sapiens-erectus* crosses would be like. These 'wise-peckers' as one might call them."

He paused again, scraped a tendril of cold, congealed cerebral matter from a monkey skull that lay beside the fire, and sucked it from his fingernail.

"And now a brief digression," he continued. "You've doubtless wondered how it is that I, a prehuman by your standards, came to speak fluent English and to acquire such a fund of botanical, zoological, and anthropological lore. The answer: Mungo Park." He waited, smiling tentatively, to see if the name meant anything to them. Bucky nodded slowly. Mungo Park, first great English explorer of Africa, the Scots physician who settled the question of the Niger, then returned to Africa and disappeared at the falls of Busa in 1806.

"My great-grandfather captured Dr. Park," Clickrasp went on. "Rather than eat him on the spot—he and his hunting party were sated with the brains of an elephant they had killed the previous day—my worthy ancestor brought Dr. Park here, as a sort of pet at first. Thus, unwittingly, we revolutionized our lives. For Dr. Park was

an exceptional man—tall, strong, very brave, and very
loving. He quickly mastered our language and taught us
his own. He inculcated us with a reverence for natural
history, and in subsequent raids we captured volume on
volume of taxonomic texts, along with works of history,
poetry, geography, geology, linguistics, mathematics, and
the like. Amazing what the British will pack along while
'roughing it.' From Dr. Park we learned who we are, and
from us he learned how to fit into Africa."

"What became of him?" Bucky asked.

"He died at eighty-seven after breaking a hip on a
butterfly-collecting expedition. I'll show you his grave
when we get home—and his collections. Our national
treasure. But I am getting too far ahead of myself. Right
now we want to discuss your, er, immediate future. It was
Dr. Park, at any rate, who finally convinced my ancestor of
the immorality of mating between Tok and *Homo sapiens*.
He was a deeply religious man, with many of the
inhibitions that came to full flower later, in the Victorian
period. But since that time, many things have changed in
the world, and we have managed to keep abreast of those
developments. The pressures of expanding tribes around
us have driven us deeper and deeper into the mountains,
and since Park's day we Tok have declined greatly in
numbers, our total population today amounting to no
more than five hundred odd souls. We are pressed on all
sides by enemies—the newly emerged African nations that
lust after our land, the ever-grasping Europeans who
desire our diamonds. We want only to live in peace, here
on our plateau, nibbling brains and watching the fair
African sunlight play through our diamond windows. But
you will not let us. So now you are going to help us, like it
or not.

"You, dear Bucky, are going to stud. You will
inseminate as many fecund Toklettes as your puny
member can handle. You are going to copulate until your
corneas fall out, as they say, and then stick a few more.
Don't worry, we have drugs that will aid you in your duties,
and believe me, Tok maidens are nubile. And you, fair
memsahib, you are going to breed as well. Our womenfolk

recently developed an herbal potion, K'zchr we call it, that speeds the estrus cycle so that a damsel such as yourself can drop a child every three months. And in most cases, the births are multiple. During an experimental run last year, I personally begat twenty-seven young from three women in a nine-month period. All of them triples." He grinned winningly. "Once the old pestle's back in shape," he said, "we'll shoot for quadruples, hey?"

"And what are you going to do with these 'mules,' as you call them?" Bucky asked. "Send them out into the real world with diamond-headed spears to get gunned down in harness? They've got cannon and airplanes and flamethrowers and machine guns out there. Your pestle is just going to produce a lot of mortar victims."

Clicky giggled. "A good pun, if a bit grim. Let me assure you, however, that I have already taken steps to procure modern armaments for my troops. Agents are at work abroad. What's more, we don't intend to range very far beyond the plateau—only far enough to set up advance lines of resistance in the event of an invasion. Our main line, naturally, will be the scarp itself. We expect to have trouble from air strikes, perhaps even lose the City of the Tok in its entirety, but our rain forest should prove every bit as protective as those of Southeast Asia were for the Vietcong. We can hold out."

"Still," Dawn broke in, "it will take years before these 'mules' of yours are old enough to fight. And from what you say, the invasion will come sooner rather than later."

"Correct on the last point," Clicky replied, "but you aren't aware of another unique feature of Tok physiology. Thanks to our 'primitive' nature, our young mature—physically at least—quite rapidly. Our infants walk within a week of birth, drop their milk teeth at four months, and reach their full height at one year. They fill out a bit later, but by my reckoning they should be able to handle firearms at nine months, at least defensively. With the warriors I have available now, once the weapons arrive, I can bloody any invader's nose and thus buy time until my first generation of hybrids comes of fighting age."

"It's awful," Dawn cried, shuddering.

"Awful?" asked Clickrasp. "Awful that a leader should devise a plan to save his people? The entire record of human affairs during the past two centuries or more, not just in Africa but in the Americas and Asia as well, is one of the persecution and extermination of so-called primitive peoples by the so-called enlightened ones. The Bushmen of southern Africa, the Hottentots of German Southwest, the Ainu of northern Japan, countless tribes of Amerinds from the Aztecs to the Zuñi, the Ik of Uganda, the Tasaday of the Philippines, the Meo of Indochina, even the Eskimos of the Arctic. If these peoples have not been destroyed root and branch, then they have had their cultures stripped from them, leaving them soulless in a world they never made." His eyes sparked verdant rage and he stood to his full four foot eight. "It was *your* people who did these things—not just the Americans and the Europeans, but all *Homo sapiens.* And to one another, not just the hundreds upon hundreds of species of 'lesser animals' like the bison and the peregrines and the whales. How dare you call *me* awful?"

He turned and scampered up a tree, climbing higher and higher into the darkness, until they saw his dim shape roll into a hammock high above the ground. Bucky could have sworn the Tok was crying.

"But we *mean* well, don't we?" asked Dawn after a while. "You know, mankind?"

"That's the propaganda, anyway," said Buck.

But propaganda or not, Bucky thought, it was his world. And this little egomaniac with the outsized pecker was out to destroy it. Don't be taken in by that "endangered species" bullshit, he warned himself. You've seen enough of politics to know that they all lie, they all try to make themselves look clean in the eyes of the world while they're elbow-deep in guts. Or money. He smiled cynically to himself as he imagined Clickrasp at the United Nations, in striped trousers and a morning coat, fawned over by Third World leaders, then dining at Lutece on what he claimed was *cervelles au beurre noire.* Clickrasp charming on the Johnny Carson show, swapping one-liners with the Great Man. Clickrasp and Abe Beame riding in a ticker-tape parade down Broadway, waving at the hooks and faggots, the mayor at last able to gaze down at a guest . . .

But it wasn't really funny. Yeah, it was a shit world back there, and Bucky had nothing to go back to. He was tired to death of the games he wrote about, his wife had left him because of his slobhood, the few women who would still have anything to do with him either spoke a different language or wanted money, which he didn't have. But it was his world—dim, smoky bars where the talk and booze were warm, the few covers still full of grouse and woodcock, the trout streams and the bookstores. Here he would be a prisoner, and a prisoner at stud, to boot. He'd done that stud bit once before—trying for months on end to get his wife pregnant, to save their marriage with a kid, coming home early from work when she called to say her temperature was right, now was the time to do it. That's when he learned to lie about his duty, at work at least, then dashing up from the Fleetwood station into the three-room apartment with the Miró prints on the walls, and those bookshelves she'd wanted from Paul McCobb, her head still full of rollers, smiling, and done her till he was raw. Then lying there in the suburban heat to hear the mothers on the playground, watching their children across the road. "Careful!"

Those voices.

Strange that he'd never knocked her up. Made a man feel he had some control over his seed, if not his jism.

Well, I'm older now, Bucky thought. Clickrasp wants a bedroom athlete, he's looked the wrong way. Thumb out my eyeballs if you want, you friggin' dwarf. . . .

Suddenly Buck had a yearning in his legs, an itch he couldn't scratch. He arched his toes, flexed his calves, scratched his ankles. Sure. The Guinea worm. He hadn't thought about the Guinea worm in a long time. If the Guinea worm were back . . .

He looked up into the tree where Clickrasp slept.

Not now. Later, maybe . . .

Dawn rolled over in her sleep, her warm curple pressing against Bucky's thigh. The fire had died down to a bed of coals. Bats swooped in the dark. Monkey skulls grinned from the shadows around the hearth. Why not take her now? I'd be doing her a service—might knock her up, give her nine months' grace before Clicky and his pronged predators have a shot at her. All I'd have to do is sweet-talk her a bit, she's scared and ready, just lie to her a bit like the pretty ones always expect. . . . But you said you'd never do that again, never betray a trust. And for all that he's a woolgatherer, a bit of a poseur, Donn trusts you. What I've got to do is get her the hell out of here, and quick.

High overhead, Clickrasp growled in his sleep.

But in the morning, the Tok chieftain's good humor had returned intact. During the march out of the jungle and across the rolling, high-grass plain that lay before the city, he chattered gaily to Dawn and Bucky about the local flora and fauna, attempting to teach them the Tok words for gemsbok and francolin and mimosa, laughing at their stiff-tongued failures, exulting whenever they got a glottal stop right. The other Tok were friendly, too, remembering Buck's miraculous cure for spitting cobra venom, no doubt. They smiled at him and a few tried to speak to him in English. He smiled back and nodded approvingly even when they got it wrong. Then, finally, the city hove into sight.

"Home again," sighed Clickrasp. "This city has been here since the beginning of time—or at least since the retreat of the last glaciation some twelve thousand three hundred years ago. When the Würm Glacier was down, the country north of here, now the Sahara, was a vast game plain. Perhaps the richest in the world. As I understand it, the glacier, which covered most of northern Eurasia and North America, blocked the flow of westerlies and forced them south, so that they dropped their rainfall on North Africa. All manner of wondrous beasts lived here then. What we see today is a mere vestige of the mammalian fecundity that obtained in Africa just so short a time ago.

I'll show you some bones and horns from that period in our family museum. But when the glacier retreated—and apparently it went fast, a mere few centuries for the retreat after some sixty thousand years of ice—the westerlies moved north, to Europe and Siberia and Canada, dropping their rain up there. The Sahara began to dry up, and our people moved south with the game. That's when we built the city. It may be the oldest in the world, or at least the oldest that has survived."

As they neared the gates, a crowd of Tok swarmed out to greet them. They clittered and grinned, dancing with joy at the return of the warriors. Some of the children—perfect physical copies of the adults except for size—jeered at the captives until Clickrasp chided them. Then they gazed awfully upward, particularly at Dawn, whose golden hair flowed in the cool breeze from the mountains. The women, Bucky noticed, were indeed nubile—pocket Venuses with tiny waists, sweepingly broad hips, and firmly packed buttocks tapering to trim, shapely legs. Clad only in hides draped loosely over their shoulders or hips, they were full-breasted as well, much more so than the only other women of that size with whom Bucky had had dealings—Japanese and Southeast Asian, mainly. Even the old women were lovely, smooth and sedate. Facially they resembled Asians, except for the uniformly green eyes. Their hair, long and black, reached generally to the waist, and was held back from their shapely small ears with clasps adorned with precious and semiprecious stones. The fire opal seemed a favorite. None of them, oddly enough, wore diamonds as jewelry. That was fine with Buck: He had a deep suspicion of diamond-bright babes.

The walls of the city, which appeared to be of stone filled in with a tan, almost rosy mortar, were smoothly finished and tall, perhaps six feet thick at the base and tapering to half that at the crenellated tops, themselves perhaps eighteen feet above the ground. Skulls adorned the poles that flanked the heavy gray beech-wood gate. Some of them had diamonds set in the eye sockets that winked playfully as they passed. Dawn shivered slightly as they entered the city, then drew in her breath at the scene that lay before them. The houses, surrounded by tall flowering trees, were low half-timbered structures with rambling wings and thatched roofs, vaguely English Tudor in style, but the windows glistened with diamonds. The gravel-paved streets wound narrow and mazelike between the houses, everything gleaming white and brown and green, cleanly swept and tidy. The scent of flowers filled the cool air.

"Beautiful," Dawn sighed. "Just exquisite."

"Thank you, my lady," said Clickrasp with a gentlemanly bow. "Of course we can't take the entire credit for it. Dr. Park had quite an influence on the architectural style of the city as you see it today. Back in 1826, by your count, Mount Baikie erupted, and though the lava never reached us, the tremors destroyed most of the solid structures of the day. Dr. Park rebuilt his house in the Tudor style, and many of the Tok followed his example out of respect and affection. Dr. Park also taught us sanitation. He had discovered an underground river that, by chance, flows directly under the town. Only about forty feet down. He dropped a sewer into it, and showed us how to build conduits that would carry our wastes away. The river rises to the surface of the plateau some six miles to the south. The plant life there is amazingly rich."

"So you have indoor plumbing," said Buck. "But where do you get your water? I hope it's not from the same underground river."

"Of course not," snapped Clickrasp. "Most of the houses have their own wells—the water table is quite near the surface this close to the mountains—but we also have three stone mains, again the contribution of Dr. Park, which flow by gravity feed from springs just north of the city. Enemies might try to poison the springs, and thus the city, but we can always fall back on the wells in that event."

They walked on through the winding lanes, Clicky stopping frequently to talk with the citizenry. There was no sense of pomp or condescension in his manner, Bucky noted, but rather a genuine aura of warmth and egalitarianism. Indeed, Clicky bowed to every older person and woman who greeted him, clapped the men on the shoulders, and picked up most of the children for a quick hug and kiss. Most of the houses had small vegetable gardens behind them, and many of the women emerged from these plots, their hands black with loam which they brushed off on their skin skirts as they hastened up. Bucky studied the gardens, but saw little that he recognized. There were gigantic purple squashlike fruits growing under broad-leafed vines; a bush that bore yellow foot-long pods bulging with what looked like baseball-sized peas or beans; leafy plants with crinkled edges that resembled certain lettuces, yet stood as tall as a man. Fruit trees were interspersed in the gardens and around the houses, some of them hung heavy with globules that resembled oranges, avocados, and papayas. Giant sunflowers marked the verges of the gardens, blazing orange and yellow around their dark-brown faces. At this altitude, Bucky thought, with this intensity of sunlight this close to the equator, why not? It's a gardener's paradise. The whiff of compost heap came to his nostrils, cutting sharply across the sweet scent of blossoms. It reminded him of his grandmother's garden back home, in his boyhood. An Austrian immigrant, she had had the greenest of thumbs. Gooseberries the size of marbles; sweet plums that she baked in a softer version of potato dough and called *Zwetschchenknödel;* cabbages big as basketballs; and always the sour, biting scent of the compost, rotting behind the garden, an intimation of death and regeneration.

Farther on they passed what appeared to be a communal bath. Wisps of steam rose from the rocky pool in which a few Tok men and women lolled, chin-deep in the hot water. A faint odor of sulfur reached them. The pool was surrounded by carefully tended shrubs and small trees, and artfully arranged piles of varicolored rock, wind- and water-worn, that glowed in the noon light. It reminded Bucky of the hotsi-bath gardens in the inns of

Japan, and indeed he noticed one Tok female scrubbing herself assiduously beside the pool with something that frothed like soap before she entered the bath itself.

"We built that bath only fifteen years ago," said Clickrasp, noticing Buck's attention. "At the behest of an American captive, who had spent some time in Japan. During the Occupation. Nice chap, a wealthy banker from Philadelphia. Can't recall his name. We took him alive down in the flats west of Lake Tok, where he was seeking a world-record beisa oryx. Taught us a lot about money matters—the gold outflow, balance of payments, your declining natural resources, that sort of thing. He finally committed suicide, though. Got bored with us and ripped his belly open with a diamond-bladed butter knife. *Seppuku,* he called it."

"You're quite adaptive to other cultural styles," Bucky said.

"Yes," Click agreed. "As you'll see when our weapons arrive." He giggled behind his hand. "Now then, here's my home. Let's go in and say hello to the womenfolk. You'll be seeing quite a lot of them over the next few months, Bucky my boy."

24
THE SPORTING LIFE

"Fork it!" bellowed Nordquist. He slapped the rifle on the butt and kicked his boot in the dirt. The wounded lion coughed as it slunk into the heavy brush of the karonga nearly a quarter of a mile away. "There must be something wrong with the ferkin' scope!" He stalked back to his motorized tricycle and stuck the weapon muzzle down into the lustrous leather rifle boot strapped to its side.

Winjah said nothing. The rifle was a Weatherby .17-caliber magnum, mounted with a costly three-to-ten power variable scope. Nordquist claimed to have killed a Kodiak bear with it up in Alaska, along with every lesser species of North American big game. At first Winjah had objected that so small a bullet—a mere twenty-five grains, seven times lighter than the smallest he used on any animal—was too light for Africa. Nordquist had exploded.

"It's movin' at 4,020 foot per second out of the muzzle," he roared, "and still going better'n 2,000 at three hundred yards. It shoots where I wanna put it—right in the goldang earhole. Sure, it's only packin' 230 foot-pounds of clout at that range, where your freakin' seven-mil mag's got sixteen hunnert plus. But 230's enough to pick the wax out of any critter's ear. What is this pussy shit about breakin' animals down? I wanna drop 'em where they stand, with the teensiest hunk of lead possible. That's what we call sportin' down Texas way."

Nordquist had indeed dropped a few animals with the popgun—a tommy, standing, at four hundred yards, and two hartebeest, one of them on the move, at lesser ranges. All had been hit either in the head or the neck. But he had hit and lost six others, mainly plains game like impala and Grant's gazelles. When they bucked and went off wounded, he never followed them up.

"Aren't you going to finish him?" Winjah had asked, that first morning, when a fine Grant's had given them the shake and split. He had seen the hairs fly on the gazelle's throat. The hollow-point bullet had probably opened an artery, or the windpipe, and the animal would run off for perhaps half a mile before it lay down to die. An easy follow-up, particularly on the cycles.

"Why?" asked Nordquist. "Gas is a helluva lot dearer out here than gazelles." He gestured at the game plain, the high Tok Plateau, over which grazed countless thousands of horned creatures. Now, though, with the lion wounded, Winjah knew he had to take a stand.

"Are you going to follow the lion in?" he asked, as politely as he could manage.

"And get clawed up for nothin'?" Nordquist asked, turning stupefied from the bike, which he had been about to kick-start to life. "That's for the adventure books. If I don't drop 'em with one shot, they don't even exist."

"But he's wounded. He's not only in pain, which I'm sure matters nothing to you, but now he's a menace to everyone who passes this way, ourselves included. If he doesn't die quickly, he may well end up crippled. When we come back out, he may choose us for dinner rather than some fleet-footed tommy or impala. And you hit him in the foreleg, you know."

"Bullshit," said Nordquist. "I missed him clean."

"Then come on over with me while I look for blood. I'm sure you hit him. Or are you getting the wind up?"

Nordquist reached for the revolver on his hip. It was a Ruger Super Blackhawk in .44 magnum, with the seven-and-a-half-inch barrel and the tanged trigger guard, onto which he had screwed grips of ivory from a walrus he shot up in the Bering Strait. Nordquist had explained at length that the highly touted .357 magnum pistol round was actually a much overrated bullet. A study by the New Mexico state police had demonstrated conclusively that the .44 mag was far superior for blowing a man's guts out his asshole, as the Texan put it. Now he stared steely-eyed at Winjah, his hand hovering a twitchy few inches above the ivory butt. "You better take that back, Limey," he said. Huey, Dewey, and Louie gripped their machine pistols more firmly and smirked. Paw was at it again.

"Then follow me into the cover," said Winjah, spinning on his heel and walking toward the draw into which the wounded cat had limped. Donn followed, his trigger finger on the guard of the .375, safety forward, his back twitching in anticipation of the Uzi bullets. He could see that Otiego, just ahead of him, was shivering his spear in preparation for a quick throw to the rear, if it were needed. But the Texans did nothing.

Lambat, in the lead, spotted the blood first. He pointed it out, wordlessly, with a stalk of grass—bright arterial blood clustered like berries in the low grass. Just about elbow height on the lion, Winjah thought. Yes, he'll end up a man-eater all right. The trail led off into the draw. Winjah ordered Otiego and Machyana to follow along the lips of the deep brush-choked gully while Lambat went in with Winjah and Donn. Red Blanket was to climb that acacia over there, as high as possible, and watch to see if the lion came out ahead of them.

"All right, duty calls," Winjah said, turning to Donn. He smiled, suddenly, for the first time since they had met the Texans the previous morning. Christ, Donn thought, he actually loves this part of it. He looks ten years younger. "Once more unto the breach."

It was hot and stale in the karonga, the air still and the smell of dead water hanging thick with the pungent stink of thorn. Even in the mottled, brushy shade there was no cool. Lambat moved at a deep crouch, slowly, some five paces ahead of Winjah, with Donn an equal distance behind. Above, to either side, Donn caught occasional glimpses of the two flanking trackers through the spiky cover. Each time it gave him a start, and once Otiego saw his fear. The Turkana smiled wisely and then made a bhangi-smoking gesture. Donn's heart began to slow and he smiled to himself. That's a helluva man, he thought.

They came to a drop in the draw, a spot where, during a heavy rain, there would be a waterfall. Below, the brush gave way to heavy sand and water-worn rocks. The lion's pad marks were deep in the sand, and there was a depression where he had lain down for a moment, punctuated by a pool of glossy blood on which the flies were already at work. Lambat whispered to Winjah and pointed ahead. The draw widened and hooked to the right. A large boulder obscured the view around the corner. Winjah shook his head, in the negative, and Lambat slid back to him for a closer, quieter conversation. Donn felt something on his boot and looked down. A dung beetle, shiny, huge, was pushing a ball of shit over his toes. He watched it while the others conferred, watched it push its valuable load against the crepe sole of the boot, straining stupendously, finally raising the ball to the curved angle of the leather, then repositioning its hind legs and pushing once more. The shit-ball rolled over his foot, then down the other side. The dung beetle dropped after it and continued the interrupted journey.

Winjah gestured and Donn went up to him.

"The simba is just ahead of us," Winjah whispered. "He's lying up just beyond that boulder. Lambat smells him and thinks he can hear him breathing. I want you to give Lambat the .375 and then when I give you the signal, to throw a rock over the boulder. Then maybe he'll come, or else he'll run farther down the karonga and weaken a bit more."

"But I want to shoot."

"Not on lion, Bwana. Not yet."

"Yes," Donn whispered. "Now or never, as they say."
He stared into the hunter's pale-blue eyes. Very hard. "I
can do it, Bwana."

Winjah looked back, equally hard. Finally he nodded.
He whispered something to Lambat, who in turn looked
closely at Donn. No smile. Lambat eased over to the right
side of the draw and picked up a rock. Winjah moved to
the far left. He raised the .458 to his shoulder and dug in
his heels, leaning forward, head up over the sights. Donn
did the same, but kept his eye on the scope at the proper
relief. The boulder just framed the sight picture, not more
than twenty yards ahead. Out of the corner of his eye, he
saw Winjah gesture to Lambat.

He never heard the rock land. Instead there came a
sound like none he had heard before, a raving,
deep-chested hiss that erupted into a jet-engine roar,
compressed and heated by the closeness of the karonga,
and the lion was around the corner. All eyes and open
mouth, the dark mane framing like black fire a grainy
apparition that grew mountainous as he saw it through the
scope, coming at them, and he felt the sear go. The blast of
Winjah's rifle slammed his eardrums, masking the
explosion of his own. He had lost the lion through the
scope, with the recoil, and frantically he sought it again,
working the bolt and feeling the second round slap home
in the receiver. Goddamn scope sights! At close range they
aren't worth shit.

"Easy, Bwana," said Winjah. "He's finished."

The lion lay on its back, headed the way it had come,
its tail twitching in short, spastic jerks. The great arch of
the cat's chest heaved once, then again, and Donn heard
air whistling through blood and broken bone. Then the
lion was still. Lambat hurled a rock at the carcass, eliciting
no response. They walked up.

"Nice shooting," Winjah said. He pointed to the two
entrance wounds, one in the throat and one on the point
of the chest. "The higher one's the .458. You put yours

right down into his heart and lungs. Very nice shooting for a scoped rifle at such close range, Bwana." He turned and shook Donn's hand, while the other trackers leaped whooping down into the gully. Above, they heard the snarl of combustion engines.

"Well," Nordquist drawled from the lip of the draw. "You collected him for me. Thanks, fellers."

"He's Donn's cat," said Winjah, not bothering to look up.

"The hail you say," Nordquist answered. "I'm the one that hit him first off. That makes him mine. First bullet—that's the rules back home. Otherwise you'd have ever' nigger in the woods plunkin' lead into your deer after you dropped him."

"But you didn't drop him, Mr. Nordquist," Winjah said. "You were going to let him go off and die on his own, don't you remember? 'If I don't drop them with one shot, they don't even exist.' "

"I was joshin' ya. Why, my boys and I were headin' over here right now to do the job. You Limehousers can't take a joke."

"I don't want the lion," Donn interrupted. "I never intended to kill a big cat. And I'd be ashamed to show the trophy in my home. He can have it."

Winjah explained the situation to the trackers, who were preparing to skin the animal out. Otiego looked up at Nordquist, fierce contempt in his blood-rimmed eyes. With his panga, he chopped off the lion's right front paw and gestured with it to Donn. "This much you keep," he said. "I make necklace for you, out of the hooks." Then he shifted his eyes back to Nordquist, the panga cocked meaningfully in his chopping hand.

"Sure," the Texan said quickly, "sure, why not? Let the Young Gavern have the claws. Hell, give him all of 'em. All I want's a head mount, anyways. Head and shoulders." He grinned wickedly. "With them big yaller choppers showin'."

When they got back to the main body of porters, the Kansduvian officer came up to Winjah looking nervous.

He pointed to the edge of the rain forest, which loomed dark and tall to their right, perhaps half a mile off.

"He says there are people moving on the edge of the jungle," Winjah reported. "Perhaps a dozen, maybe more. At first he thought it was baboons or chimpanzees, but they walk erect and carry spears. He thinks it's the Tok."

"The Dorks, hey?" said Nordquist. "Well, let 'em come. We're locked and loaded, ready, willin', and able, ain't we boys?"

"You bet, Pa," chorused the ducklings.

Nonetheless, the Nordquists tented together that night with the cycles gassed and parked at their door. They kept a Coleman lamp burning inside the tent, and left it up to Winjah and Donn to keep an eye on the night guards. Sitting beside the fire, sipping a cold Coors, Donn could hear their voices twanging dolefully over the crackle of the logs.

"I thought you said all Texans were brave?" he said to Winjah.

"These ones prove the rule," the hunter replied. "It will be interesting to see the outcome of this internal struggle. Avarice versus cowardice. I'll bet you right now that avarice wins."

Donn smiled into the dark, remembering the lion. Now he saw it clear: the difference between the good hunter and the bad hunter. Now he knew his side.

25
BUX FUX

"Aha, fair Ticklette, I saw thee looming from afar!" Bucky clattered in his heavily accented Tok. "Thou art larger than the fang-nosed one, larger even than the two-toothed snouter." The girl entered shyly, bowing and smiling under a cascade of long black hair. It was good form, Buck knew, to address a Tok of either sex as if they were gigantic. Comparisons with the rhinoceros and the elephant were the grandest of compliments. This young lady could scarcely top four feet, yet she beamed with delight at his greeting.

Bucky sat in the main room of his house, reclining on a pile of soft-cured hides before a fire of juniper wood. The fire smelled like a boiled martini. In his hand, a skull goblet of brandy distilled from the curious Tok fruits—he couldn't tell which, but it didn't matter. Buck naked, he told himself again, as man was meant to be. The paintings on the stucco walls depicted scenes of sex and

violence—hippopotami beheaded on the shores of reedy
swamps, maidens impaled on the prongs of humanoid
dragons, group gropes of the grossest nature—all
rendered with the finesse of a cave-dwelling Modigliani. If
you turned your head at just the right speed, squinting as
you did so, you got—he had remarked earlier to
himself—a cross between network and educational TV,
with a porn flick thrown in for free.

Starlight broke against the diamonds of the
windowpane. Each window was built differently, with
jewels of varying size and color set at odd angles within
frames of wood or translucent cartilage. The play of light
on the wall paintings and floor hides—zebra, okapi, oryx,
bongo—moved slowly, changing all the while, under the
cruder, more violent roistering of the fire. Clearly the Tok
valued hallucination as an adjunct to lovemaking. Or
perhaps on even a broader level, as a spice of life. Bucky
knew they'd laced his booze with something strange, that
was for dang sure. He'd copulated regularly for two days
now, with scarcely a need for respite. Now and then a nap,
occasionally the need for a pee. Once he had taken time
out to wander back through the winding corridors of the
low cool house—it was midday, he recalled, judging by the
sunlight on the diamond windows (but how could you be
sure?)—to the hole-in-the-ground crapper. The graffiti
were just fine.

Every third girl brought a tray of food, crisp young
vegetables plucked moments before from the garden
behind the house, green onions and fresh tomatoes,
mainly, along with a steaming bowl of soup that looked like
vichysoisse but tasted far stronger, thickened perhaps with
brains. With an appetite fiercer than any he had known
since childhood, Bucky devoured the food, washing it
down with long drafts of ice water, or lesser gulps of the
sweet, guava-tasting wine that the girls offered in chilled,
crooked kongoni horns. For ten minutes they encouraged
him to eat. Then they went to work.

Tok women were strangely built below the waist. They
were equipped with a natural skin skirt—the *tablier*

egyptienne, Clickrasp had told him it was called, during one of the chieftain's few visits since the mating had begun—that dropped loosely from the top of the pubic mound and covered the front of the genitalia. "It's found also among the Bushpersons of southern Africa, or the lady Bushmen if you prefer," Clicky had winked. "Damned if I know what it's supposed to do. Perhaps it was a failed attempt to reduce female sexuality, by keeping the genitalia covered and thus removing a source of temptation. Could have come in handy in days when early man could not afford frequent pregnancies. Desmond Morris and Robert Ardrey make much of the labia and vagina as surrogate lips. This *tablier egyptienne* might well be our species' equivalent of the Moslem veil."

"Yeah," Buck had answered, "but it kind of puts a damper on the old missionary position."

"Not really," Clickrasp replied. "They don't mind it a bit, belly to belly. The whole thing just kind of shifts up toward the navel. I think they get a bit of a thrill out of the crinkling."

By now, though, Bucky had done them every which way—frontward, sideways, upside down—and he knew from experience that they liked it any way they got it. By itself that was a revelation to him. What's more, they were teaching him the language. Like most good things, it happened quite by chance.

"*X'gt'kqhl,*" exclaimed the first Toklette he penetrated.

"What does that mean?" he asked, a bit fearful that he might have hurt her.

"Nottink a-much," she had replied, gazing up lovingly at him. Fortunately she spoke a bit of English, as did most of the Tok, though none so fluently as Clickrasp. "Only tat iz feel gootz."

"I mean, precisely," Buck continued, pressing her now in more ways than one. "That word. Say it again and tell me, if you can, exactly what it means."

She had done so, repeating it every time Buck thrust into her, then falling back into her heavily accented English during the respites between thrusts. Later she relayed the word of his linguistic turn-on to the other females who were awaiting his services. Each one taught him a few more words. With the influence of the drugs that kept him sexually eager working also on the level of intellectual curiosity, he soon had a vocabulary of workable Tok phrases, and a vague idea of how their language was structured. Not to mention the creatures themselves.

His favorite was the girl he called Ticklette the Tocklette. Her name actually was X'zqk', but it came off her palate like a tick. At first Bucky had felt bad about making jokes to himself with the Tok language, but soon he realized that if he took them too seriously, he would not be able to fulfill his function—not just as stud, but as sincere believer in their tiny revolution. Tick, as he first called her, spoke much better English than the others, and loved it when Bucky applied the diminutive to her name.

"Sounds like Chicklet," she laughed, reaching for his crotch. "But who chews whom?"

She was the grand-niece of Clickrasp, a princess of the Tok, and thus much better educated in the ways of outlanders than the other women. After their first coupling—all mating had been carefully timed by Mrs. Rasp, Click's number one wife, to coincide with the height of the estrus cycle, the "heat" as Clicky called it—Buck had thought he might have seen the last of her. But Clicky had asked him if any of the ladies deserved a return engagement.

"I feared it might get boring, just one after the other," he said. "You're doing extremely well so far, much better than I'd expected, so if you find any one of these fair creatures compelling enough, don't hesitate to ask for her again."

Buck had said that he would like to see Ticklette at least once a day, whether they "made it" or not. He liked her company. And she taught him good words.

"You too loom large," she laughed now, walking up to him as he lay on the hide bed, "at least as large as the buffalo's horn." She stood before him, ankles together, pert as an Olympic gymnast. Her smile was wide, and the hair sprawled loose across her smooth shoulders, vaguely masking the luminous, pale-pink nipples that stood erect under the caress of her fingertips. Bucky's eyes flicked to the wall. He squinted and cocked his head slowly. His focus lay on a mural that depicted a coupling, female astride, her head tossed back, mouth agape, hair flying down her back and across her neatly turned shoulders.

He raised his arms slowly and opened them. Ticklette the Tocklette bestrode him as she might the balance beam.

"Teach me a few more phrases," he groaned.

Later, when Ticklette had gone, Bucky decided to take an evening stroll. The night was cool so he donned a heavy woolen greatcoat, cut in an early-nineteenth-century manner, that Clickrasp had given him. It had been Mungo Park's greatcoat, the Tok chieftain said, and Bucky was pleased to see that it fit him perfectly. Park had been a big man for his day. He walked down the winding road toward the village square, passing a few Tok along the way. They bowed and smiled, as he did in return. Two of the women made eyes at him, and he recognized them as former clients of the Blackrod Stud Service ("Satisfaction Guaranteed or You Can Have My Head for Breakfast.").

At the far corner of the square, over a low, sprawling, half-timbered house with leaded diamond windowpanes, through which glimmered a million shafts of multicolored lamplight, hung a sign that represented the Moor's Head Inn. It was the only public house in town. The sign was a wish fulfillment of Dr. Park's, who had built the inn in 1826. It showed the severed head of a beturbaned and ugly despot—that very Ali, ruler of Ludamar, who had held Park captive during his first visit to Africa and nearly starved him to death before the good doctor managed his escape. "Unchristian as it may seem," Park wrote in his Tok Journal, "I would like nothing better than to see my small compatriots glutting themselves on the brains of that Moorish fiend. Even today, I sometimes wake in the middle watches of the night and imagine myself once more hopeless in his tent. May he and his kind spend all eternity staked out over an anthill—and may God forgive me my thirst for vengeance."

Though that thirst remained forever unslaked, Park's less vengeful taste for strong English ale had been amply satisfied. No sooner had he arrived in the capital city of the Tok, initially as their captive and later as their valued sage and friend, than he taught them how to brew beer. "I had with me some few grains of the native corn, *Holcus spicatus,* and in this salubrious clime it was but a matter of two months before a healthy crop stood ready for malting. My botanical training enabled me to discover a local root containing a bitter principle, which I employed in lieu of hops. Stored in hardwood casks of my devising, it is as fine and strong and frothing a brew as any to be found in Britannia."

How right you are, Good Doctor, thought Bucky as he pushed through the low oaken door of the Moor's Head. Inside, the pungent smoke of a juniper fire mixed with guttering yellow light from oil lamps. The customers, Tok warriors and elders, greeted Buck warmly. Three of them interrupted their dart game to come over to the bar and inquire, not unsolicitously, as to the state of his, ah, love life. The innkeeper, a plump, elderly Tok named Tschamm, drew a stoup of ale from the barrel behind the bar and slid it across the dark, scarred, teakwood surface. "Lead in your pencil," he said, deadpan, and they all laughed.

Bucky took the tankard to a low table in the corner of the inn, under an oil lamp. It was an early-nineteenth-century lamp, of the sort that was designed to burn whale oil, but Park's version was fueled instead with shea butter, a compressed vegetable fat from the nut of the karite, or shea tree (*Butyrospermum parkii*), which the great man himself had discovered and named. With bark like a chestnut and leaves like a pear, the shea tree produces a peachlike fruit the flesh of which is eaten, while the fat surrounding the nut is pressed and strained into a hard white butter which keeps a whole year without turning rancid. The nut has the color, taste, and aroma of

cocoa, whose odor in the inn now mixed with that of
woodsmoke and beer. Other Parkian memorabilia
adorned the inn—portraits in oil and watercolor of various
Tok warriors and chieftains, of strange plants and animals
peculiar to the high country of Kansdu, a self-portrait
done late in his life which showed the explorer gazing
steadfastly over a huge bushy beard at a panorama of
thorn veldt through which wound the mighty river—was it
the Kan, or the Niger? In the yellow light, Park's eyes
looked huge, beatific. Bucky studied the face as he himself
chewed absently on a gingerbread cake. Actually, it wasn't
gingerbread, but another Parkian invention. Using the
berries of the Rhamnus lotus, a thorny shrub that bears
sweet yellow fruit, he had dried them, ground them in a
mortar to separate the flour, mixed this with water, and
baked cakes that tasted much like gingerbread. Park
himself believed that the Rhamnus was the very lotus
mentioned by Pliny as the food of the Libyan "Lotophagi."
Bucky was not about to gainsay him.

From the pocket of the greatcoat, Bucky slid a heavy
leather-bound ledger. In it, with the spiky well-formed
hand now so well known to him, Park had recorded his
final journal. It picked up shortly after Park's
"disappearance" under native attack at the Busa Rapids of
the Niger, early in 1806, and ran up to the morning of his
death on September 10, 1858—his eighty-seventh
birthday. Bucky had read most of it, caught up in the
explorer's calm, thoughtful style, admiring him his
courage and refusal to give up hope in even the most
desperate situations. When Park had been swept down
Busa Rapids and then washed ashore far below with
broken ribs and a badly fractured tibia, and seen
crocodiles approaching him in the mosquito-thick gloom,
unable to move, he had recalled a trick his guide, Isacco,
had used in a similar situation. When the first croc got
within reach, he grabbed it and stuck his thumbs in its
eyes. The crocodile slithered away, leaving a wake of
reeking, disturbed muck that nearly suffocated the
explorer. Then, when a hunting party of Tok discovered

him the following morning, and he thought he was hallucinating, he almost wished the great saurians had finished him. But no—the Tok proved gentle, binding his wounds and giving him herbs that eased his suffering. They carried him on a litter deep into the rain forest, then out onto the veldt. For weeks, it seemed, they marched deeper, deeper into Africa. Then they climbed to a highland that reminded Park of his Scottish home—cool, green, pungent with crushed heather underfoot.

The years of his captivity—which soon shaded into willing house arrest, and finally into a commitment to live out his life with these wondrous people—were studded with botanical and zoological discoveries. In return for their kindness, Park repaid the Tok with his medical, botanical, and architectural knowledge. He taught them how to build sturdy cottages to replace the drafty caves and mud huts in which they had previously lived. He taught them sanitation and preventive medicine. He taught them how to play Scots bagpipes and sing Scots ballads. He taught them the warmth of good, strong nut-brown ale and the companionship of the public house. He taught them tea and gingerbread and darts. But he could not teach them Christianity.

"That is my sole regret," he wrote in his last journal entry, to which Bucky now had turned. "Yet it is not so great nor grievous a regret as once I might have felt. After all, when I chose to return to Africa, knowing the hardships and dangers unto death that I needs must face, I did so from motives then obscure to me but which had nothing to do with the conversion of the heathen, nor the opening of the continent to British commerce, as the Africa Association and Sir Joseph Banks anticipated. I must now admit that I came to see the elephant, as it were, to see this power, this heady mix of life and death, for one last time—and, yes, to perish here. There is that in Africa, as in some narcotic, that addicts one for good or ill. Much as I miss the green hills of home, the winding Yarrow and the tidy cottages of Foulshiels where I was born, much as I miss my loving Ailie and my companions, Walter Scott with whom I rode the moors, my dear brother Arch, the good doctor Anderson who taught me surgery—much as I miss them, I missed this more when I was away. The celebrity which followed the publication of my Narrative only sickened me. The palliative was obvious—the hot sun, the fierce colors, the life-in-death of Africa.

"Here I must come, here I must stay, here I must die. It is a compulsion that overpowers even that of the Christian God, or the Muhammadan for that matter, the African compulsion. Here, I believe, and the Tok would seem to bear me out, man first blinked in wonder and comprehension of the world. Here, under this pounding sun, amidst these fangs and claws, with the blood of men and animals mingling to beauty—the ultimate beauty of the world—here is the only life. Untrammeled by the sordid competitions of commerce, unsullied by the crass pursuit of fame, unmarred by the deceits of politics and power-mongering. How fortuitous that I should have arrived among these people. Unlike the Moors and the tainted tribes I met along the Niger, the Tok, for all their initial ugliness, are pure. The Natural Man of whom the French Revolutionary Rousseau was writing when last I was in Europe. And I, the Man of Science, had something to give them, as they gave me their purity in return. Yes, the only life worth living. And the only death worth dying. Africa. Amen."

Bucky sat back and pulled at his tankard of ale. So that's where the torch was lighted, he thought. Ironic. The whole tradition of which Winjah was a final representation had begun here, with this one man, Mungo Park. The tradition of teaching, of bringing light to the so-called heathen. But it had been perverted along the way by commerce and the jealous demands of the Christian God. If only there had been more Mungo Parks.

Hell, he thought suddenly, I can be one!

He smiled and stared at the diamond-dance of the windows.

"Ahem!"

Tschamm, the innkeeper, was standing at Bucky's shoulder, clearing his throat hesitantly.

"Sorry, guv, but there's a young lady outside says she's an appointment wif you. Up at the 'ouse." Bucky rose and fumbled in his pocket for money to pay the tab, then suddenly realized where he was. The Tok had no money. He clapped Tschamm on the shoulder, winked at the other men, and slipped the book back into the pocket of his greatcoat—Mungo Park's greatcoat.

"Work, work, work," he sighed with mock exasperation. "If it's not one chore, it's another."

The men were laughing as he walked out into the night.

26

AVARICE

Two bodies lay beside the ashes of the campfire. Only one was headless. The other, minus its legs from the hips downward, wore the penises of both as a dire bouquet that bloomed from its mouth. A note was pinned to the legless man's nose.

"I regret to sey that my ordres require me to return to Palmerville if Tok get too tough," the note read. It was signed "Abner Kodobe, Lieut., K.A.F."

"Dumb frock can't even spell good," grumped Nordquist as he scanned the missive. He picked his teeth with the thorn that had pinned the note. "What it means, he's *yaller!*"

The troops were gone, along with their weapons. During the night, after the guards who remained alive had found the bodies, the Kansduvians had decided to decamp. At this point in the campaign, they had been advised back in Palmerville, it could only get worse.

"At least they left all the gazarene," said one of the ducklings.

"Well, we ain't goin' no further anyways," another replied.

"Oh yeah?" asked the third, probably Heber. Proudly, the lad gazed at his daddy.

Nordquist *père* plucked his teeth.

"The bogus is still out there," he said after a long pause. "We gotta stay quick now, cautious."

Winjah glanced over at Donn, who was reclining against the tire of one of the ATCs. Donn winked back at him. Greed and gumption, sure 'nuf. Two days before, the morning after the lion hunt, they had come on fresh buffalo sign near the edge of the rain forest. All day they followed it, catching sight of the herd only infrequently in the heavy low brush that edged the jungle. No one had seen the Diamond Bogo himself, but the tracks indicated a few enormous bulls tagging after the main body. That night the Tok had taken the first guard. They must have moved with incredible stealth, as the man was found not ten yards from the spot beside the fire where Winjah was sleeping. The guard had been beheaded and emasculated.

The next day, still working northward, they had come on the buffalo herd in the open, at the edge of the brush. There were perhaps fifty animals, mostly cows, calves, and young bulls. The big herd bulls were no doubt still lurking in the jungle edges. They waited patiently for an hour, two hours, dead quiet, hoping that the big bulls would show themselves. The herd moved slowly through the tall grass, browsing as it went, lying up for sometimes half an hour at a time under stands of whistling thorn and juniper. Occasionally they caught glimpses of large dim shapes moving ahead of the herd, in the thick brush beyond the grass, but they saw no horns, no gleam of stone.

I'll bet my butt he's in there," Nordquist hissed finally. "What we oughter do, we should set up the recoilless rifle that the troops brought along and just cut loose in there, along through that brush. Or maybe a fifty-caliber machine gun. Yeah, let's do that!"

"The main herd is in your way," Winjah said. "If you try to work your way around them, the big bulls will spook."

"Well, shee-it! We can't just sit here doin' nothin'." He whispered for the Kansduvian officer to come over to him. "Set up that fifty of yours," he said. "Maybe the herd will move aside and we can get a shot." The officer looked at Winjah, who cold-eyed him, but obeyed.

"How far do you make it to the edge of the brush?" Nordquist asked Winjah.

"About four hundred yards," Winjah lied. "Give or take." It was more like six hundred, but in the hard equatorial light at this altitude the Texan would be unlikely to notice the difference. Nordquist hunkered behind the air-cooled gun, adjusting the sights and checking the long brass-tipped bullets in the feeder belt. He cocked his Aussie hat down over his eyes and squinted through the sight.

"Maybe I'll just give 'em a leetle squirt," he whispered. The main herd, only two or three hundred yards in front of them, was growing restive. The cows with calves were on their feet, staring back at the grassy draw in which the men lay. Tickbirds flapped and fluttered in consternation. The calves began a low anxious bawling. Nordquist hit the trigger.

The machine gun roared for a full twenty seconds, bright brass flickering at blinding speed up into the snapping steel maw of the block, the barrel traversing madly right and left. Cows and calves leaped only to fall, kicking, under the clout of the heavy bullets. A cacophony of bovine bellows echoed back over the racket of the gun. The balance of the herd bolted toward the jungle, then suddenly pivoted and came charging back.

"Cripes O'Grady!" Nordquist hollered, dropping the trigger grip of the gun. "They're comin' back at us!" He turned to run back toward the cycles but tripped over an ammo box. Winjah jumped up to the edge of the draw, facing the charge, and fired at the leaders—by now just a hundred yards away. At the sight and sound of the man, the herd spun once again and angled off to the left. Black bodies, whirling dust, an insane bellow, and the very earth shook to the hoofs. The wind carried the dust toward them in a gray billowing wall.

"They're turned," Winjah said.

"I knowed they would," Nordquist said. "I was goin' to get one of the bikes and try to herd 'em, Texas-style." Then the wave of blowing dust washed over them.

From up the line, in the dark whirl of dirt, came the snap of gunshots and a chorus of screams. Then the dust blew through, and in the hanging haze they saw small figures leaping, dancing, spearing. Tok. Winjah raised his rifle again but one of the ducklings slammed into him, running back to get his own weapon. Then the Tok were gone, lugging heavy burdens as they fled.

Four Kansduvians lay headless at the tail of the draw. A fifth, blood bubbling through spear holes in his chest, lay face down and moaning over the body of a dead Tok. Other Kansduvians pulled the wounded man off, threw him roughly aside, and fell on the Tok body with their knives. Soon the wounded man stopped bubbling. The blood had redyed his camouflage shirt.

That was only yesterday, Donn thought. Then last night, two more guards. No wonder the officer decided to pull out. This was war. Hell, with casualty rates like that, it was almost as bad as automobile racing.

"So you're going to continue after the buffalo?" Winjah asked.

"We'll give it another day, anyways," Nordquist said. "There's nine of us, with you and your boys. We'll just have to keep low, noses to the wind, and hope them Dorks ain't a helluva lot braver than they been so far. I mean, they been sneakin' in at night, and usin' that dust cloud yesterday. They don't want no direct confrontation with our firepower. Also, we got a pretty good idea where that bogus is now. If we can just sneak on up around the herd and get a decent shot at him . . . Damn, I wish they hadn't of took that machine gun!"

"We've still got these," chanted the ducklings, waving their Uzis on high.

"Yes," said Winjah, "but so do the Tok. They've got the guns they took from the guards and those five they killed yesterday."

"Them little monkey-men will never figure out how to shoot 'em," said Nordquist. "Or if they do, they'll prob'ly end up shootin' one another. Why, them ain't real people. Them's some kind of animals. Next to them a goddamn nigger's a Albert Einstein."

Winjah shrugged and said nothing. He knew the Tok were merely biding their time, to what end he wasn't sure. What he was sure of, though, was that the Tok could already have killed them all if they chose. The best bet, now that the troops had fled, would be for him and Donn to take off on their own, work out from the camp at night while the Nordquists slept, pick up the Tok trail and follow them back to their main camp, and there to seek Dawn and Bucky. Only by moving quietly, stealthily, using his bushcraft to its utmost, could they hope to avoid the Tok and effect the rescue. He dared not tell Nordquist, though. The Texan would certainly kill them rather than let them go off on their own. Yes, he thought. Avarice.

They hunted out toward the edge of the forest that day, leaving the ducklings behind to guard the camp, with its valuable gasoline, cycles, and ammo. Again they picked up the herd, but with the machine gun incident still fresh in the buffalo mind they could not approach close enough for a shot. All afternoon they followed at a distance. The wind, which had blown strong from the northeast the previous two days, had died to faint whispers. It backed and eddied on them, sending their scent to the herd whenever they seemed to be making a fair approach. Each time the herd panicked and fled another half mile before calming and browsing again. Tsetse flies swarmed around them, stinging through their sweat.

"Consarn it," grumped Nordquist, swatting viciously at the flies, "I'll never shoot me a bogus."

"You killed seventeen yesterday with the machine gun," Winjah said.

"Them don't count. I was just tryin' to clear 'em out of

the way so I could get a shot at my trophy bogus." He
swatted and flapped some more. "Anyways, the nig-nogs
et all that meat. They carried it off with them when they
headed for the barn this mornin'. Yeah." He smiled
reminiscently. "That was fun. Reminded me of the old
army days, over in Frozen Chosen. Was you in Korea,
Winjah?"

"Yes," the hunter replied. "For most of it."

"You Limeys was pussy over there," Nordquist said.
"Now, them Greeks and them Turks, they was somethin'.
But not the Limejuicers."

Winjah said nothing. He had been in a special
commando. It had been the first time he had killed men
with his bare hands. It won't have been the last, he
thought.

Just then the wind backed, gusted briefly, and the
herd bolted again. They all stood up, watching the black
mud-caked rumps bounce out of sight. The sun was
swinging low now, and they would have to head back.
Then, just as they were about to turn, they saw it.

The Diamond Bogo stepped from the edge of the
jungle, half a mile ahead of them, huge as a house. He
stared in their direction. The westering sun picked the
facets of the great stone. It blazed at them for a long half
minute.

Nordquist stood with his mouth hung wide. A tendril
of saliva rolled over his cracked lower lip and disappeared
into the stubble of his beard. His eyes, behind the tiny
glasses, were bright as the bogo's diamond.

Then the buffalo turned and the jungle swallowed
him up.

27
"SAVED BY THE BELT!"

Dawn reclined on her cushions, awaiting Clickrasp's
nightly visit. At her side, purring like an outboard motor
with a ragged carburetor, lay Kricket the Caracal. The
Tok, generally speaking, were not pet fanciers. A few of
the children kept dassies, captured in the rocks and hills
behind the city, and every house had its share of virtually
tame lizards, which spent the evenings on the ceilings and
walls, hopping on disk-cupped feet and cleaning up
whatever insects strayed into the dwelling. But only
Clickrasp had a caracal. The caracal is the African lynx, a
long-eared, long-legged cousin of the North American
wildcat, with a thick, soft, almost wine-red coat unmarked
by spots or stripes. Kricket had taken to Dawn right from
the start, rubbing her forehead briskly against Dawn's legs
the moment they met.

"It's not really affection," Clicky had said. "They have
scent glands between their ears, and they rub against
things—furniture, rocks, trees, people—so that they can

recognize them. Own them, in effect. It's like dogs
urinating on trees and fence posts to mark their territory."
But Dawn didn't care. She stroked the cat behind its tall
tufted ears, then down its slim brawny neck. When she sat
down, the cat eased into her lap, purring for more.

"Her name is Kr'tzk'," Clicky said. "It's onomatopoeic.
Notice now loud she purrs."

"I'll call her Kricket, if you don't mind," Dawn replied.
"How come you people have no dogs? All human beings
love dogs . . ." She trailed off, fearing she might have
offended him with the unwitting remark.

"We too love dogs," Clickrasp said graciously. "Too
much, I'm afraid. Frankly, we eat them."

"Oh."

She gazed absently around the room, painfully aware
that the chitchat had ended. Trophies of the chase
adorned the walls. The hide of a leopard that had to
measure a good nine feet, its tail curved in a wicked,
snakelike sweep, but sadly truncated by the absence of its
head. A set of rhinoceros-hoof wastebaskets. The forelegs
of antelope, bent at the ankle, serving as wall-mounted
spear racks. Against the far wall, serving as beams to hold
the fireplace mantle, stood two enormous tusks, fully eight
feet tall, she estimated, but straight, not curved like those
of the elephants she was familiar with.

"Those are the tusks of a long-extinct elephant that
once lived in the Sahara," Clicky explained. "An ancestor
of mine saved them. He must have killed the brute some
twenty thousand years ago. I suppose it was the largest
ever taken, and that's why he kept the ivory. The tusks
weigh 256 and 262 pounds respectively."

"He must have been quite a hunter," Dawn said,
desperately seeking to prolong the conversation. "To kill
that big an animal with only a spear."

"Not really," Clicky answered, taking the bait.
"Judging by the paintings that have survived, they used
fire to drive the animals over cliffs, or into bogs, where
they could spear them with impunity as they struggled in
the muck and mire."

"Have you killed elephants that way?" she asked.

"Not lately," Clicky said. "The elephants around here are a bit too clever, too fierce. I feel it's unsporting to use fire, or to drive them even if they could be driven into pits or bogs. And it's too costly to hunt them straight. We are short of warriors as it is—or was, now that you and Bucky will be working in our behalf." He smiled and actually twirled his seedy moustache.

"I . . . I admire elephant hunters," Dawn chirped, cursing to herself as her voice broke. "Winjah is a great elephant hunter. I would certainly admire you a lot more if you killed an elephant for me."

"We shall see," said Clicky. "Now, let's get down to business." He began to unstrap the bamboo splints that held his wounded member. Once they were off, he tested it for tensile strength, wincing slightly but clearly satisfied with its recuperative powers. "Yes, not quite tickety-poo just yet," he said. "But it should do. In case you've wondered at the, er, constant rigidity of the member, it's not due to any great lust on our part. We're not actually 'satyrs,' in the usual sense of the word. There are two cartilaginous uprights, as it were, that extend the full length of the shaft. Your well-aimed blow of the other evening managed to sprain one of them. Had I not been so carried away with 'brain fever,' as we call it, I would easily have avoided the chop. The organ seems usually to have eyes of its own. That's how we can run through the thorn nyika so easily, without seriously injuring ourselves. Though I must admit that the, shall we say, retractable mating gear of your species seems a far superior adaptation to a hunting way of life." He smiled suavely and sat down beside her.

"I wish we could put it off for tonight," Dawn said. "Just tonight. I'm fully aware that I'll have to give in to you sooner or later, and really, I've come to like you a lot. I really love the city, and the good taste you've shown in your interior decor. But I . . ." She cast wildly about for another excuse. "I . . . I've got a splitting headache tonight and . . ." She stopped. "Really."

Clickrasp had laughed. He stood and restrapped his splints.

"You're right," he said. "I shouldn't rush you. We've plenty of time. I was crude the other night and I vowed I wouldn't act that way again. Tomorrow night, Fair Dawn Lady." With that, he left.

But now it was tomorrow night.

"Oh, Kricket," Dawn purred to the lynx, "what can I do?"

Her eyes fell on a diamond-bladed knife that lay on the low table from which she took her meals. If I killed him . . . No, they'd kill me right back, or worse. At least Clicky is kind, sort of. Should I kill myself? Too melodramatic, and besides it hurts. She thought of the Philadelphian who had built the hot bath and then committed seppuku. Her stomach cramped. Then she heard the front door open. Footsteps nearing her room. Heavy breathing. The beaded curtain that masked the door snickered to a faint breeze. The lynx arched its back and hissed.

"Good evening, my dear," said Clickrasp as he entered. "I thought we might sup before we continued our little tête-à-tête." He carried a tray heavy with steaming bowls and cutlery. A single green and orange orchid floated in an opalescent bowl.

"What is it?" Dawn asked, sniffing the delicious aroma that rose from the serving dish.

"Just a little dish I whipped up for your delectation," Clickrasp replied, swiftly and surely setting the table for two. "I won't tell you precisely what it is. Let's make a game of it. You tell me what it is." He whisked the top from the dish. "*Voilà!*" he said. Then he began serving.

It's some kind of stew, Dawn thought, tasting. Large squares of a pale sweet meat, no doubt simmered in a white court bouillon, then stewed in something like Madeira. Covered with a wonderful garnish—let's see, quenelles, perhaps of veal. Mushrooms. Blanched olives, it would seem. Yes kidney. And a freshwater crayfish? Yup. What's this—truffles! How marvelous! And this little gizmo? Yecch! It looks like a rooster's comb. Hmm, but it doesn't taste so bad. Not bad at all. Tongue, yes, and of course the inevitable sliced brains.

Clicky waited expectantly, a half-smile on his face as he watched her sample the stew. He rolled a bowl of white wine absently in his cupped hands as he watched.

"I'd say it was *Tête de veau à la financière*," Dawn said finally. "Or something very much like it."

"Spot on!" exclaimed Clicky. "Marvelous. You guessed it right off. Actually, though, it's not really calf's head. We don't have any such creatures available to us. It's the head of a young oribi, but just as good to my palate." He helped himself to a plateful of the stew and began eating. "I've underrated your culinary perspicacity," he said between eager mouthfuls. "I can't tell you how delighted I am to learn that we have this in common."

Dawn ate hungrily, glad to have pleased Clickrasp and proud of her gustatory knowledge. Had Clicky told her that the dish was actually prepared from the head of a Kansduvian recruit named Phillip Tabatote, killed yesterday by his warriors, her appetite might have left her. But the dish would still have tasted as good.

A salad of Tok lettuce and avocado vinaigrette, followed by a bowl of mixed fruit in a sweet wine, concluded the repast. Clicky then produced another surprise—coffee.

"I've been saving it for a special occasion," he admitted. "Took it just a month ago from an Arab caravan we raided up north of here, so it should still be fairly fresh. If you're a good girl tonight, I'll have some more brewed for our breakfast."

"I didn't realize the caravan routes ran that close to Kansdu," Dawn said quickly.

"Oh, yes. The main route from the Upper Nile to Timbuktu passes not a three-day march from here. We go out the back way, not the way I brought you in. It's bloody fierce desert out there, but we know all the spots where water can be dug in the sand rivers. Better even than the Arabs. But there I go, boasting again. Forgive me."

"It's quite all right," said Dawn, fanning herself as she finished her coffee.

"Yes," Clicky observed solicitously, "it is a bit warm in

here. Shall we retire to the garden for some air?" He
poured two goblets of brandy from a pottery decanter and
stood.

A cool breeze fanned through the garden, carrying
the scent of night-blooming flowers and a faint hint of
woodsmoke to their nostrils. The moon, just easing up
over the low rolling mountains to the east, varnished the
already waxy leaves of the surrounding trees. Frogs piped
on the verge of the spring in Click's backyard. A bat flicked
past, its wings golden in the pale wash of the moonlight,
and Dawn ducked involuntarily, spilling a splash of her
brandy. She laughed. Clicky put an arm around her,
reassuringly. My God, she thought with a barely contained
shudder, the top of his noggin only comes to my armpit!

"There's nothing to fear, my love," he whispered up at
her. She saw the moonlight glinting on the silver hairs of
his moustache, on the ultrabright of his small clean teeth.
His arm was terribly strong.

Then she was on her back in the greensward, Clicky
between her thighs. She saw that the terrible machine was
unsheathed, unsplinted. Clickrasp stared down at her,
smiling gently, as he reached for the top of her
leopard-skin skirt. She could hardly breathe, and her heart
raced wildly up toward her throat. That was it!

Clickrasp pulled the skirt free and stared down,
between her inner thighs. A look of puzzlement crossed
his face. Then it contorted into one of disgust. He leaped
to his feet, gagging, and dashed into the shrubbery. She
could hear him retching as he ran, his footsteps pounding,
pounding, out of the yard, into the fading distance.

What the hell?

She looked down at herself. The insides of her thighs
were dark with blood. Omigosh! she thought suddenly.
That's what the cramps were. I'd forgotten—yes—it's right
on time. She began to laugh, slowly at first, then with
increasing hysteria until she was in tears. Exhausted,
finally, she rose to her feet and went inside, fumbled in her
shoulder bag, and came up with her pads and belt.

"That's something," she said aloud as she slipped into

it. "Winjah would enjoy the pun. Saved by the belt."

A few moments later, Mrs. Rasp bustled into the room. A plump shy woman with graying hair, she averted her eyes as she spoke.

"So sorry about the embarrassment," she said. "You see, we have strong taboos against women in, ah, your condition. Very strong. It is silly, I know, and so does my husband, but it is our way and we cannot help it. If you will please get your things together, I will escort you immediately to the Pool of the Bleeding Ladies. You'll be quite comfortable there, lots of other ladies to talk with, plenty of time to rest and read. Clickrasp said you could take any books you wanted from the library, if you promise to bring them back. Now please, hurry."

"Be right with you," Dawn said.

Kricket wound around her ankles, purring joyfully.

28
ON THE RUN

"Only about an hour of moonlight left," Winjah said as they stopped for a breather. "But we're nearly there now." He looked to the rear, into the tall grass that glowed bone-white under the night sky.

"Still behind us?" Donn asked.

"Bloody yes, they are." The hunter cursed. "Six or eight of the bastards."

The hyenas had picked up their scent just out of the Nordquists' camp and stuck tight for two hours now, all the way to the edge of the rain forest. They kept well out of gunshot range, but their heavy awkward shapes showed every now and then in the near distance. Occasionally a whiff of them blew past on the vagrant breeze—sour swampy rot.

"They'll leave us when we go into the forest," Winjah said. "That's the best place to lie up for the rest of the night. All the predators are out on the veldt right now, as I hope the Tok are too. Come morning we'll look for Tok sign and trail it back to their camp. Then, by God, we'll bust your Fair Dawn Lady loose, and Bucky too if he's still amongst the living, and cut the hell out of this godforsaken country. Clout us a few Tok headhunters along the way. Hey, Bwana?"

"Yeah," said Donn. "You bet."

If we live through this mad-ass run, he added to himself. It was spooky to run through the African night, even with a heavy rifle in your hands. Everything had teeth. The thorns, barely visible under even so bright a moon as this. The rocks, leaping out to nip at your shins. The animals—hundreds of them, it seemed—that slunk away at the pounding approach of their boots. Silver-backed jackals that yapped and scuttled, then turned to stare back with the light encasing them in liquid steel. The small spotted cats—servals, sand cats, the ubiquitous African wildcat with its blurred spots and long striped tail. At one point they ran past a pride of lions, heard the low groaning growls, then the resumption of teeth slicing through bone and muscle of a kill. Mainly, though, the damned hyenas hulking everywhere, standing slope-backed and gazing with those big stupid eyes, their heavy jaws hung open, tongues lolling limp over brutal teeth.

"Otiego says we should pop one of the damned fisis," Winjah said as they rested. "Then the other ones would stay back to clean him up. What you you say?"

"Wouldn't a shot draw the Tok?" Donn asked.

"Perhaps. But we're only a hop, skip, and a jump from the woods right now. A shot would also spook off anything that's lying up between us and the trees, and that edge there is really the most dangerous part of the journey."

"Okay by me."

Winjah took the .375 and waited until one of the dim shapes circling in the grass stepped into the clear. The shot sounded flat, like the slap of a giant hand. The hyena leaped and began to run in circles, snapping at the hole in its paunch. Donn saw a fat white tube emerge from the

wound. The hyena swung its thick wedge-shaped head
and the tube became a length of hose. Other hyenas
emerged from the grass, cackling gleefully, and dove on
the wounded one.

"Let's move out," Winjah said.

They ran for the jungle, listening to the raucous,
gut-ripping racket behind them. Otiego was giggling as he
ran. It was quite a joke, the fisi devouring its own guts.
Better than TV, Donn thought.

Thorn, gullies, more thorn and tall grass that cut the
forearms. More creatures of the night fleeing their
approach. Once a hoarse, angry grunt—a bulbous shape
that Winjah said was a bush pig. Donn would have sworn it
was a buffalo, or maybe even a rhino. Then they were into
the forest, walking easily on the open, spongy turf beneath
the impenetrable canopy. The mammoth tree trunks
shone dully through the dark, like the pillars of some
Olympian temple, Donn thought. Yes, it's a church in
here, a cathedral to some ancient, awful god.

They lay up finally, half a mile into the rain forest,
under the trunk of a fallen giant. The trackers scampered
up a huge juniper and cut boughs for them to use as
mattresses. Donn unrolled his sleeping bag and pulled the
bandoleers from his shoulders.

"We daren't light a fire, I'm afraid," Winjah said. "But
there's really no need to. A bit chilly in here, under the
gloom, but the bags should keep us cozy enough. I'll have
the lads take turns at the watch. Take a turn myself, right
now, I suppose. You get some kip, Young Gavern. I'll
wake you at first light."

Donn slid into the bag and tucked his boots under his
head as a pillow. He lay on his back, staring up into the
canopy. His eyes, adjusted now to the dark of the forest,
saw the trees in fine detail. The leafy sky, shot through in
spots by pricks of starlight, shifted rhythmically to a high
wind. Like the sea, he thought. The rain forest has its own
tides and currents. The trunks, thick and gray, smooth
where they were not wound with shaggy vines, seemed to
nod, one toward the other. They're alive, he thought. As

alive as I am. And sentient, too, but in ways I can't begin to perceive. A faint horripilation moved up his spine, up his neck. I wonder if they think. His eyes slid closed and he slept in the temple.

Donn dreamt that he and Winjah had gone north to Alaska. They were sitting in a saloon on the banks of a roaring salmon river. Cold gusts blew through the knotholes in the log wall. Donn was interviewing a boy who claimed to be the illegitimate son of Jack London. He was a short, blond, wide-shouldered young man with acne and tan teeth, and he claimed his name was Sam London. He had just come off a king-crab boat out of Kodiak and was using the money he'd saved to buy a trapline from an old Indian whose legs had gone bad. An ancient jukebox, its lights winking pale and pastel, played in the corner—Johnny Horton songs. Donn doubted the boy's veracity but was afraid to say so. The kid looked tough. When he finally screwed up enough courage to ask him about Jack London, the kid leaped to his feet and swung. . . .

Something hard and heavy smacked Donn across the bridge of his nose. He sat up in the sleeping bag and cursed. Sure, the rain forest. Overhead, a strong wind arched the canopy into a chaos of ripping leaves and groaning branches. Deadwood fell among the leaves—whole branches as big as the trees back home. A hunk of wood had bounced off Donn's face.

"You'd better get over here," Winjah yelled above the moaning of the wind. "In the lee." The hunter was crouched near the roots of the downed tree under which they had slept, coaxing a small wood fire over which a pan boiled. He was singing to himself as he fed sticks into the flames. "North to Alaska."

"You're in good voice this morning," Donn said, rubbing his skinned nose.

"Just so bloody glad to get shut of those damnable Texans," Winjah said. "I can't stand that sort of thing. All that bloody boasting and one-upping and playing so

bloody tough when all they really are is a fragile
membrane of scum on the Great Pond of Life. Yellow
scum at that. Ah, well, it all evens out in the fullness of
time." He pointed to the fire. "Care for some brekkers?"

Buffalo ribs roasted in the coals at the edge of the
blaze. Donn noticed that the trackers were hunkered back
under the tree trunk out of the wind, eating and watching
him. Back there in the shadows, their eyes and teeth
flashing from the gloom, they appeared to be chewing on
three-foot-long spareribs—Harlem gone berserk. Donn
took a rib and whittled the meat from it with his Gerber
lock-blade knife while Winjah poured him a cup of coffee.
It began to rain.

"Perhaps we'd best lay low today," the hunter said.
" 'Tain't a fit day out for man nor beast."

"Yeah, but that means the Tok will probably be lying
low, too," Donn said. "I don't mind the weather if you
don't."

"Done," said Winjah, finishing his coffee. "Let's get
packing."

They followed the game trails at the edge of the
forest, finding old Tok sign everywhere but nothing very
fresh. Here and there they came on the skeletons of
monkeys and other small game, all of the bones
distinguished by an absence of skulls. This was the Tok
hunting ground, all right. The storm grew more furious,
with lightning snapping high to the east of them and fierce
blasts of rain slashing the upper canopy. They continued
moving north. Out on the plain, they saw a mixed herd of
wildebeests and zebras stampeding in panic at the constant
bowling-alley roar of the thunder.

"Everything's moving because of the pyrotechnics,"
Winjah said. "We might keep our eyes peeled for the Big
Bogo. He could well be charging around out there with the
others. Oh, I'd dearly love to shoot him out from under
those Texicans!" He sniffed the air, sharp with the taste of
ozone. "I feel lucky today, Bwana. Bloody lucky!"

Toward midday, with the storm at its peak, they
spotted a herd of buffalo milling on the prairie beyond the

edge of the forest. A lobe of the jungle extended westward just here, running out into the grassland up a long shallow valley, then dwindling to thick brush. The buffalo were some three hundred yards out into the plain from the wooded edge. Rain slashed sporadically, obscuring their vision.

"I don't know if he's with them," Winjah said, "but I'm sure that's the herd we've seen him with. I recognize one of the askari, the one with the broken right horn tip." He scanned the herd thoroughly through the four-power scope. The rain abated briefly. "Wait a minute . . . Yes, he's in there, Bwana! Yes. I see his great bloody diamond winking at us. Like the bloody lightning itself. Yes." He turned and looked at Donn, his eyes shining. There's the real lightning, Donn thought.

They circled back into the deep woods and ran, low, out along the extension of the forest, their passage covered by the racket of the storm and the wild tossing of the foliage. When Winjah figured they were parallel with the herd, they eased back out to the jungle's edge. The herd was still there, milling in a circle, bawling under the howl of the wind. It sounded to Donn like Gregorian chant, in counterpoint to a mad organist. A Kyrie, he thought. A Dies Irae.

"They're still too far for a shot," Winjah said. "A good three hundred yards. And the Big Bogo's masked by the others. We'll have to belly on out there. I think I see a way." He spoke to Lambat and took the .458. Donn already was carrying the .375. "I want the lads to stay here while you and I make the stalk," Winjah said. "That way, if the herd breaks before we get close enough, the lads can follow them out for us. Let's go."

They crawled on elbows and bellies through the wet grass, Winjah in the lead, Donn a body length behind. Just like a war movie, he thought. Stalking the wily Nips. After about a hundred yards, Winjah stuck his head up behind a thornbush and looked ahead. He turned to Donn and nodded, smiling. Still there. They were in a shallow depression that snaked out toward the herd. Rainwater lay clean and cold in the lower spots. Donn sipped some. He was very dry.

Winjah crawled to the top of the depression and slid the rifle barrel out in front of him. With his hand flat, he signaled for Don to crawl up beside him. The herd was barely seventy-five yards ahead of them, huge in the blued-steel light of the storm, heads and horns tossing in stark silhouette against the bone-white rage of the sky. The wind, from herd to hunters, carried the scent of wet cow dung and the sound of the bovine fear. Donn saw the Diamond Bogo, looming above the others. The great stone flashed. He was nearer the edge of the herd now, the milling of the others having carried them somewhat apart from him. Any moment now the shot would come clear.

"Line him up," Winjah whispered. "Point of the shoulder, the way he's standing now. We both shoot at once. When I say so." Donn put his eye to the scope and waited. His balls felt tight against his crotch. But the cross hairs did not waver.

They barely heard the pop. It sounded like a twig snapping, against the bellow of herd and storm. The Diamond Bogo leaped and tossed his huge head angrily, fell to his knees, and then turned to bolt with the rest of the herd straight for the woods.

"What the fuck?" said Donn. He hadn't shot and neither had Winjah. Then they heard it.

"Ah hit 'im, Ah hit 'im! By Gawd, Ah hit 'im!"

It was Nordquist. He stood with his ducklings at the edge of the forest, some three hundred yards from them, waving the .17-caliber Weatherby over his head, his voice thin and tinny over the loud distance.

"God-bloody-dammit-to-bloodyell," Winjah said. He looked to where the herd was disappearing into the heavy cover of the valley. "He *did* hit him, too. Oh shit, oh dear."

29
CRUSADER

"I can't!" yelled Bucky. "Can't, can't, can't! I need a vacation, Clickrasp. I'm too pooped to pop." They stood in Clicky's study. Outside the storm was breaking up. The garden dripped and shone in the aftermath of the rains, the blue skies blazed behind the flowering trees. Clickrasp stood leaning on the haft of a heavy two-handed broadsword, his chin just resting on the worn steel pommel.

"But you were doing so well," he lamented.

"Yeah," Buck said bitterly. "Eight, ten, twelve times a day. I'm worn to a frazzle, a nubbin, and my nerves are going fast. It's all that dope you're sticking in my chow."

"Now wait a minute," Clickrasp said angrily. "I've put nothing in your food. No stimulants, no aphrodisiacs, nothing. I want you for the long term, my lad. Do you think I'd risk good breeding stock on harmful drugs, for nothing but a brief, flashy performance?"

196

"You mean . . ."

"Yes, you did it all on your own." Clicky smiled. "Didn't know you had it in you, eh?"

"No," Bucky grumped, blushing nonetheless, "it's not that. It's just that I need a break now and then. You've heard the phrase 'too much of a good thing'?"

"Certainly, certainly. Well, I suppose, in light of your good record to date, a spot of holiday would not be out of order. How long had you in mind?"

"Oh, just a day or two. I thought maybe you could spare me a couple of your warriors—you'd want them with me as guards anyway, I suppose—and I'd head up into the mountains, maybe do a bit of fishing or bow-hunting. I notice you've got bows and arrows around"—he gestured to the walls of the study, on which hung arms of all nations—"and I reckoned maybe I could shoot me a bit of game."

"I don't know," Clickrasp said. He rubbed his heavy chin. Could Buck be planning an escape? He had had the strong feeling that Buck was enjoying it here, actually liked the Tok, and Clickrasp foremost among them, perhaps was even glad to be helping the cause. But you never could tell with these subhumans. Their minds worked in devious, inexplicable ways. "Say, I've got an idea. Why don't you join me on an elephant hunt? Dawn told me the other night that she would like some ivory, killed by yours truly, and I'd dismissed the idea just then. But perhaps we could go together—kill two tusks with one stone, as it were."

"Great," said Bucky. "How is Dawn, by the way? I've been too busy, thanks to you, to look in on her. You two, uh, hitting it off okay?"

"Swimmingly," Click replied, looking away and gritting his teeth. "Just swimmingly. She needed a bit of holiday, too, and I've sent her up to a little spa we maintain in the foothills. A natural hot springs. Something of a health resort for the ladies of our people."

"Good," said Buck. "Well, when do we hit the trail of the tuskers?" He took a short, recurved bow from the wall.

It was backed with bone and sinew, impeccably wrapped, with a well-waxed string that seemed to be woven of muscle fiber. He placed the tip to whose end the string was tied on the outside of his right foot, stepped through between bow and string with his left leg, and bent the bow to slide the looped end of the string into its notch. The bow was powerful. With it strung, he held it at arm's length and drew. Christ, he thought as his forearm quivered slightly, that's a good eighty pounds of pull.

"Right now," said Clicky. "That's why I'd taken down this sword. I've never killed an elephant with a sword and was thinking about giving it a try. This weapon belonged to a Crusader, a German who wandered into our country some seven centuries ago on a futile quest for the lands of Prester John. He slew many of us before our people subdued him. And all for nothing. Legend has it his brains were too sour even for stew. Well, that's neither here nor there. Let's go hunting." He bellowed orders in Tok to the guards who lolled outside the study. They sprang to their feet like bird dogs at the sight of a shotgun.

An hour later, trotting behind Clickrasp and the rest of the Tok hunting party, Bucky felt like a kid on the day school lets out. A full quiver of arrows bounced on his hip and the bow felt heavy, solid in his hand. Poking through Click's collection of cutlery as he armed himself, he had come on a sheathed Buck knife—property of the late suicidal Philadelphian—and the Tok chieftain had given it to him as well, a memento of the hard days and nights just past. It flopped against his opposite hip.

They were running through the rain forest southeast of the city, along the fast white-water arm of the upper Kan, where the river debouched from the snow-topped mountains. Click's hunters had been watching a small herd of elephants that had fed for the past few days in the bamboo stands not far from town. Elephants were protected under Clickrasp's regime but the hunters were always aware of their proximity, if only for safety's sake. Many a Tok had gone into heavy cover after wounded small game only to be stomped flat by hiding elephants he had foolishly failed to notice. This particular herd was notorious for its ferocity, especially that of the dominant bull, whose ivory Clickrasp estimated must go over one hundred pounds the side. Not gigantic, but big for nowadays.

They came on the fresh elephant trail just two hours out of town. Mounds of dung steamed in the afternoon heat. The trail was ten yards wide—ripped, stripped branches, uprooted shrubs, footprints pressed deep in the spongy forest floor, filling slowly with the seepage of groundwater. Clicky stuck a finger into one dung pile and then withdrew it, shaking the digit like a thermometer. "Still hot," he rasped, in a throaty whisper. "They came down out of the bamboo, probably because of the storm this morning, and now they're heading to the edge of the forest. Can't have passed here more than fifteen minutes ago."

He flashed signs with his fingers and hands to the other hunters, who immediately spread out and began a slow, still stalk along the fresh trail. "From here on we don't talk," Click whispered to Bucky. "I realize you don't know our hunting sign language yet, but just stay close to me. This means 'elephant,' this means 'stop,' this means 'circle' either 'right'—like so—or 'left.' " He demonstrated the various signs. "And this"—he made a forward snapping motion with his index finger—"means 'shoot.' "

"And what if we wound him and he comes for us?" Bucky whispered.

Clickrasp grinned and flashed him a middle finger. "That means 'go climb a tree,' " he said.

A short way up the trail, one of the point men froze, then made the sign for elephant—a drooping of the hand from the nose, fingers bunched downward. Bucky stopped and peered ahead, but could see nothing. He nocked the heavy steel-headed arrow tight on the bowstring. Clickrasp signaled 'circle right' and Buck followed him, slow and quiet, pausing every two or three steps for as long as a minute. It seemed an eternity between steps. During one pause, a giant bumblebee swung up from the orchids and buzzed them, circling around Clicky's head. The Tok remained dead still. The bee landed on his nose. It crawled up his face, into his eyebrows, its legs furrier than the landing site, then back down his nose. Bucky stifled a sympathetic urge to sneeze. The bee probed Clickrasp's nostrils with its forelegs, then stuck its head in. Buck closed his eyes—he couldn't watch. When he opened them, the bee had flown off and Click was signaling "follow me."

They stopped again, in the midst of what appeared to be a clump of giant rhododendron. Clicky signaled "elephant," very slowly. Buck stared out through the waxy leaves. Nothing. Just the empty forest, gray, brown, slightly steaming. Then Clickrasp signaled "shoot."

The spears appeared out of the surrounding brush like bolts of diamond-tipped lightning. A scream like that of an ocean liner broke directly overhead. Buck looked up and saw the elephant—not five yards ahead—suddenly clear, all of him, raging tall above him. Its tusks flashed golden in the late light. The tiny eyes blew fire at the earth, and the great ears flared wide. He felt his thumb at his cheekbone and heard the bowstring twang. The arrow took the elephant in the throat, buried to the fletching, and then he had another arrow out and nocked. Drawing . . .

And Clickrasp was out in front of him, out of the bushes with the broadsword bright, upright, bright as the elephant's tusks, darting in under the trunk that swung at him like a giant baseball bat, the elephant rearing with the spears dangling—toothpicks from his wrinkled, jungle-gray side. Clickrasp leaped and slammed the sword deep into the elephant's throat. He hung there for an instant, working the blade, then dropped free and darted between the elephant's legs. Another ocean liner blast as the sword dug deep into the elephant's gut. Its head turned and Buck released his second arrow. It disappeared into the elephant's earhole.

The beast staggered forward two steps and then teetered. Clickrasp appeared around the elephant's stern.

The bull fell forward to its knees, moaning, the trunk slashing blindly in the foliage. Clickrasp poised, sword held high, his eyes gleaming wildly as he watched. Then he kicked the elephant's ass. The bull toppled with a slow bubbly sigh. Only then did Clicky turn and grin.

"Jesus," said Buck, his throat dry, his ears humming with adrenaline, "you're some Crusader!"

Clicky's grin rearranged itself into his customary, self-deprecating smile and he began to frame a reply. Just then, from close at hand, they heard the roar of a gun. Voices came faint, excited, through the underbrush. In English. Then another shot.

Clickrasp signaled "stop." They waited a long silent moment. Clickrasp shook his head with worry.

"Your friends," he said to Bucky, avoiding his eyes. "They have met with the Diamond Bogo."

30
HOME FROM THE HILL

It was always this way, Winjah thought. The waiting to go in. It was this way in Korea, up on the MLR, on those nights when we went in for prisoners, waiting in the dark behind the cold bags full of dirt with the star shells turning the wire to neon. And later in Malaya, waiting to go into a camp full of Chinese, picking the leeches off your legs from the walk through the swamp, and hearing the Chinese voices up and down out there while you checked the Bren to make sure there was no mud in the muzzle. And then during the Emergency in Kenya, up in the bamboo with the moon shining on the ice at the top of the mountain, and the fires of the Mau Mau dancing up ahead, the men in their long greatcoats and slouch hats hunkered around the fires, talking happily in Kikuyu and eating bush pig, not knowing you were about to do the lot of them.

But it was different with buffalo, this way, in that the

buffalo knew you were coming. Oh how they knew.

Winjah and Donn and the three trackers were squatting at the edge of the cover into which the Diamond Bogo had fled. It was an irregular lobe of the forest that projected into the grasslands like a mashed thumb. Marula trees and whistling thorn, edged by tall elephant grass and termite mounds. Rainwater ran down the declivity that bisected the lobe, and already the peeper frogs thronged in the small pools that had formed, their incessant chirrup masking any sounds that might come from the cover. The Diamond Bogo's tracks, splayed and deep, led around the largest of these pools and disappeared into the heart of the thicket. Somewhere in that tangle, a quarter of a mile long by a hundred yards wide, he was waiting for them.

Winjah checked the five bullets carefully before sliding them down into the magazine, ensuring that none was the least bit bent. A bent bullet meant a jam, and a jam in cover like this meant finished. Then he checked the gaffer tape that he had wrapped around the floor plate, just forward of the trigger guard. The floor plate was the bottom of the magazine, and with a heavy-kicking rifle like the .458, the floor plate had been known to fall off at the jolt of a shot. Rather embarrassing when a buffalo was on top of you. It had happened to an acquaintance of Winjah's, a hunter named Talbot, down in the Mara a few years back. During the autopsy, the pathologist had extracted Talbot's testicles from a lodgement just north of his liver.

There was still time to wait, time to let the Bogo stiffen where he lay, and Winjah found himself thinking a bit morbidly about buffalo accidents. There had been many of them during his time in Africa, tossings and tramplings mostly, but plenty of crushings and punctures and outright dismemberments. Bad animals. They killed more hunters than lions and leopards and elephants put together. And sometimes they did so quite ironically. Winjah remembered an elderly hunter named Bryce-Armytage who had come out to British East during the twenties with, as he liked to recall over a cold Tusker's at the Long Bar, "naught but five quid in me pocket and a shotgun over me back." He thrived, as all of them had, during the hunting boom of the fifties, piling up the nicker until he owned his own farm above Nanyuki, on the slopes of Mount Kenya. Finally he invited a younger brother out on safari, free of charge, a birthday safari for a younger brother who had now turned sixty, having worked all his life as a clerk in the Admiralty. It was to have been a jolly good hunt, the Big Five, in the very best blocs Bryce-Armytage could secure. They would start with buffalo, up on the Tana River. Yes, jolly. The brother had wounded the bogo, they had gone in, and the bogo had jumped them of course—the usual story. Bryce-Armytage had fired his .460 Weatherby magnum as the buff charged through, and the animal had fallen. Beyond it, his brother lay dead. In a one-in-a-million shot, the heavy bullet had gone clean through the bogo and taken the birthday boy's chin off. Back in Nanyuki, Bryce-Armytage burned all his guns, sold the farm, and emigrated to Australia.

Winjah's closest call had come one sultry morning out near Kakamega, west of the Rift Valley. Control work for the Game Department. In control work, the locals complained that wild animals were destroying their crops and killing their wives and children, and the Game Department dispatched a hunter to those parts to kill the naughty beasts. The fact that the locals had despoiled the previous tract of land "controlled" by another hunter, ruining it with wasteful agricultural practices and copulating themselves into another near-starvation crisis, was not considered naughty. Now, having moved farther into the bush in their ravenous manner, their needs must be protected. Winjah had caught up with the corn-trampling culprits, a herd of some fifty buffalo. He had killed twenty-seven in the morning's shoot, cows and calves and herd bulls alike, but when the twenty-eighth had come at him the gun jammed. Overheating. It was a small bull, a young one, with perhaps a three-foot spread of horns. It could kill him with one punch. Now he recalled the terror of that moment, the helplessness, the nightmare sludge of it as the bolt refused to move forward, the bull coming at him head high with those piggy black eyes shining under the scaled bulge of boss, over the sucking caverns of nostril.

At the last moment, his dog—a Brittany spaniel bitch named Belle—had leaped in and grabbed the bull by the nose. While he swung her, Winjah had cleared the jammed cartridge, slipped in a fresh one, and blasted the bogo to the ground. Yes, old Belle, Winjah thought. Old and gray and full of sleep now, her teeth nearly gone, groaning as she moves to her conclusion. I should put her out of it, but I can't. She saved my life.

"I think you'd best sit this one out, Bwana," he said to Donn as he rose to his feet. "It won't be nice in there."

"I'd like to go in."

"You won't be able to do much," Winjah continued. "With the scope on that rifle, you won't be able to sight very quickly up close, and it will be close when it happens."

"I'd rather go in."

"You'll just be a distraction to me, Bwana. It's much better for the hunter to do this alone. Selfish, I suppose, but then he doesn't have the added worry of what's happening to the client."

"Am I a client?" Donn asked. He looks very grim, Winjah thought. "I'd like to go in there with you, Bwana. Whatever happens."

So he's made his choice, Winjah thought. He can see it now, the difference between client and hunter, between men who kill animals and men who truly hunt them. Of course he's seen it.

"Right, then," Winjah said. "We don't know for certain that he's in this bit of cover. If Nordquist didn't hit him hard, he may well have run right on through and into the forest beyond. But if he's in there, he will have doubled back outside his trail. He'll be lying up there, watching his track and waiting for us to pass him. Then he'll come out and flank us. They come very fast for such a large creature, and they are very rude when they arrive. I'll have Lambat and Otiego ahead of me, and you just behind me.

Then Red Blanket and Machyana bringing up the rear.
Our best chance is that one of the lads will spot him before
we pass him. Then it's sit tight, don't move a bloody
eyelash, until I've shot. Breathe through your mouth so
that there's no hissing of nostrils to alert him. If you have
to fart, do so now or forever hold your peace. If on the
other hand he comes out behind us, get to one side—out of
my line of fire—before you even raise your rifle. I don't
want to have to shoot through you to hit the bogo. It
doesn't tickle, not with a .458. And finally, if by chance he
knocks me down after I've shot, don't shoot in a panic. I'd
rather be slightly squashed by a dying buffalo than killed
by a well-meant rifle bullet. Understood?"

Donn nodded.

They walked down through the wet elephant grass
into the scrub thorn at the edge of the darkness. My heart's
pounding, Donn thought, but then he realized that it was
the sound of his footfalls. The earth here must be hollow,
volcanic, like the skin of a dead, dried bug. But his heart
was indeed pounding as well, his mouth dry, as it had been
before a race. He tried to shift his mind into that neutral
he had found, motor racing, before the green flag
fell—the calm that observed the storm. The neutral that
took imagination out of gear. If you could keep
imagination in neutral during a race, while the other gears
howled and whirled and drove you even into death, then
the horror of it was very interesting. Even the pit wall at
Riverside, coming your way at 160 miles an hour, knowing
it would soon tear the car in half, and you with it. Very
interesting to be out of control.

But Donn could not find neutral. Walking past the
ponds, with the peepers going silent as they passed and
then resuming their screech a moment later, avoiding the
wait-a-bit thorns, looking into the cavernous tracks of the
bogo still filling with clear rainwater, he felt as he had in
childhood, when he first discovered the concept of the
moment. This moment is now, it is all that is real, what
happened is no longer real, what is yet to happen is
unrealized. The world seems to balloon at such moments,

to bulge frighteningly into so vast and inexorable a thing that reality itself becomes unreal. That is true fear, Donn thought. The moment. The lie of sequence, with its promise of careful cause leading to benign effect, is much more reassuring.

What in the fuck am I babbling about? I should be looking for the bogo. He peered ahead, searching the maze of dark and tangle for a blacker patch—a fragment of buffalo hidden to right or left, dead quiet, waiting. They were moving quite slowly, a step followed by a ten-beat pause, sometimes longer. Their heads turned like the turrets of tanks in ultra-slow motion. The eyes of the Africans were slits, their lips compressed, and Donn suddenly realized that it was to minimize the bright flash of eye and tooth that might alert the buffalo. The air was heavy, unmoving, not a breath of breeze, and Donn could smell the miasma of sweat and rancid fat that Lambat, just ten yards ahead of him, left collapsing in his wake. Butterflies flickered ahead, in the gloom, disturbing his concentration. They were skippers, mainly, the shade-loving *Ypthima* and *Precis,* with a few of the poorly represented Lycaenidae thrown in for good measure. And what the hell am I lepidopterizing for? He almost laughed at a sudden image of Vladimir Nabokov dancing into the thicket, butterfly net at full tilt, pale legs squirting from the dim mouths of his mountaineering shorts. Pnin on the prowl, uttering elegant puns in impeccably translated Russian.

Otiego's long hand pointed earthward, the grass stem indicating a bead of blood on the wet black leaves. A scarlet pearl, bright blood, arterial. It was the first blood they had seen on their way in. A neck shot, Winjah thought. Could be superficial. Could be he's gone out the back door. Could be he's halfway across the Sudan by now. Yes, could be, but you know damned well he isn't. That bullet just enraged him, like a banderillero's sticks in the neck of a fighting bull. He's bloody in here and he's bloody vexed. Winjah felt the hair prickle on the back of his neck. He could feel the buffalo's eyes on him, it seemed. His own eyes cast back and forth, to right and left, probing, stabbing at the dark spiked tangle, checking each still shadow again, and yet again. He felt the cold lump swelling in his stomach and willed it to shrink, but it wouldn't. He surrounded it with rage, hoping the heat might neutralize it, but it was too cold. The rage went warm, then lukewarm, then became part of the fear.

All right, then if it's to be ice, let it fill me. Let it freeze the nerves to numbness. Then let him come and I will kill him stone-cold dead.

And then the Diamond Bogo came, black and awful in the instant. He came from behind them, out of a patch of thorn that seemed scarcely large enough to hide a house cat. He came in one great silent rush, moving the heavy air before him like a bow wave. He came with a shivering of the very earth. He came like a truckload of death. Spinning, Donn saw Red Blanket rise through the air, mouth wide with hair and brown teeth, his back snapped at right angles, ribs popping through the shiny skin of his crushed chest. And the Diamond Bogo kept coming, under the arc of Red Blanket's orbit, his head up, nostrils like stovepipes, the tiny eyes brighter even than the stone that led his charge. Donn was still bringing the .375 up when the boss struck him. He saw the horn tip flash past his face, polished ebony, and then the bogo's knee took him in the stomach and he too was airborne, his nose filled with the taste of blood and cattle. As he flew, he saw the Diamond Bogo move on Winjah.

Winjah stood waiting, legs braced, until Donn was thrown clear. The .458 was up and out, the blue eye hard and wide back of the iron buckhorn. The ice filled him now: An icicle of death sprang from his eye down the sighting plane. The bogo's head filled the world. He could see the veins around the eyeballs, the moss on the rough boss, the light winking blood and black from the facets of the stone. The sear snapped—a blossom of flame. The five-hundred grain solid-cased bullet moved out at 2,130 feet per second. In precisely 1/426 of a second, it crossed the five feet that separated muzzle and buffalo. When it got there, it delivered a punch that measured 5,040 foot-pounds of momentum. It delivered this punch directly up the right nostril of the Diamond Bogo. The bullet, tearing through mucous membrane and cartilage, burst into the Diamond Bogo's brain cavity and ran a circle of lightning around the banked wall of the Diamond Bogo's skull, smashing brain matter into dead pulp. And the Diamond Bogo kept coming.

Dead, totally dead by any means measurable to magic or science, the Diamond Bogo smashed into Winjah—a full ton of black moving death. Winjah felt his right thighbone crack, heard the pop like a pistol shot, as he moved on the boss of the horns, the diamond digging into his ribs, smelling the barn as it fell on him. The breath went out of them both with a great roaring whoosh.

And then, lying there stunned under the huge hot body, both of them twitching and Winjah yelling— "*Hapana! Hapana!* No more bullets!"—he had heard the cycles roar up.

Nordquist appeared over the mountain of the bogo's shoulder. He had the pistol out. He smiled at Winjah, his eyes tight behind the rimless glasses, and cocked the hammer.

"No," Winjah said, looking up at Nordquist. "Don't shoot again. He's done, finished."

"The hell you say," Nordquist answered. "I gotta put the last bullet into him. You're the guys who made up that rule. Remember the lion? This'n will make that diamond my very own." He smiled down at the pinned hunter, but avoided the hard blue eyes.

"You'll kill me if you do," Winjah said flatly.

"Naw," said Nordquist. "It won't even tickle." He squeezed and the hammer dropped. The Ruger Super Blackhawk .44 magnum banged once, very loud.

The dead buffalo flinched as the heavy bullet tore through its body. Winjah's eyes widened, then fixed on eternity.

Nordquist holstered the pistol and grabbed the bowie from its sheath on his hip. Straddling the bogo's nose, he began hacking at the horns around the diamond.

Then Donn raised his rifle. Nordquist's face

ballooned at him through the scope, round and pitted like
a photo of some distant moon, eyes bulging under the
glasses: strange creatures of another planet, dwelling
under domes. Donn—who loved peace and poems, who
until a few short days ago had never killed a big-game
animal, who had scorned all hunters but had learned to
respect at least one—Donn squeezed off.

Nordquist's head came apart in a whirl of snot and
teeth and brains and broken glass. The Diamond Bogo
raised his great ruined head and stared at Nordquist.
Winjah was staring too, but his eyes were fixed on nothing
in particular.

The moment stretched and stretched deep into
timelessness. Donn heard the ducklings' three motors
start, heard them grumble out of hearing. He heard a
hawk scream high overhead, and heard the raindrops
spattering down as a breeze worked the treetops. He saw
butterflies alight on the bogo's wound and drink the blood.
Then Lambat and Otiego and Machyana came out of the
trees and walked slowly up to the buffalo. He saw them
grab its legs and roll it over on its back. Then they knelt
behind it, looking at Winjah, and he heard Otiego crying.

He could not bring himself to move.

Two more figures emerged from the wood. Bucky
and a Tok. Bucky wore a zebra-striped kilt and carried a
recurved Tartar bow in one hand. His hair was bound
back with a strip of rawhide, his face grave beneath the
grizzled beard. The little man with him carried a sword
nearly his own height.

Bucky surveyed the tableau. The shattered body of
Red Blanket began the path of carnage, angled and awful.
Then Donn, propped up on his elbows, his nose mashed
flat again, black with blood, his eyes still wide with shock.
Before him, the rifle. Then the mountainous body of the
buffalo, quiet save for the tortoiseshell ticks that crawled
on its cooling testicles. Then the three Africans standing
hopeless, helpless, over the quiet form of Winjah. Beyond
lay the body of another man, head smashed and leaking. A
ray of sunlight hit the diamond in the buffalo's forehead

and sent a slow moving beam of radiance over the dead hunter's chest. Bucky watched it sparkle on the bloody hole in Winjah's starched corduroys. Then the beam moved on.

It was too big for them, Bucky thought. Too big even for him. Too strong, as it always has been, for everyone. Africa.

He walked over to Donn and helped him to his feet, brushing the wet black leaves from his shirt, wiping the blood from his face with a damp bandanna. Then he put his arm around Donn's shoulders and walked him toward the edge of the thorn thicket, where the light sparkled— bogo bright, he thought.

Clickrasp moved to block his path.

"Where are you going?" he asked in a solemn voice. His eyes shone, dull green behind the lidded eyes.

"I'm taking him home," Bucky replied. "Donn and Dawn both. Home from the hill."

Clickrasp's hands tightened on the haft of the broadsword. For a moment it seemed as if he was about to strike. But then he averted his eyes and held the sword out to Buck, haft first.

"Take this," he said. "It is my laisser-passer, my gift of freedom to you all."

31
OUT
OF AFRICA

They walked out swiftly, saying little. No one stopped
them. No animals impeded their progress. The
broadsword seemed a specific to peace. When Buck had
raised it to the Tok women at the Pool where they had
found Dawn, the women fell back in silence. Bands of Tok
warriors who crossed their path on the march to the scarp
detoured at the flash of the blade. Even the game—lions,
oryx, buffalo, a lone bull elephant—only stood and
watched as they passed.

At the scarp they paused and studied the plain below.
Clouds of dust snaked across it—trucks on the move. The
occasional slam of a rifle shot or the clatter of automatic
weapons echoed up to them. Men in uniform crawled like
bugs down there, killing the game. It was always that way
when African troops moved into an area.

In the Butterfly Glade where they had lambasted the
Lepidoptera, rib cages and backbones picked clean by the

ants gleamed in the cool green gloom. A machine-gun emplacement stood on the knoll that housed the Skull Cave; the Africans manning it munched giant spareribs of eland and giraffe. At the Rope of God they found a Volkswagen "Thing" with two impala draped over its hood. The driver, a portly man in lederhosen and a camouflage shirt, was photographing the graffiti on the rock spire. Buck spoke to him in German.

"He says there must be nearly a thousand hunters here already," Bucky reported as they moved on. "From all over the world—Americans, Frenchmen, Germans, Britons, Yugoslavs, Japanese, even a bunch of Brazilians. The Kansduvian Army has sent in a regiment of askari with automatic weapons to protect them from the Tok. They're all after the Diamond Bogo. I wished him luck."

At White Legs, they found the trucks and the remainder of the staff waiting and anxious. They wept at the news of Winjah's death but quickly regained their composure and began striking the camp. Bucky made his farewells.

"You'll be in good hands all the way back to Palmerville," he told Donn and Dawn. "By the end of the week, you'll be back on the Wandering Y, wondering why in hell you ever came here. I've got to go back up there." They all looked up toward the scarp. Rain clouds boiled slowly over the blue mountains. "Clickrasp will need his Crusader's sword."

"I understand," said Donn.

They shook hands. Bucky took Dawn in his arms and kissed her on the cheek. For the first time since she had met him, he didn't smell bad. Then he walked back down the plain, toward the river and the plateau.

EPILOGUE

Dawn heard the pickup truck crunch ice in the driveway.
She went to the window. The sleet, which had been falling
since morning, had turned to snow and the beech trees
that lined the road up to the house were coated in ice. It
was beautiful to look at, the limbs sheathed in clear fire,
trees carved of diamonds, but she knew that when the
wind sprang up behind the snow, the trees would break
and shatter. Donn got down from the truck with the
shotgun over his shoulder and Lil, his yellow Labrador,
leaping and snapping at the four dead grouse that dangled
from his hand. He allowed the dog a sniff and then walked
over to the side of the woodshed to hang the birds, heads
down, under the protective eave. He'd clean them tonight.

"There's a package for you," she said after he had
stomped the snow from his boots. "From Africa."

It was a large flat manila envelope, reinforced with
cardboard inside the wrapping, and it bore many stamps.

Donn poured himself a cup of coffee and opened it, Dawn hovering over his shoulder. He pulled out a gigantic postcard, two feet by three, with the photograph of a Cape buffalo on the front. A chip of diamond bigger than the one in Dawn's engagement ring had been glued between the buffalo's horns. Donn turned the card over.

"Dear Donn and Dawn," he read. "Ah yes, we remember it well. The S.O.B. And we'll get even with its kin in the fullness of time! We all miss you up here in the lonely land of the Tok. I hope this card gets to you sooner rather than later. I'm turning it over to a mercenary who is leaving shortly for French West and he promises to forward it as quickly as he can, but as you damned well know, that could mean months in this slow-moving continent. First off, let me assure you that both Clickrasp and I are alive and well and waging a hell of a war against the outlanders. As I told you before we said good-bye, I've always wanted a war of my own and now I've got one. It isn't exactly heaven, but it isn't hell either. In our case, it's necessary. If we didn't fight now, the Tok would be gone in a matter of months and this whole plateau would be one huge diamond mine.

"As you've probably read in the newspapers, we've gotten support from a number of nations, mainly Israel, and next month we're planning to send a delegation to the U.N. Clickrasp will head it, and I'm sure he'll make a hit with the media, if he gets a decent tailor. Of course, General Opolopo Bompah, the dictator of Kansdu, is furious. But as the Tok say, his time is not long. Click says he'll call you from New York when he gets there. I know he's eager to see you—particularly his lost love, the Fair Dawn Lady. Funny thing. The other day he was musing about his unrequited romance and he ended up blaming it on the stars. 'My chart for that month predicted danger from water, darkness, and mysterious disappearance,' he told me. You two must go to the same astrologer.

"I also discovered a few more things about Clickrasp that we didn't know when you left. For years he'd been selling Tok diamonds outside the country under the pseudonym of one Nikolas Rokoff, and it was he who had planted the stone in the Diamond Bogo's horns. It was a carefully planned lure, thrown out into the big world in order to draw hunters into his realm. He knew that the first ones in would be the boldest and best, if they survived the buffalo. And those were the ones he wanted for his master plan to save the land of the Tok. Very clever, these superhumans.

"Clickrasp also used the money from the diamond sales to stock his library and to purchase the weapons for the war, which began arriving over the mountains shortly after the two of you departed. When the first wave of invaders hit the River Kan, we repulsed them quite bloodily. Then Opolopo Bompah sent in more troops, but they couldn't take the scarp. So far we've had fairly light casualties—only fifty-odd dead and wounded in the five months of fighting. We took quite a pounding from the air, right at the beginning, but since the Israelis came in to build the airstrip and man the interceptors, it's been virtual peacetime up here against the mountains. The major loss in town was the Moor's Head Inn, my favorite watering hole, but we're rebuilding it. At least the ale remained largely intact. And the paintings.

"Along the way, though, we've taken some painful personal losses. I'm sorry to report that Lambat is dead, killed by mortar fire in a fight near the Skull Cave. Machyana was seriously wounded leading a reconnaissance-in-force in the area of the Rope of God. He was taken prisoner and we haven't heard from or of him since. Knowing Opolopo's tendencies, I fear the worst. Otiego, though, is doing very well. He's taken a hareem of Tok wives and they keep him out of trouble when he's back here on his infrequent leaves. He often reminisces, when I see him, about the Bhangi Bwana and smiles nostalgically in memory of the highs.

"Well, I see I'm running out of space on this gigantic postcard, which an Israeli intelligence aide printed up for me from one of the film rolls you left behind. Oh—the fate of the ducklings, as you called them. Apparently they fled on the ATCs until they ran out of gas, then wandered on foot through the Nyika. Tok hunters, following up the sound of gunfire, found two of them dying of gunshot wounds, apparently after a fight over the water left in a canteen. The Tok ended their suffering quite swiftly. The third boy made it to the Pool of the Bleeding Ladies, but the Tok women who were there at the time said he couldn't bring himself to drink the water. He shot himself instead. That night, the Tok dined on *cervelles des canetons à l'orange.*

"I buried Winjah beside the grave of Mungo Park. It seemed appropriate—the First Great African Explorer and the Last Great White Hunter. The skull and horns of the Diamond Bogo, with the stone still gleaming at the boss, serves as headstone for them both.

"So that is that. Take care and, as Robert Frost said of his apple orchard, keep cold. Love, Bucky."

Written in a tiny, almost indecipherable scrawl was a postscript:

"P.S. Ticklette had triplets, wouldn't you know! And I got me another Guinea worm."

Donn sat back and tasted his coffee. It had grown cold. "I don't know," he said, "maybe we could have stayed. . . ." His voice trailed off. Outside, the wind worked on the ice-sheathed trees.

Any moment now they would hear the pistol shot of breaking branches.